T0197310

JOSEPH

JOSEPH

— Son of Jacob —

Reverend John B. Alumbaugh

JOSEPH
SON OF JACOB

Scripture quotations marked NIV are taken from the Holy Bible, New International Version®. NIV®. Copyright © 1973, 1978, 1984 by International Bible Society. Used by permission of Zondervan. All rights reserved. [Biblica]

Certain characters in this work are historical figures, and certain events portrayed did take place. However, this is a work of a biblical novel. All of the other characters, names, and events as well as all places, incidents, organizations, and dialogue in this novel are either the products of the author's imagination or are used fictitiously.

iUniverse books may be ordered through booksellers or by contacting:

iUniverse
1663 Liberty Drive
Bloomington, IN 47403
www.iuniverse.com
1-800-Authors (1-800-288-4677)

ISBN: 978-1-5320-7111-9 (sc)
ISBN: 978-1-5320-7112-6 (hc)
ISBN: 978-1-5320-7110-2 (e)

Library of Congress Control Number: 2019903477

Print information available on the last page.

iUniverse rev. date: 03/26/2019

Contents

Contents

Assumptions

Many facts and names are not found in the Bible. I have made the following assumptions in writing this biblical Historical Novel.

1. All of Jacob's children (except Benjamin) were born during the seven years he worked for Rachel and the six years he worked for his flocks and herds (Genesis 29:28). The average age of weaning a child was two and a half to three years. The boys were listed in the Bible according to the position of the wife in the family and girls were always listed last. I have assumed the following ages at the start of the trip to Canaan.

    Wives: Leah 30, Rachel 28, Concubines, Bilhah 27 and Zilpah 26
    Leah's children:
      Reuben, (conceived during the wedding week) 12 years 3 months
      Simeon, 10 years 2 months
      Dinah, 9 years
      Levi, 7 years 10 months
      Judah, 6 years 4 months
      Issachar, 2 years 9 months
      Zebulon, 4 months
    Zilpah's children: (Leah's handmaiden married Jacob when she was 14)
      Gad, 9 Years 5 months
      Asher, 5 years 3 months
    Bilhah's children: (Rachel's handmaiden married Jacob when she was 14)
      Dan, 9 years 6 months
      Naphtali, 6 years 3 months
    Rachel's Children:

Joseph, 6 years 2 months

Benjamin was born when Joseph was 14 years old

2. Laban's sons were too young to be shepherds when Jacob arrived. In Genesis 30:35 and 31:1 he had sons. I have given them the names and ages as follows; Azbuk, 24; Lod 21; Miphkad 18; Hodevah 15.

3. A pace is five feet.

History

1. Joseph was born in 1915 B.C. (NIV Old Testament Chronology; The NIV Study Bible by Zondervan Publishing Co, copyrighted 1995)

2. Joseph was 17 when taken to Egypt in 1898 B.C. The Pharaoh was Amenemhet II. He ruled from 1921B.C. to 1895 B.C. Amenemhet II was ill for the last three years of his life. He appointed his son Senusret II as co-ruler until he died.

   a. The vizier for both pharaohs was Lord Siese
   b. The royal engineer for both pharaohs was Lord Khentykhetywer (ken tyk' hety wer)

3. Senusret II was Pharaoh from 1898 B.C - 1878 B.C

4. Joseph was 30 when he interpreted the dreams for Pharaoh Senusret II in 1885 B.C.

5. When Joseph died, he was 110 years old. That would have been in 1805 B.C. At that time a rare female Pharaoh, Sobekneferu was ruler. She ruled from 1807BC. To1802 BC.

6. The Hebrews word for 'talent' is "Kikkar" which means circle. The Egyptians used rings of gold, silver and bronze as money. Since Egypt was the major nation and commercial center, I have used rings as the medium of exchange. Shekels and rings each weighed 2/5 of an ounce.

7. Hebrews told directions as if they were looking at the sunrise. Forward is east; back is west; right or going toward Egypt is south and left or going toward Hittite is north.

8. The Egyptians called the hippopotamus a water cow.

9. Canaan had a twelve hour day, from sunup at six A.M. to sunset at six P.M. A person could tell time by his hands. With the thumb bent under, looking to the eastern horizon and by moving the hands one on top of the other, there would be six hands from sunrise to noon and six hands from noon to sunset. The four fingers equate to the four quarter hours.

10. God appeared to Abraham (Gen. 17:1) as El Shaddai. El Shaddai is now translated as "God Almighty".

11. An Egyptian "deden" weighed 93.3 grams.

12. An Egyptian Heqat equals 4.8 liters.

13. Talmudic Midrashes are explanations of Hebrew traditions. Midrash Prave Bata 15 explains that Dinah, Jacob's daughter who was raped by Shechem, became Job's second wife.

14. A Midrash by Rabbi Rashi explains why Dinah was married to her brother Simeon. She is listed in Genesis 46:10 in Simeon's family as "that Canaanite woman". Her son Shaul is also listed there. She is called that Canaanite woman because she had a son by Shechem.

15. The apocryphal book of 'Divir Iyov' lists Uzit as Job's first wife.

16. The Midrash of Rabbi HaYarshar lists the name of Potiphar's wife was Zuleikha.

17. The pseusepigraphic book of Jubilees lists Noah's wife as Emzra, the wife of Japheth as Adeleteneses, Shem's wife as Sedeqetelebab and Ham's wife as Na'eltema'uk.

The Hebrew Calendar
during Jacob's Time

Number	Name	Our Date	Season	Crops and Activities
1	Abib	Mar 16- Apr 15	Latter Rains	
2	Ziv	Apr 16- May 15		Barley Harvest Shearing Sheep
3	Sivan	May 16- Jun 15	Dry Season	Wheat Harvest Shearing Goats
4	Tammuz	June 16 – July 15		First Figs
5	Ab	July 16 – Aug 15	Summer Heat	Grapes, Olives and Figs
6	Elul	Aug 16 – Sep 15		
7	Ethanim	Sep 16 – Oct 15	Former Rains	Date Harvest; Late Figs
8	Bul	Oct 16 – Nov 15		Plant Wheat and Barley
9	Kislev	Nov 16 – Dec15	Winter	
10	Tebeth	Dec 16 – Jan 15	Rains begin	
11	Shebat	Jan 16 – Feb14		
12	Adar	Feb 15 – Mar 15		Almond Trees in Bloom

Every six years a month of second Adar is included to align the calendar with the sun

CHAPTER 1
THE JOURNEY BEGINS

Jacob was in a state of semi-sleep. He wasn't sure if he was awake or asleep. He knew the night was cold; he had wrapped his heavy woolen cloak around him as he lay in the entrance of the temporary sheepfold. Jacob had been dreaming of his time with Laban. His dream reminded him how he got his wives and their children. Laban had promised him Rachel as a wife; then had given him Leah. After he finished his week of marriage with Leah, Laban gave him Rachel as his second wife. Jacob had wanted only Rachel as his wife, but after his marriage to her, he found her cold, indifferent and very moody before her moon time. He was glad Laban gave him Leah as she was warm and responsive to him.

Jacob remembered that after the fourteen years were completed, Laban and Jacob made another agreement. Laban asked Jacob what wages he wan ted, Jacob told Laban not to give him anything, I will go through the flocks and remove every sheep that is dark colored, and the female goats that are speckled or spotted, these shall be my wages.

Laban agreed but sent his sons to go through the sheep and goats and remove any that should have been Jacobs. He had his sons take the sheep and goats three days from the main flocks and herds. In this way Laban cheated Jacob out of his wages.

God would not allow Jacob to be cheated so He told Jacob to take branches of fresh popular, almond and plane wood, and to peel the bark off exposing white stripes on the branches. Jacob was to place the branches in front the sheep when they came to drink. The results that the sheep and goats bore spotted speckled young was not magic; it was God performing a miracle.

Jacob's dream continued Leah was very fertile; she conceived during the first week of marriage. When a boy was born, Jacob names him Reuben. When Reuben was two years and one month old, Leah had another boy. He was named, Simeon. Then a daughter was born one year and two months later, she was named Dinah. Two years and two months later Leah had another boy and he was named Levi. When Levi was one year six months old, Leah had her fourth boy and he was named Judah. Then she did not have any more children for several years.

After Simeon was born, Rachel was in a foul mood, because she could not conceive. She told Jacob, "give me a child or I will die!"

Jacob responded, "Am I in the place of God who has kept you from having children?"

Rachel called Bilhah and told her, "I am giving you to Jacob as his third wife. Go into his tent and consummate the marriage."

Jacob and Bilhah left. That night Bilhah conceived. A boy was born and Jacob named him Dan. After the birth of Dan, Rachel told everyone, "God has vindicated me. He has listened to my prayer and has given me a male child through my handmaiden."

When Leah saw that Bilhah had been given to Jacob as his wife, she gave her handmaid, Zilpah to Jacob as his fourth wife. Zilpah had a boy and Leah said "what good fortune," so he was named Gad

Bilhah had another child three years after Dan was born and delivered another boy. Rachel said, "I have had a great struggle with my sister and now I have won," so the boy was named Naphtali.

Then four years and two months after Gad was born, Zilpah had another son and she said, "How happy I am. Now women will call me happy," so he was named Asher.

During wheat harvest when Reuben was seven years old he went out to the field to help. He was picking up arms full of wheat and tying them into bundles by wrapping a few strands of wheat around the bundle to tie into a sheath. During the lunch break, he wandered into a field of trees. There he found some mandrake plants. Women thought the mandrake plants would help them get pregnant. Reuben took the mandrakes plants to his mother. When Rachel saw the mandrake plants she asked Leah for some of them. Leah replied, "Isn't it enough that you have taken my husband from me, now you want my son's mandrakes."

Rachel told her, "give me some of your son's mandrakes and I will tell Jacob to sleep with you tonight."

When Jacob came home, Leah told him, "You have to sleep with me tonight. I have hired you with my son's mandrakes." He slept with her and she became pregnant.

When another son was born, Leah said, "God has rewarded me for giving my handmaid to my husband and now he has given me another son." He was named Issachar. Two years and five months later she had another son. He was named Zebulun.

Four months after Zebulun was born Jacob was with the flock. He and his under shepherds had built a sheepfold earlier out of rocks and brush in the area. The sheep were securely inside. That night Jacob was lying in the entrance to keep predators, both the four-legged and the two-legged kind, from bothering the sheep. Jacob sensed another presence with him. Suddenly a man stood before him. The man glowed as if a bright light shone from within. "Peace be to you" the being said, "I have been sent from El Shaddai to give you instructions. Laban and his sons have turned their faces from you. You are to start your herds and flocks for your home today. If you delay, Laban and his sons will do you harm." The being disappeared as soon as he finished speaking. Jacob lay silent for a few minutes. He didn't know if he had been dreaming or if he had been visited by an angel from God.

Either way, he reasoned, I have been warned so I had better go home. I have been gone twenty years. I wonder if Esau is still angry with me. Oh well, I won't have to face him until I get there.

Jacob realized that the day was beginning to dawn. Oohdal, Jacob's assistant, was up and had a small fire started to cook their morning meal.

"Good morning Jacob," Oohdal called cheerily, "I suppose we'll be turning the flocks towards the main camp today. It'll be good to see our families again. We have been gone over two moons."

Jacob said good morning to the shepherds and under shepherds. Taking Oohdal aside he said, "No, we will be going toward Egypt for a few days" I want you to take the flocks to a pasture just forward of Halab. Here is a bag with 100 silver rings and 100 bronze rings. Give a bronze ring to each shepherd and schedule him to have a day off in Halab. Don't tell them where we are going. We are going to Canaan! This morning a messenger from my God told me to go back to my home. We are going! When you get to the pasture, leave Moric in charge. Go into Halab. Find the great left handed warrior, Ater. Offer him three gold rings to accompany us to Canaan."

"I have heard of this great left handed Hittite warrior," Oohdal said. "He was a personal guard to the king until one of the king's concubines tried to seduce him. He was found to be not guilty but the king still banished him. But my Lord," Oohdal continued, "We have fifty men who can use the spear and the sword. Why do we need Ater and his warriors?"

"A group of peoples from toward the setting sun have captured the island of Cyprus. The king of Cyprus and about 200 of his soldiers escaped. They are coming down the Euphrates River. They are attacking and plundering small towns and caravans along the way. If we should meet up with them, we will need trained soldiers. Tell Ater I will expect him to train my men. Rent enough pasture for the sheep, cattle, camels, donkeys and goats. I will be sending them to you in the next two or three days. I am going to Reuben who is in charge of the camel herds, and then on to Simeon, who is in charge of the donkeys. After I get Levi started with the goats, I will go to Laban and tell him we are leaving."

They had boiled crushed barley for last night's supper. What had been left had congealed into mush. This morning they heated flat rocks, rubbed them with mutton fat, and baked the leftover mush on the hot rocks. Each cake was turned with a stick they had flattened on one end so the cake could be turned and baked on both sides. After breakfast Jacob took Oohdal aside again and gave him instructions on moving the sheep. "When the sun is one hand high, move the sheep," Jacob told him. "Move them faster than normal. Move them at the pace we call half graze. Keep them moving until one hand before the sun reaches its highest point. Let them graze and rest for two hands. Then move them out again until the sun is one hand from setting. Follow this pattern until you reach the pasture at Halab. I'll see you there."

Late in the evening of the fourth day Jacob arrived at Laban's camp. He went directly to Laban's house. As he was about to knock on the door he heard Hodevah, Laban's youngest, and Miphkad talking.

Hodevah was telling Miphkad, "I wish father would let us kill him. Jacob has gotten everything he owns from our father and has gained all his sheep and goats from what belonged to our father."

Miphkad replied, "I agree with you but father says that he is our relative and that Jacob has come under his protection. Perhaps we could slip out some night and kill him without telling anyone else."

"That's a good idea," Hodevah answered excitedly. "We could slip upon him in the night and kill him and no one would know it was us."

Amazed at how their attitude toward him had changed, Jacob retreated into the darkness. He had intended to stop by Rachel's tent for the night. Now he thought it better that Laban's sons not know he was in the area. His camp was two fingers time away when walking rapidly in the daytime. It was dark and walking was much slower. Jacob decided to find a place to sleep. In the morning he would go to the camel herd and send Reuben to get Leah and Rachel.

In Jacob's camp work went on as usual. A boy trudged slowly up the hill. The sun beat unmercifully on his head. The sweat ran down his face and back and into his eyes. The load he was carrying was almost too heavy for him. The boy's name was Joseph, the only son of Jacob and Rachel. It was his responsibility to carry water from the well to the plants in the garden.

Joseph had passed his sixth birthday two months earlier. The trip to the well and back took the length of time for the sun to move the distance of two fingers. Jacob had made a wooden yoke that went across his shoulders so he could carry two leather buckets of water at a time. His three half-brothers, Judah, the fourth son of Jacob and Leah; Naphtali, the second son of Jacob and Bilhah; and Asher, the second son of Jacob and Zilpah, were also working in the garden. These three were weeding and hoeing. Judah was about two months older than Joseph so he was in charge. Naphtali had his sixth birthday three months earlier and Asher was nine months from his sixth birthday.

As Joseph came to the garden with the water, the other three boys came for a drink. As they approached, Joseph told them, "Reuben is home!"

"Are you sure?" asked Judah. "Father would never allow him to leave the camels in the middle of the day. Father is the best herdsman in this area. He says the reason Laban's flocks did not increase faster is that his shepherds took the flocks to the well at noon and kept them there the rest of the day. Father says this keeps the sheep from grazing long enough to gain the weight they need to produce lots of wool and healthy lambs."

"I know," Joseph replied. "That's what bothers me. Something important must be happening."

Asher interrupted Joseph to say, "Let's go to camp and see what's happening!"

In a flash the four boys were running down the hill to the camp. When they arrived they saw Reuben talking to Leah and Rachel. Leah was standing in the shade holding little Zebulon, her sixth son who was four months old, while Issachar her fifth son, who was two years and nine months old was holding onto his mother's skirt. Rachel was standing a little behind her. Reuben was saying, "Jacob wants you to come to meet him. He says it is important that he talks with you. You are to leave Zilpah and Bilhah to watch the children and servants. Zichre has brought two camels for you to ride. We can get started as soon as you are ready."

The four boys expected Reuben to reprimand them for leaving the garden. Reuben was the first son of Jacob and Leah. As he was over twelve by three months he was considered a young man and could discipline the younger children. When he saw the boys, he called them to him.

He said, "Don't worry about the garden, but be sure to bring the tools in and clean them, especially the bronze hoes that Father bought for you. Help anyway you can and watch that the servants don't steal anything while we are gone."

Zichre was Jacob's servant that worked with Reuben and the camel herd. He and two of his sons had brought camels for the women to ride. The camels were kneeling when the women came over to them. As was the custom, the saddles were behind the hump. Whenever a man rode a camel he would sit behind the hump and use a long pole to guide the camel. The rider would tap the camel on the side of the head opposite the way he wanted the camel to turn. One of Jacob's craftsmen had fashioned a seat that faced backwards, with a canopy over the head of the rider so the woman would not be in the sun. Zichre's sons would lead the camels. As soon as Leah and Rachel were seated, the camels got up and with Reuben leading the way the little party headed for the meeting with Jacob.

Jacob had directed the herdsmen to move the flocks and herds towards

Halab for the last few weeks. At the time he didn't know why he had them moved in that direction. The pastures seemed better and water was plentiful. The herds had crossed the Balikh River a few days earlier.

Jacob had ridden a donkey to within a hand's time from the camp so the women didn't have far to ride. Jacob was sitting under a tamarisk tree when Reuben led the group to him. The camels were made to kneel so the women could get off. Jacob told the servants to take the camels to the stream and allow them to drink and graze until he sent Reuben to get them. He sent them so that they would not hear what he wanted to tell his two wives.

Jacob began," when I arrived your brothers were not old enough to be shepherds. When I first came they were glad to have me as a shepherd. Now I see that your father's attitude toward me is not what it was, but the God of my father has been with me. You know that I've worked for your father with all my strength, yet your father changed my wages ten times. God has not allowed him to harm me. If he said," 'the speckled ones will be your wages,' "then all the flocks gave birth to speckled young, and if he said," 'the streaked ones will be your wages,' "then all the flocks bore streaked young. So God has taken away your father's flocks and herds and given them to me."

"In breeding season I once had a dream in which I looked up and saw that the male goats mating with the females were streaked, speckled or spotted. The angel of God said to me in the dream, "Jacob" I answered, "here I am." And he said, "Look up and see that all the male goats mating with the flock are speckled, stripped or spotted. I have seen all that Laban has been doing to you. I am the God of Bethel where you anointed a pillar and where you made a vow to me."

Then Leah replied, "Do we still have any share in the inheritance in our father's house? Does he not regard us as foreigners? Not only has he sold us but he used up what he set aside as a bride price for us. Surely all the wealth that God has taken away from our father belongs to our children. So do whatever your God has told you to do."

Jacob told them, "last night an angel of El Shaddai came to me. He warned me that if I stayed here Laban and his sons would do me much harm. The angel told me to return to my homeland. I am ready to go."

Jacob continued, "I was 77 years old when I came here. I have been working for your father for twenty years. I am now 97. It is time for me to return to my own land. Now is an ideal time as your father and your brothers will be away from home for three weeks shearing sheep. I have started moving the herds and flocks towards Halab. They have already crossed the Balikh River. Start breaking camp as soon as you get back. I will send Levi to you with carts, oxen and donkeys to the pull carts to haul everything and camels for you to ride. Try to be packed and ready to travel by the time the sun reaches its high point the day after tomorrow." Reuben led the way back to camp.

As Reuben was leading the way back to camp, he saw his father moving towards the flocks. As soon as Reuben got to camp, he called a meeting of all the camp. Reuben told them, "Jacob has said we are to move to another camp tomorrow. Zichre and Mesha will have the carts, camels and donkeys here. Be ready to load by the time the sun is two hands high. I have ordered the oxen and carts to be here this afternoon so we can began loading the heavier items. Today you—"

"But what about the garden?" Joseph interrupted. "We have worked hard watering, weeding and hoeing it. It won't be ready to harvest for some time."

"Joseph!" Reuben scolded. "You are not to question orders from father! You and the other boys are to clean the gardening tools and get them ready to load. Then you are to help pack in any way you are told. As I started to say, today you must pack as much as possible so that we can get started before the sun reaches its high point the day after tomorrow. Levi will come to camp early the day after tomorrow so he can guide us to father."

Early the morning they were to leave, Rachel went to visit her mother. She was not intending to tell her that they were leaving for Canaan but she wanted to see her mother one last time. When she got to her mother's house, her mother was not home. Rachel sat on a camel's saddle to wait. As she was looking around the room of her childhood, she saw the household gods that she had worshipped until she married Jacob. Jacob would not allow her to worship idols. Jacob worshipped a God he called El Shaddai, also called God Almighty. He was the God of his father and his grandfather. He was the God that Jacob had worshipped by pouring oil on a stone at a place he called Bethel, which means 'the house of God'. He was the God who had given Jacob all of the property he now owned. As she looked at the silver idols of Tammuz and his sister and helpmate, Anath, she remembered that her father had spent one hundred silver rings for the idol of Tammuz and sixty for the idol of Anath. This money came from the dowry that Laban had set aside for her and Leah. Rachel also remembered how often Laban had taken a kerchief and a ram and had gone to worship with one of the temple prostitutes that served Tammuz and Anath.

Rachel remembered her father telling her the story of the god Tammuz. Nimrod married Semiramis and had a son named Tammuz. When Tammuz was a young man, he went hunting and was killed by a wild boar. His mother was distraught and built a temple to Tammuz. She told everyone that Tammuz had ascended to Baal, his father. The people came to worship Tammuz as the god of herds and flocks. Tammuz became one of the main gods of the Mesopotamia valley and of the Canaanites, the Hebrew calendar has a month named for him.

She knew that the Hittites ruled the land in which she lived. Their law said that the owner of property could give his property to anyone he chose. He would signify this by giving the family idols to that person. This was usually the oldest son but it could be to anyone. Rachel thought that by taking the idols, after Laban's death, all of his property would belong to Jacob and his children. She took the idols and hid them in her cloak and returned to her house to finish packing.

After they finished packing all the personal belongings and while the servants were loading the carts and donkeys, Leah, Rachel, Bilhah, and Zilpah, along with some servants, went to Laban's camp to say good bye to old friends and to tell them they were moving camp to be closer to the pasture Jacob wanted to use.

Laban's shepherds had been poor workers when Jacob arrived. They took the sheep and goats to the wells at noon. They liked to sit in the shade, talk and play games until evening. They did this because they were hired shepherds and did not care if the flocks increased or not and Laban was a poor supervisor. This practice stopped when Laban hired Jacob as chief shepherd. Sheep did not graze during the heat of the day. They were watered and allowed to rest until it was cooler. Laban's shepherds would stay at the well until evening. Jacob made the shepherds take the sheep back to the pasture after two hands of time when the heat had lessened and then stay until evening so the flocks could have more time to graze. With more grazing time, the sheep grew fatter, had more wool, and healthier lambs. When some of the lazy shepherds complained and would not follow his orders, Jacob fired them and hired others. When Jacob became chief shepherd, Laban had four small flocks. Now he had twenty very large flocks with a shepherd and two helpers tending each flock.

A week later, Jacob, and all his people had crossed the Euphrates along with the flocks and herds, were camped about two days from Halab. Jacob called the camp together and told them. "We have crossed the Euphrates without losing any of the animals. You did very well. Now is the time to tell you where we are going. An angel of the God I serve has told me to return to the land of my birth. We are going to Canaan."

Jacob waited for the time it takes the sun to move half a finger's width across the sky before he continued, "in two days we will be forward of Halab. We will stop and rest for a day when we get there. Those hired servants who do not want to go to Canaan may draw their pay. Those who will accompany us will get a small bonus for the trip. Anyone who is not needed to keep the flocks and herds in temporary pens will be allowed to go into town for the rest of the day. Be sure you are back at camp and ready to leave before the sun is one hand high in the morning sky the next day. That's when we start again. We will stay about two hands width of time from the edge of the desert. The way is smoother and there is enough water for us and the animals."

All the women were very excited about the prospect of going into a town as large as Halab. Rachel started the conversation "I hear that they sell beautiful material in the market. They may even have some material from a land very far toward the rising sun. I can't wait to go to the market for some new material. Joseph needs a new cloak since he has outgrown his old one."

Leah replied. "Oh! That's all you think about, fancy clothes, earrings, bracelets and necklaces. Don't you care that we are running low on supplies? We need wheat, barley, peas, flat beans, lintels and salt for the trip. Maybe I can even find some fresh fruits and vegetables. Maybe we can find some squash, black radishes or muskmelons. It will be so nice to have something fresh to cook and eat."

Bilhah joined the conversation, "If it is alright with you, Mistress Rachel, I would like to go with you. Dan needs a new pair of sandals and

Naphtali wants a new belt for his tunic. I haven't been to a town for three years. It will be so exciting to see so many markets."

The wives and servants continued talking as they prepared the evening meal. Many of the servants came to ask if they would be allowed to go into Halab. The good news was that Jacob had said that anyone who was not needed at camp could go into town. The camp soon took on a festive mood. Everyone was excited about the trip and about going into a large town.

As they were sitting around the fire after supper, Joseph spoke to his father, "Father, please tell us the about how our great-grandfather, Abraham, was called to leave Ur and travel to Canaan."

'I will start at the beginning, of how El Shaddai created the world." Jacob replied. But just as he was about to start, they looked up and saw Oohdal and a group of soldiers coming toward camp. Jacob went to meet them. When he approached, Ater placed his hands on Jacob's shoulders. They touched cheeks, Ater's left cheek to Jacob's right, and then they did the same with the other cheeks. This was the normal kiss of greeting.

Jacob told Ater, "I am very glad to see you. I am afraid of the king of Cyprus and his army. I heard they are coming down the Euphrates River."

"Yes", Ater replied. "They are a well trained army. No town has been able to stand against them. However, they are one moon's time up the Euphrates from here. We don't need to be alarmed."

"I'm happy to hear that," Jacob replied. "Have your men set up camp. I was about to tell the children how El Shaddai created the world. If you or any of your men want to listen, they would be welcome."

After Ater and his twenty-five men were settled, Jacob called the children together to tell them how the world was created. "Alright," Jacob began. "Where should I start? We will have many nights to tell the old stories so I think I should begin at the beginning of the story of how God created the world and everything in it."

Leah asked. "My Lord may the women and girls listen as you tell our history?"

"Yes," Jacob answered. "I think it would be good for them to hear the truth about God. When we live in Canaan, they will meet many people who worship false gods. In fact, any God but El Shaddai is a false god. When people know the truth, it is harder to deceive them."

Leah asked Jacob to wait until she told the girls they could sit near the fire to listen. The women would listen while they continued cleaning up.

Jacob started the story, "In the beginning God created the heavens and the earth. Now the earth was formless and empty, darkness was over the surface of the deep, and the Spirit of God was hovering over the waters."

"On the first day God created light. He knew that the humans He would create later needed light to see. God said, 'let there be light, and there was light' He called the light 'day' and the darkness 'night'. This was the first day."

"Then God caused an expanse to form between the waters that were on the earth from the waters above the earth. God called the expanse, 'sky'. He did this on the second day."

"God gathered the waters under the sky into lakes, seas and rivers. This caused the dry ground to appear. God called the dry ground, 'land'. Then God knew that we would need food so He caused the land to produce seed bearing plants and trees bearing fruit with seed. God did all this on the third day. God saw that all he had created was good."

"God created the sun to rule the day and the moon to rule the night. He set them in the sky to serve as signs to mark the seasons, months and days. God also created the stars. God put the sun, moon and stars in the sky to give light so the people he would create would have light. On the fourth day God did all this and saw that this was good."

"God said, 'let the waters have living creatures, and let birds fly through the sky. God created all the fish and other creatures in the waters, and all the birds that fly in the sky. God told then to increases in numbers and fill the waters and the sky. That was the end of the fifth day."

"On the sixth day God created all the living creatures, livestock, wild animals, and all creatures that move along the ground. Then God wanted something that could choose to worship him or ignore Him, so He created mankind in His own image and gave us free will. God set man over all His creation to maintain it and to rule over it. He set us over the livestock, the wild animals, the birds, the fish and all the sea creatures and all creatures that move along the ground. God blessed them and told them to be fruitful and increase so that they would fill the land."

Then God told them that He had given them every plant and its seed as food. He also gave the plants for food for all other animals and creatures that He had created. God saw that everything He had created was good. This happened on the sixth day of creation.

"God created the heavens and the earth in six days. God finished all His creating by the end of the sixth day. On the seventh day God rested from all the work He had been doing. God blessed the seventh day and called it holy, because he rested on the seventh day. On the seventh day we are to rest and worship God."

After Jacob finished telling how God created the earth he sent everyone to their tents, reminding them that tomorrow would be a long, hard day.

Jacob spent the night with Rachel. "When we get to Canaan and meet Esau, do you think he will be glad to see you again?" Rachel asked.

"I really think he has forgotten about how angry he felt when I left to find you." Jacob answered. "He never could remain angry with me for very long. I'm sure he has mellowed by now. He probably has large herds and flocks, and many servants of his own."

Jacob left Rachel's tent before sunrise. He was organizing his twenty shepherds for the journey. Each shepherd with their under shepherds had 100 ewes with their lambs besides the twenty or more rams in each flock. After assembling all the shepherds and herdsmen, he went over his plan. "You are all to lead your flocks and herds at the pace we call half graze. We are going to Canaan. I am going home. Anyone who does not want to go may draw his or her wages and leave with no hard feelings. I will give every shepherd and every herdsman three bronze rings besides their wages if they stay with me until we get there. Every under shepherd and helper with the herds will get one bronze ring.

The cattle will go first with the camels following them. What donkeys we are not using will follow the camels," Jacob told them. "During this weather you will need to water the camels every seven to nine days. As the weather gets hotter, you will have to water them more often. Each herdsman should carry a leather bucket to draw water for his livestock." Jacob gave the first herdsman a bag of barley cakes and a jug of water. "You haven't had breakfast yet, so you and your helpers can eat these as you are walking. Start looking for a place to camp when the sun is one hand from setting."

Jacob continued, "As soon as the cattle, camels and donkeys have started, Hezron will lead his flock first. He will lead it half way between the desert and the hill country. You will find much grazing and water there. Mamre will wait while the sun has moved the width of one finger. Then he will lead his flock one finger's width forward of Hezron's flock. Gaal will leave just after Mamre. He will lead his flock one finger's time back of Hezron.

Asher had been watching Jacob organize the shepherds. "Father," Asher said. "I don't understand how Mamre could go forward of Hezron if Hezron left first?"

Jacob laughed and told Asher, "Son, we tell directions as if you are facing the rising sun. Therefore, when I told Mamre to go forward of Hezron, I was telling him to go on the side toward the rising sun. When I said for Gaal to go in back of Hezron I meant for him to go on the side of the setting sun. If you were to go to the right you would be on the side towards the land of the Egyptians. The left would be on the side toward the land of the Hittites. Does that help?"

"Yes papa, thank you." Asher replied."

Hezron and his helpers left. In a few minutes they heard the sound of his pipes as he led his flock away from the group.

The rest of the shepherds were organized in the same way with each group of shepherds leaving one finger's time after the group ahead of them. The goats were organized the same as the sheep and departed last. As soon as Jacob had gotten all the herds and flocks organized, he went to Leah's for breakfast. Leah asked Jacob, "Will we be allowed to shop while we are in Halab?"

Jacob told her, "Yes, I am going to sell some fleeces while I am there. You can buy all that you think we will need for the trip. If you think the children need anything for the trip you should buy it for them. I should get a little over two silver rings for each fleece. I sold over a thousand fleeces in Haran before we left and I still have over a thousand left to sell. I got a little less than two silver rings for each fleece in Haran. They pay more for a fleece in Halab than in Haran."

After breakfast of bread and leben, Leah told the other wives what Jacob had said. They camped by Halab the evening of the second day.

CHAPTER 2

—— MARKETS IN HALAB ——

After a walk of two fingers time they came to Halab. While still a little way from Halab they saw a wonderful sight, the east gate of Halab. The east gate was the main entrance to Halab. It was in the form of an arch, as tall as ten men standing on each other's shoulders. All around the arch was white and black stones alternating over the top of the arch there was a smaller arch the height of five men, this arch was made of light tan rocks. Inside this arch was a two leaved polished wooden door with carvings of battle scenes, animals and their gods and goddesses. The entrance, shining in the sun, was the most beautiful sight the travelers had ever seen.

When they walked through the gate, they were in a large room with two heavy wooden doors on the opposite side. The side walls were made of rock with windows so arches could shoot arrows at enemies if they got inside the first gate. The doors were open and they could see a long straight street, longer than a person could walk in two hands of time. On both sides of the street there were booths for the sellers to show their merchandise. The booths were three stories high. The booths were grouped by product with the best on the ground floor. They didn't know there could be so many booths in the whole world. Halab was the main trading center for caravans going from Egypt to the ports that served India and also for the caravans from the great sea to the east.

Leah, Zilpah and Dinah went to the market to purchase wheat, barley, beans, chick peas, flat beans and lentils. Leah was also looking for fresh vegetables like black radishes, leeks, onions and squash. Leah had to go to several booths and bought all their available food products. Leah told the merchants, "my husband is the man that owns all those sheep, goats and other animals you have seen pastured forward of Halab. He has gone to the fleece merchants to sell about a thousand fleeces. When he gets here, he will pay you and bring carts to carry the foods." The merchants were very glad to accommodate her. Then Leah, Zilpah and Dinah went to the leather merchants and purchased twenty pairs of sandals and ten belts. Turning to Zilpah, Leah said. "With about 250 people in our camp, I know we will need several pairs of sandals and belts to replace those that are broken or lost."

Rachel and Bilhah walked through the markets. When they came to a booth that sold exotic cloth, Rachel said to Bilhah, "I want to get some beautiful cloth to make Joseph a cloak." The merchant asked, "What are you looking for? I have some very special cloth from a country far toward the rising sun. I have been told that they spin the threads from the cocoons of worms that live in mulberry trees." He took a bolt of light brown material that was very shiny and had been woven with patterns of many colors.

Rachel really liked the material. She thought it was very pretty. She told the merchant, "I'll take enough to make a full cloak for my son. How much will enough material to make a cloak for a man cost?"

"This is very costly material," the merchant replied. He measured out the material. Before he cut it, he told Rachel, "That will cost two and a half silver rings."

"No." Rachel said. "I'll give you one silver ring and five brass rings."

"This is very expensive material and it comes from far toward the rising sun. I couldn't let you have it for less than two silver rings and five brass rings and I'll give you the thread to sew it," the merchant told her.

"That's still too high." Rachel told him. "I'll give you one silver rings and seven brass rings."

"My wife will complain that I sold it so cheaply, but I'll let you have the material and the thread for two silver rings." he said.

"I'll take it," Rachel told him.

With the dealing completed, she laid two silver rings on the counter. The merchant cut the material, folded it and handed it to Rachel.

Bilhah told Rachel, "Mistress, Dan lost his knife crossing the river when he saved that small herd of goats. May we go to the bronze merchants and get a new knife for him?"

"Yes." Rachel replied. "I think Naphtali is also old enough to have a small knife. I think I'll get a knife for Joseph while we are here".

After walking past several booths in the market, they came to the area where bronze items were sold. The first booth they came to had many cheap knives. When Rachel and Bilhah looked at them they decided they were not good quality so they went on. At the third booth they saw knives they liked. This booth had many beautiful bronze knives with goat skin sheaths.

Rachel liked the looks of one of the knives. It had a silver looking blade with stones set in the handle. "I would like to see that knife" she said.

The merchant replied, "The lady has a very good eye for fine knives. This knife is made of iron, a new material that is much stronger than bronze. Only the metal workers in Hittite know the secret of iron. That knife was made by one of the finest armories in all of Hittite. It has a special iron blade with stones set into the handle. It is worth one gold and five silver rings."

Rachel answered, "I want two more knives. Bilhah, which knives do you want for your sons?"

Bilhah pointed to a bronze knife with a few stones set in the handle. "May I get that one for Dan?" She asked, "Could I get that smaller bronze knife for Naphtali?"

"How much is the price of these three knives and their sheaths?" Rachel asked the merchant.

"I need two gold rings and seven silver rings," he replied.

Rachel told him, "I'm tired of haggling over prices. I'll give you two gold rings and no more. I'm sure another merchant would want my money." Then she turned to Bilhah and started talking about getting back to the carts. The merchant looked at her and decided she wasn't bluffing.

"My wife will most likely skin me alive for selling my knives so cheaply but you drive a hard bargain. I'll take your offer," he agreed. He picked up the three knives and their sheaths. When Rachel laid the two gold rings on the counter, he picked them up and looked then over carefully. He weighed them in his hand, and being satisfied they were real, he handed her the knives.

Leaving the bronze area, they looked at booths in the market until they left to go back to the camp. They bought some bracelets for themselves and a necklace for Rachel. When they got back to camp, Leah and her servants had lunch ready.

They had baked bread and made a thick soup out of lentils boiled with a goat leg. They made a salad of endives, leaf chicory, mallows and caraway roots and seasoned with cumin. Leah had her servants spread many tanned hides around the eating area. A pot of the goat meat and a pot of the lentil stew, a bowl of salad and a stack of bread were on each skin.

Jacob arrived then and he was in very good spirits. He had gotten two silver rings and four brass rings for each fleece. Leah told him that he would need to take three carts into the market to pick up the supplies she had ordered.

Everyone found a place to sit on one of the hides. After Jacob gave the blessing, they started to eat. They tore the bread into pieces and folded it so that it made a scoop. Then they picked up a piece of meat or scooped out some of the lentil stew with the bread. Everyone sitting on a hide ate from the same dish. Though they were in a festive mood, this meal was eaten in silence as were most meals.

When the meal was finished, Jacob asked, "Is everyone through shopping?" When there was no reply, he continued, "Leah, Zilpah and I will ride in the carts to get the supplies Leah has ordered. The rest of you will break camp so you will have three hands of time to travel a little before sunset. Rachel, Bilhah and the children may ride in carts. Make camp about one finger's time before sunset. Build a large fire so Leah and I will be able to find you." Having said that, he, Leah and Zilpah got into the carts and the men led the oxen toward town.

Rachel and Bilhah gave the knives to the boys. Joseph was overjoyed with his fancy knife. Dan and Naphtali started making fun of Joseph and his fancy knife. Rachel interceded for Joseph and told Bilhah's two boys, "That knife is just right for the leader's favorite son."

Bilhah told her boys to go help with the packing. Rachel told everyone to start packing. The packing had to be done quickly so that they could leave within two fingers time. Tent pegs were quickly pulled, the tents rolled and put into a cart. The tent poles were tied together with their tents and placed in the carts.

The other supplies were either placed in carts or tied on the backs of camels or donkeys. They had not packed a camp for some time so the packing went slower than expected. They got moving a little late but they made good time without the livestock.

As Jacob had told them, they stopped one hand of time before sunset and set up camp. The boys were sent out to find wood for the fire and the girls were put to the task of grinding grain for the evening meal. The meal was a simple one. The women took the ground barley, added water and baked the bread on heated stones. One of the slave girls had found some savory herbs growing along their way so they had picked some. The women put up a tripod and hung a leather bag of water on it. When the water began to seep through the leather and make beads on the outside of the bag, the bag was moved over the fire. As long as water seeped through the bag it would not burn. When the water was almost to boil, the herbs were thrown in. After the tea steeped for a while, everyone took their cup and got a hot refreshing drink. Rachel, Bilhah and Jacob's children had some honey in their drink.

About two hands of time after sunset, Jacob and the three carts rolled in. Jacob said, "I'm sure glad you made a big fire. We had passed the camp, but when we topped that hill just back of here one of the men saw your fire."

Bread and drink was brought for them. As he was finishing his meal, Jacob said, "We need to get to bed soon. We will be getting up before sunrise. I want to be packed and moving in three fingers time." He told his servant, "Don't put up my tent tonight. I am going to sleep in Leah's tent."

The campers were up long before daylight. They ate a hurried breakfast of leftover barley bread. While the fire was hot, the women put water on to boil. Into the water they added some coarse ground barley. The grain boiled while they finished packing. The gruel was put in large jars. It would be eaten cold with barley bread when the sun was overhead. The group made good time without the animals. They continued traveling while eating the bread and gruel. As they traveled, the children picked up wood and dried animal dung and put it in a cart so they could build fires when they stopped. They came to a small hill about one hands time before sundown. They stopped for the night. A small stream at the bottom of the hill gave them water.

The campers were up early the next morning and were on their way almost immediately. They ate a cold breakfast of barley bread as they loaded the tents. Jacob set the course slightly toward the rising sun. Just after the sun passed its highest point, Jacob saw where the animals had passed.

The grass was chewed short and scat was everywhere. By looking at some of the scat, Jacob could tell that they were about one hands time behind the goats. He told everyone, "The last flock passed through here about one hands time ago. We should overtake the herds and flocks long before sundown. As soon as we overtake the leading herd, we will stop and set up camp. Some of the young men will go to watch the herds and flocks so that the herders and shepherds can come in, have a meal and relax for a short time."

Just as Jacob had estimated, his group reached the first herd about one and one half hands time before sunset. The word was passed to stop and let the flocks and herds graze and rest. Everyone who could be spared helped build the temporary pens. These pens were made by placing brush in a circle with an opening so the animals could go in and out. The shepherd would lay in the opening to keep the predators from getting to the animals.

The herdsmen and shepherds were glad to see the help arriving and to get to come to the main camp for a meal. One of the shepherds had a ram that had gone lame. Jacob had it dressed and the women boiled to for the evening meal.

While it was boiling, the women added lentils, leeks, a little garlic and wild onions and enough cracked grain to the broth to make a stew and seasoned it with caraway seeds and endives. The women spread hides around and placed pots of meat and soup and stacks of fresh barley bread on each hide. Jacob stood and raised his hands toward the heavens and prayed. "Oh God of Abraham, and fear of my father, Isaac, I thank you that you have brought us safely this far. I ask You to bless this meal and protect us for the rest of our journey. Amen."

The next evening as Jacob and Ater were talking, Oohdal came over to them and said. "Master, one of the herdsmen and one of the shepherds has seen a band of men watching the herds and flocks for the past two days. They think they may be from a tribe of Bedouin raiders that live in this area. They think we may be attacked soon."

Ater responded. "I think my men will become shepherds and herdsmen tonight. I will leave sergeant Samon, my second in command, with four men to stay with your camp. I have not seen any danger to your camp. If any trouble comes, Samon and his men will lead the attack. You and your men will follow. Have your men take orders from Samon. My men and I will leave after it gets dark. The raiders will most likely have someone watching the herds. It is my opinion that they will attack one of the forward flocks of goats or one of the forward herds of camels. The only use Bedouins have for sheep or cattle is to steal them and take them to a market. I will put two of my men with each of the forward herds. One man will be put with each of the forward flocks. Two men will scout the area to find their camp. Then they will watch for any activity that could mean an attack is coming. We have a system of wolf songs that we use to communicate. I have found that the enemy does not notice wolf songs and a wolf song carries a great distance. The two scouts will start the attack from the rear. They will probably take down four to six raiders before they are noticed. By then the ones coming from the other herds and flocks will be there to attack from the sides. The rest of my men and I will be in position to make a frontal attack with our slings. If need be, we will finish with swords."

After speaking and laying out his plan, Ater left to get his men ready. No one saw or heard them leave. Jacob sent a message to the herders not to get involved. If an attack comes, leave the animals and run, the message said.

Two hours after dawn the next morning, Ater and his men heard a wolf song. It told them the attack would be on the second forward herd of camels, and would start in two fingers time. The wolf song was passed up and down the flocks and herds. Ater and his men lay down and in their light brown cloaks and they were almost invisible. Ater watched until he could clearly see fifteen men on camels. When they were a little way in front of him, he gave a wolf song and the two scouts started slinging stones. They each threw three stones. Five attackers were knocked off their camels before the leader noticed anything was wrong. When the leader turned to face the two men, he heard another wolf song and men appeared on both sides slinging stones with deadly accuracy. Ater and the men with him were close enough to sling stones. In very little time all the attackers were knocked down. Ater's men went through the raiders and killed any who remained alive.

Ater called his men together. "You may take anything you want as spoils of war," he said.

One of the scouts spoke. "Captain, if you want spoils, their camp is about two hands time from here. There are camels, donkeys, tents and women."

Ater replied. "Well men, what are you waiting for, let's get more spoils."

Ater's men caught the camels and mounted them. Ten had to ride double. They had taken the cloaks and turbans from the attackers and put them on so they would not be noticed as quickly. Ater and his men were in the center of the camp before anyone noticed that they were not their men. Two older men had been left to guard the camp. They were quickly killed. Ater called the camp together and said to them. "We have killed all your men when they came to steal our camels. You and all of this camp now belong to us. You will break camp. You may use the camels and donkeys to transport your tents and supplies. My men will help you."

The women had all been taken in raids and had been ill used by the Bedouins so they were not sad to know the raiders were dead. They showed Ater where the wine and gold was hidden. The men began drinking the wine. The women started preparing a meal. They wanted to start their new life on a positive note. Whenever one of the women saw a man looking at her, she would lead him into her tent. Many lasting relationships began that morning, and Ater's camp increased by seventeen women, many children and much goods. One of the women came to Ater and said, "My son and some other boys are keeping a flock of the sheep in the land just past the desert. Mydul and his men stole them from many shepherds. He intended to take them to market, but when he saw your camels, he decided to take some of your camels to market with them. Can we get our sons when you get to the sheep?" "Yes," Ater told her, "you may have your sons, but we will take the sheep as spoils of war."

Oohdal sent one of his young men to report the outcome to Jacob. Jacob had broken camp and was beyond where he had camped when the young man caught up with him. When Jacob saw the man running toward them, he stopped to wait for him. The courier was out of breath and tired from running. Jacob ordered food and drink brought to him.

While waiting for the food, the young man blurted out, "Ater whipped them fast and good, my Lord." Jacob told him to wait until he had rested and eaten before continuing. The rest of the camp wanted to hear the news so they crowded around.

After a short rest, the courier continued with a complete account of the short battle. "Yes my Lord, Ater's plan worked like magic. Fifteen raiders were seen riding up on camels when all of a sudden those in back started falling from their camels. One of the raiders yelled that something was wrong. As the leader turned to look, Ater gave a wolf song and the soldiers on both sides started slinging stones. Ater and his group stood up and started slinging stones. Boy! Could they sling stones fast and hard! The stones they threw were about as big as my fist! In the blink of an eye, all the raiders were down. Ater's men quickly finished off the ones that were still alive. Then they put on the turbans and cloaks from the raiders and mounted the camels and rode off. That's all I saw. That's when Oohdal sent me to you."

Jacob was pleased that the threat to his camels was over. He told the courier to rest for one hands time and then to return to Ater to inform him where Jacob would be camping that night.

Jacob's camp stopped a little early that night. As the sun was tipping over the western horizon, a band of men riding camels came into view. Samon, his four men and twenty of Jacob's men formed up between the incoming camels and the camp. When the band got a little closer, they could see that women and children were leading camels and donkeys loaded with supplies. Within the time it took the sun to drop half way past the horizon, Jacob recognized Ater in the lead. Then he remembered the courier telling him about the camels. As Jacob reached them, Ater got off a camel and they greeted each other with a kiss. Ater was quick to tell Jacob about the battle and all the spoils they had gotten. He told Jacob about the women and how they had been introduced to his men. He then told Jacob about all the sheep, camels and donkeys, the gold and silver and supplies that he had taken as spoils. Ater finished by saying. "Of course, all these spoils belong to you."

Jacob answered. "You and you men deserve the spoils. God has given me all I need. You and your men divide the spoils. Only be sure to give the men who stayed here an equal share."

"Yes," Ater replied. "We always divide the spoils equally, but this time the men who went with me have selected the women they want. Samon will get his pick of the two women who are left if he wants one. The gold, silver, animals and supplies will be divided as you said."

Jacob asked Ater and his men to eat with them. They were all invited including the new women and children. They had all gathered for the meal when Jacob called for everyone's attention, "for the benefit of the newcomers I want to tell you that we serve the one true God, El Shaddai. He tells us to be kind and respectful to everyone. I want you to know that we don't care about your past. We accept you as friends of Captain Ater and his men. You are welcome to walk freely about our camp and make friends with us."

During the meal one of Leah's servants came running up to her along with another woman. "Mistress Leah, Mistress Leah! This is my sister. She was kidnapped five years ago. We didn't think we would ever see her again but here she is! Her name is Noma."

"It's good to meet you, Noma." Leah replied.

"I'm so happy that the soldiers killed all those raiders. They kidnapped me and two of my friends. They were very cruel men. They killed one of my friends in a terrible way because she tried to run away. They made us watch as a lesson to all of us."

"That's terrible." Leah said. "I hope your life gets better now."

"I think it will. I have become the wife of a very good man. He has already given me more than my previous man did. See the gold bracelets and nose rings he has given me. I think he will be a good mate for me." The two women went away talking happily.

Ater came over to Jacob and said. "I want to show you how responsive my men are, and to show you how quickly they can meet a threat. I would like for you and some of your men to try to sneak into my camp before sunup tomorrow morning. Don't tell me when or from which way you will come."

Jacob agreed, "That will give me an opportunity to see for myself if what I have heard about you and your men is true."

Jacob invited Ater to eat with him. Jacob asked Ater how the training of his men was progressing. Ater replied, "Most of them are learning very well but three seem to resent me telling them how to fight as an army."

Jacob told Ater, "Send them back to camp next time they disobey or do not follow your instructions."

Ater said, "I have the men standing by." He motioned for the three men to come to him. He told Jacob, "These are the three men who are disrupting training."

Jacob looked sternly at them. He recognized them as recent hires. He hadn't had time to properly train them. Jacob inquired of them, "Do you want to continue working for me?"

Mibsam replied, "Yes my Lord, I like working for you. You treat us fairly."

Another one spoke up, "yes my Lord, my brother and I feel the same way. If you will give us another chance, we will do all we can to follow the Captain's orders."

Jacob turned to Ater, "do you want to give them another chance or do you want me to fire them?"

Ater looked at them before replying, 'Well, Jacob, two of them would make good soldiers if they would follow orders and work with the rest as a team."

Mibsam answered Ater. "If you please my Lord, give us another chance. I have been a soldier. I was under Captain Seggre for five years. He spoke very highly of a Captain of the King's guard, a Captain Ater. Would you be that Captain Ater?"

Ater replied, "I think so, Captain Seggre and I were sergeants in the same company before we became officers. He is a very capable officer."

"I'm very sorry I didn't know who you were." Mibsam said. "If you give us another chance, I will prove my ability to you. I was a corporal in Seggre's company. I didn't like the place we were stationed so as soon as my time was up I drew my wages and went to Haran looking for work."

Jacob told Ater, "If it is alright with you, we will give them another chance. If they disobey one more time, you can fire them." Jacob dismissed the three men, Ater stayed for the evening meal.

Very early next morning, about three hands time before sunup, Jacob and five of his men left camp. They left on the opposite side of camp from Ater's camp. They walked in a circle around both camps. After walking two finger's time they came to a dry stream bed that led past Ater's camp. They walked down the stream bed. Looking from the top of a small hill they could see the embers of Ater's camp. Telling his men to be very quiet, Jacob led them down the stream bed until they were close to Ater's camp. They had just cleared the stream banks when they heard a wolf song. Before the sound of the wolf song stopped, twenty-four men were standing in formation with shields and swords. Sergeant Samon called out "Stop and announce yourself, whether you be friend or enemy."

Jacob and his men were taken completely by surprise by the suddenness of the action and the firmness of the challenge. He called out, "It is Jacob and five of his men."

The sergeant called out, "Come forward and be recognized, Jacob and your men."

Ater came into the formation. He called to Jacob, "Come in Jacob. How did my men respond?" He then called to the guard. "How long ago did you see them?"

The guard answered, "I saw them when they went up that small hill to look us over. I didn't give the alarm until they came over the bank toward us."

Jacob told Ater and his men that he was very impressed and pleased with the response to his coming into camp unannounced. Ater told his men to return to bed. Jacob and his men went back to camp to sleep.

The next morning the camp was up and on the way very early. The next ten days passed quickly as they developed a routine. Up early, eat a quick breakfast, eat a cold lunch, and travel until evening.

CHAPTER 3

THE PURSUIT

That year Laban was going to start by shearing the largest of his flocks. His sons Abzug, Lod and Miphkad were assisting with the shearing of the other flocks. Laban had learned that the hired shearers could not be trusted. They would steal some of the fleeces if they were not watched.

Hodevah was to stay in camp to relay messages. The flocks were kept a hand of time apart and the shearing would take about three weeks. Laban, his three sons and some of the servants would move from flock to flock to do the shearing. Laban had been shearing for over half a moon when he saw Hodevah running toward him as if he had important information. As he ran up, Laban said, "Stand quietly and catch your breath while I finish shearing this sheep. Then you can tell me why you are here."

Hodevah stood quietly while Laban finished that sheep. Then Hodevah told Laban, "Jacob has left. He has broken camp. He has moved his flocks and herds across the Euphrates River. They are going toward Egypt as fast as the animals can travel."

"How do you know this?" Laban asked.

"Three days ago I went to Jacob's camp to see if I could get a handle for a hoe that had broken. All the pens were empty, everything was gone, and nothing remained! Then two days later a caravan of traders, on their way to the Persian Gulf, stopped by for some water. They said a week earlier they had seen a man with several herds of sheep, goats, camels and donkeys traveling toward Egypt as fast as they could go. They said that the man had four wives and eleven sons. The man told them they were going home to Canaan. I came as fast as I could."

"You did well my son," Laban replied. "We are almost through shearing. We have been at it for over a half of a moon. Stay with me tonight and tomorrow I will send you to your brothers. I will tell you where they are. You are to tell them to finish shearing as quickly as possible. If they are not through in five days, they are to load the fleeces on carts and take them to our camp. We will have to trust the hired shearers to finish."

Laban and his sons finished shearing in four days and returned home to celebrate. When Laban entered his house, he saw that his idols were gone. He thought that Jacob or one of his men had stolen them. He called his relatives and friends together. He told them that one of Jacobs's people had stolen his gods. The group decided to prepare that day and leave early the next morning. They could easily overtake Jacob since he had to travel slowly with the flocks and herds. Next morning, a little later than expected, they took off riding camels. They took camels and donkeys to carry the tents and other supplies. There were sixty in the group, besides Laban; there were nineteen of Laban's relativities, ten friends and thirty servants.

Laban set a fast pace. That day they crossed the Balikh River and were almost to the Euphrates. Two days later they had crossed the Euphrates and were at Halab. Laban wanted to keep going but most of his relatives wanted to spend the day in town. They pitched their tents and the men went into town. They went to a tavern to drink beer and enjoy some time with the women.

As they entered the tavern they saw some women grinding barley. While they were watching the process, the woman that ran the tavern came to them. "Are you here to drink beer or just to watch my women make beer?" she inquired.

. Zerea, one of Laban's older relatives answered her, "we are here to drink all of your beer and try some of your women but we are interested in how you make beer. Do you make it the same way as the women in Haran?"

If you will take that long table I will bring you three jugs of beer and our special beer mugs. One jug of beer is two silver rings. One jug will fill twelve mugs. I will send some women over for you," the owner told them.

The beer mugs were different than most mugs. The handle was on the back of the mug. This allowed the drinker to pick up the mug and pour the beer directly into his mouth from the spout. The spout had sides that slanted down from the mug but no top. At the back of the spout small holes had been drilled in the mug to allow the beer to flow through and to strain out pieces that were left from the beer making process.

The men were on their third jug of beer when the owner came over, "If you fellows are interested in how I make my beer, I will tell you. First we soak barley until it starts to sprout. That's called malting the grain. Then we dry the malted grain and when it is dry we grind it to flour to make loaves. After the loaves are baked we soak them until they melt into the water. This is called the wort. We add yeast, dates, figs, pomegranate juice or honey to sweeten the wort. The wort is heated to boiling and boiled for half a hand of time. When it has cooled we place it in jars for three days. We have special stoppers for the beer jars. The stoppers have a small hole in the center to let it breath. While the wort is working, it bubbles. We place a cloth over the stopper to keep out dust. The beer you are drinking was made three days ago. Beer will not keep very long. So every day we make only what we will sell in three or four days."

The men had finished their fourth jug of beer and were feeling it. The women were encouraging them. The women were leading any of the men that wanted to go with them into their sleeping areas. Each woman charged two silver rings. It was dark when they left the tavern. They staggered through the streets. It was nearly morning when they finally reached camp. They slept until late afternoon. When they awoke, it was too late to pack and leave. They vowed to get an early start the next day.

One of Leah's servants came to her and said, "Mistress, I have something terrible to tell you." "Well," Leah said harshly, "Then tell me!"

The servant continued, "This afternoon my sister, Noma, came to tell me that the older boy of the leader of that gang of raiders has left. He told some of the younger children that he was going to tell one of his uncles about his father being killed. I'm afraid this will lead to a blood feud between my master and the tribe of Bedouins."

"I'll send you to Jacob and Ater so you can explain the problem to them," Leah told the woman. Then she called one of her young men and sent him with a message. When he came to Jacob and Ater, the servant shared the information. Jacob said, "Bring Noma to me."

In less than one fingers time they were back. Jacob asked Noma, "how far is it to the camp of the boy's uncle, and how many men will he have?"

"The tribe had four clans," Noma began. "The one that tried to steal your camels was the smallest. Each clan has about as many more men as the fingers on two or three hands. It will take at least five days for the boy to reach the closest camp."

"Thank you, Noma. If you can think of anything else that might help us, you may come directly to me or to Captain Ater," Jacob told her.

Jacob and Ater sat in front of Jacob's tent to discuss this problem. Ater told Jacob, "If they have that many men, we could be facing s many as fifteen hands of warriors. I will need all of your men to defeat a group that large."

"You will have them," Jacob assured him. "I will send untrained men to handle the supplies and tents so that you and the soldiers can concentrate on fighting. How long do you think it will be before they arrive?"

Nine days later Oohdal sent one of his helpers to Jacob to tell him that he and some of the other shepherds had seen a dust cloud about two hands of time from the herds and flocks. "He sent me to look at them," the young man started. "I saw five or six double hands of Bedouins on camels. I stayed out of their sight."

Jacob sent for Ater and told him the story. Ater said, "It looks like they got here a day or two early. We will need to meet this threat head on. I will take my men and yours and we will talk to these fellows."

Jacob sent for the fifty men Ater had been training. He told them about the raiders that were riding parallel to the flocks and herds.

Ater turned to the man who had been a corporal for his friend Seggre. He said, "Mibsam, you have had battle experience, so you will be the sergeant in charge of Jacob's men. I will tell you of my battle plan when we see what we are up against. Be ready to march when the sun has moved the width of two fingers. I will bring my men through here at that time. You are to fall in behind us. I will set a fast pace. Try to keep up with my men!"

At the appointed time Ater and his men marched through the camp. As soon as Mibsam and Jacob's men got in line, they left at a trot. As soon as they cleared the camp, Ater picked up the pace to a fast trot. After about one hand's time, Mibsam and Jacob's men started falling behind. Ater called a short rest stop. He came back to Mibsam and said, "I am going to pick up the pace for my men. You and your men can follow at a slower pace. I want to get there before the sun goes down so I can see where this dust cloud is and which way it is moving. You should be able to follow our tracks. Get there as quickly as possible without tiring the men too much." With that he and his men left at a fast trot.

Mibsam and Jacob's men got to the first forward herd of camels about two hands of time after Ater. Ater was nowhere to be seen. The herdsman told Mibsam to wait with the herd until Ater returned. When the sun came up, Mibsam saw Ater and his men sleeping about a stone's throw from the herd. He hadn't heard them arrive during the night.

Ater called all the men together and told them, "We went out to see the raiders. They seem to be three bands joined loosely together. The three leaders look like they have the same father. They set up three separate camps with very little talking between the camps. The leaders got together for a meeting. There was a lot of disagreement between the brothers. It appeared that the youngest didn't want to continue with the revenge. The middle brother was not as ready to continue as the elder brother. If the oldest brother was taken out, I think the other two would be easily discouraged. Here is my plan. We will get ahead of them and make a "V" shaped formation. Two men and I will sit in their path with our hoods over our heads so that from a distance we will look like large rocks. When they get within a stone's throw, I will stand and challenge the oldest brother to a fight. The rest of you will stretch out about two arms lengths apart. You will lay on the sand with your light brown cloaks covering you so you will not be easily noticed. Jacob's men will be placed with two between each of my men. I tell my men what to do by wolf song. Follow the lead of my men and do what they tell you to do.

They took off at a fast trot at an angle that would lead them to a place in front of the raiders. They arrived at a place that Ater thought would put them in the path of the raiders. Ater deployed his men as he had told them. In about two fingers time, they could see the dust cloud from the camels coming towards them. Ater and two of his men sat on the ground with their hoods over their heads. The oldest brother saw what he thought was three rocks in front of them. His other two brothers were riding beside him. He said to his brothers," I don't remember that rock formation, do you?"

"Neither do I," the youngest replied.

"I don't either, but you know how the wind blows sand away and rocks appear," the other brother said.

"Well I think they would be a good place to rest. We could sit upon them for a drink," the oldest replied.

They went on talking until they were a stone's throw from the rocks. Suddenly, one of the rocks turned into a man. The leaders believed in magic. They thought that the stone changed into a man by magic. Ater held up his hand for the leaders to stop.

"Where are you going and whom do you seek?" Ater asked them."

"We will not tell you where we are going and whom we seek," the oldest brother answered.

Ater replied, "I know where you are going and I am the man you seek. I am the man who killed your brother. You are seeking revenge. Get off your camel and fight me for that revenge if you are man enough."

The three brothers got off their camels and started toward Ater. The rocks on either side of Ater stood up. Ater and his two men dropped their cloaks and stood in their uniforms. They had swords drawn and shields ready.

Ater sang a wolf song and all his men stood, and took a position within easy stone's throw. Ater called to the rest of the raiders. "This fight is between your leaders and us. It was their brother I killed. If anyone of you gets off your camel, my men will believe that you will attack. You will be killed by their slings or by their swords. After we kill all of you, we will backtrack to your camps and take all your women, children and everything you have as spoils of war. You are to sit still until your leaders kill us or we kill them. If you understand, raise your right hand." All the raiders raised their hands.

The three brothers were very angry at what Ater had said. They pulled swords from their sheaths and came forward to engage Ater and the other two men. The leaders had never met a man they could not make back down or beat in an unfair fight.

Ater and his men knew that their opponents were not in condition for a long sword fight so they went on the defensive. They let the three leaders swing their swords all they wanted. They caught the blows on their shield or on their iron swords. After less than half a finger's time the leaders were winded and breathing with their mouths open. Ater watched for a sideways swing from his opponent. When it came, he pushed the sword farther to the side, and raised his sword to the height of his opponent's mouth. Then with a thrust he drove his sword into his opponent's mouth so hard that the point came out the back of his neck. This separated the spinal cord. The oldest brother was dead before he hit the ground. Seeing Ater kill his opponent let the other two soldiers know it was time to kill theirs.

The soldier on Ater's right pushed his opponent's sword to the side and shoved his own sword into the stomach of his opponent. The soldier on Ater's left, took a blow on his shield, and then spun around and struck his opponent's neck so hard with his sword the man's head was severed from his body.

The rest of the raiders were amazed to see their leaders killed so easily. They didn't know what to do. Ater called to them, "You can stay and fight and be killed or you can turn around and go back to your families. The choice is yours. We do not want to kill you but if you do not leave, we will. I will tell my men to draw back to give you room to turn around. If you do not turn around, I will tell my men to attack."

Ater gave a wolf song and the men went back about a stone's throw. The raiders paused for a moment. Then they turned around and left as fast as the camels could run. Ater assigned three of his men to follow them for two days.

When Ater and the men returned, they told Jacob and the others about the fight. Jacob was pleased that Ater did not have to kill all the raiders. Jacob's God had said that life was in the blood. Therefore Jacob hated for any blood to be spilled needlessly.

Jacob set a fast pace; he was fourteen days into the trip before Laban left Halab. On the tenth evening after leaving Halab, Jacob stopped early to give the animals more time to rest and graze. Everyone was relaxing and enjoying the leisure time. Leah came to Jacob and said. "The children would like to hear another story about the beginning of our people."

As soon as supper was over, Jacob called all the children together. The adults that were not working also came to listen.

Jacob began the story, "God formed the man from dust of the ground and breathed into his nostrils the breath of life and the man became a living being."

"God planted a garden in the east, in Eden, and there He put the man he had formed. God made all kinds of trees grow out of the ground, trees that were pleasing to the eye and trees that were good for food. In the middle of the garden were the tree of life and the tree of knowledge of good and evil."

"God took the man and put him in the Garden of Eden to work it and take care of it. God commanded the man, 'you are free to eat from any tree in the garden, but you must not eat from the tree of knowledge of good and evil, for when you eat of it you will surely die.'"

"God said," 'it is not good for man to be alone, I will make a helper for him.'"

"Before God made a helper for Adam, He had Adam name all the animals. Whatever Adam called an animal that was his name. Adam knew that God wanted him to have a helper. He kept looking at all the animals that God sent to him. When an orangutan came swinging down toward him, Adam thought, could this be my helper? Next a hippopotamus lumbered by and again Adam wondered if that could be his helper. Finally all the animals were named."

"But no helper was found for Adam. God caused the man to fall into a deep sleep, and while he was sleeping, He took one of the man's ribs and closed up the place with flesh. God made a woman out of the rib he had taken from the man, and He brought her to the man. God used a rib as He wanted her to be equal with Adam and stand beside him."

"The man said, 'this is now bone of my bones and flesh of my flesh; she shall be called 'woman,' for she was taken out of man."

"For this reason a man will leave his father and his mother and be united to his wife, and they shall be one flesh. The man and his wife were both naked, but they felt no shame."

"Now the serpent was craftier than any of the other wild animals the Lord God had made. He said to the woman, 'Did God really say, you must not eat from any tree in the garden?'

"The woman said to the serpent," 'We may eat from the trees in the garden, but God did say, You must not eat fruit from the tree that is in the middle of the garden, and you must not touch it, or you will die.'"

'You will not surely die,' "the serpent said to the woman." 'For God knows that when you eat from this tree your eyes will be opened, and you will be like God, knowing good from evil.'"

"When the woman saw that the fruit of the tree was good for food and pleasing to the eye and also desirable for gaining knowledge, she picked one and took a bite. She also gave one to her husband, who was with her, and he ate it. Then the eyes of both of them were opened and they realized that they were naked. They sewed fig leaves together and made coverings for themselves."

"Then the man and the woman heard the sound of God walking in the garden in the cool of the evening and they hid among the trees of the garden. But the Lord God called to the man," 'Where are you?'

"He answered," 'I heard You in the garden, and I was afraid because I was naked, so I hid.'"

"And God said," 'Who told you that you were naked? Have you eaten from the tree that I commanded you not to eat from?'"

"The man blamed the woman," 'The woman you put here with me, she gave me some fruit from the tree, and I ate.'"

"Then the Lord God said to the woman," 'What is this you have done? '"

"The woman blamed the serpent," 'the serpent deceived me, and I ate.'"

"God cursed the serpent." Because you have done this, cursed are you above all the livestock and all the wild animals! You will crawl on your belly and you will eat dust all the days of your life. And I will put enmity between you and the woman, and between your offspring and hers; he will crush your head, and you will strike his heel.' "

"To the woman he said," 'I will greatly increase your pains in childbearing, with pain you will give birth to children. Your desire will be for your husband and he will rule over you.'"

"And to Adam He said," 'Because you have listened to your wife and ate from the tree about which I commanded. You must not eat of it. Cursed is the ground because of you. Through painful toil you will eat of it all the days of your life. It will produce thorns and thistles for you. You will eat the plants of the field. By the sweat of your brow you will eat your food until you return to the ground since from it you were taken, for dust you are and to dust you will return.'"

"Adam named his wife Eve, because she was the mother of all living."

"The Lord God made garments of skin for Adam and his wife and clothed them. And the Lord God said," 'The man has now became like one of us, knowing good from evil. He must not be allowed to reach out his hand and take also from the tree of life and eat, and live forever.' "So the Lord God banished them from the garden of Eden to work the ground from which they had been taken. After He drove them out of the Garden of Eden, He put cherubim and a flaming sword flashing back and forth to guard the way to the tree of life."

"Adam lay with his wife Eve and she became pregnant and gave birth to Cain. She said, 'With the help of the Lord I have brought forth a man.' Later she gave birth to his brother, Abel."

"Now Abel kept flocks, and Cain worked the soil. In the course of time Cain brought some of the fruits of the soil as an offering to the Lord. But Abel brought fat portions from some of the first born or his flock. The Lord looked with favor on Abel and his offering, but on Cain and his offering He did not look with favor. So Cain was very angry, and his face was downcast."

"God said to Cain, 'Why are you angry? And why is your face downcast? If you do what is right will you not be accepted? But if you do not do what is right, sin is crouching at your door, it desires to have you, but you must master it.'"

"Now Cain said to his brother Abel, 'let's go out into the field,' and while they were in the field Cain picked up a big rock and with it he attacked his brother Abel and killed him."

"Then the Lord God said to Cain, 'where is your brother, Abel?' "
'I don't know,' he replied. 'Am I my brother's keeper?'"

"The Lord said, 'What have you done? Listen! Your brother's blood cries out to me from the ground. Now you are under a curse and driven from the ground that opened its mouth to receive your brother's blood from your hand. When you work the ground, it will no longer yield its crops to you. You will be a restless wanderer on the earth.'"

"Cain said to the Lord, 'My punishment is more than I can bear. Today You are driving me from the land, and I will be hidden from Your presence I will be a restless wanderer on the earth, and whoever finds me will kill me.'"

"'I will not allow anyone to kill you,' God said to Cain. 'If anyone harms you I will punish that person seven times harder than they harmed you. I will put a mark on your back, a red mark like a lions paw, and I will cause you to learn the trade of an armorer. No one will kill an armorer so you will be safe.'"

"Cain went to the land of Nod, east of Eden, and lived many years."

"Adam slept with Eve again and she had another son. She named him Seth. We are of Seth's line."

Jacob finished this part of the story and sent them to bed. The next ten days were all the same. Everyone would get up before sunrise, eat a quick breakfast, travel until the sun was at its highest and eat a cold lunch as they traveled. The travelers would stop just before sunset and set up a hurried camp. Sometimes Jacob would tell about the olden days. He told them about the longevity of their ancestors. He said. Adam lived 930 years, his son Seth lived 912 years, Methusela, the eighth generation from Adam lived 969 years. He lived longer that anyone. Methuselah's grandson Noah was 600 when the great flood came. He promised to tell them about Noah and the great flood."

Three days later and after what seemed like an eternity to the travelers, Jacob called the camp together. "We have been on our way one turning of the moon, less the fingers on one hand," he told them. "We are camped a short distance from Mizpah. Tomorrow Leah and I will go into town to get more supplies. If you need or want anything, tell Leah or me and we will try to get it for you. We will reach the land of Canaan in a few more days. Then we will travel slower and let the flocks and herds graze longer."

That evening Jacob told the children about Noah. "The people between Seth and Noah lived to be very old, and they became very evil and wicked. God saw that the people had become very wicked; only Noah was blameless, a righteous man. When Noah was over 500 years old he had three sons, named Shem, Ham and Japheth. Japheth was born to Noah and his wife, Na'amah, the sister of Tubal Cain, when Noah was 503. Shem was born when Noah was 506 and Ham was born when Noah was 510"

"The earth and everyone in it except Noah, and his sons, and their wives were very wicked and no longer followed Gods laws. The earth was corrupt and full of violence. God told Noah, 'I am going to kill all living on the earth, and everything that has the breath of life will die.'"

"God told Noah 'you are to make an ark. Make it 450 feet long, 75 feet wide and 45 feet high. Make it with three floors, a lower, middle and an upper. On the upper floor, you are to finish it to within eighteen inches of the top and put windows in it. Put a thatch roof on it. Everything on earth, except you and what you have in the ark with you will die. But I will establish my covenant with you. You are to bring two of every living creature, male and female into the ark.'"

"It had never rained on the earth. Water came in streams and fog watered the land. Noah did everything God told him to do. He built the ark just as God had told him to build it. He and his sons gathered every kind of food for all the animals. It took Noah and his sons 100 years to build the ark and gather the food for the animals. During this time the people came to see what Noah was building. When he told them he was building an ark, they would ask why? He would tell them that God was going to send rain. They asked him, 'what is rain?' He would tell them that it was drops of water falling from the sky. The people thought Noah was crazy. 'Whoever heard of water falling from the sky,' "they would say. For the entire time Noah was building the ark the people thought he was crazy and made fun of him. The people continued to live their wicked lives even thought Noah warned them to change their ways or they would die."

"When Noah was 600 years old, God told him to take his sons, his wife and Japheth's wife Adeleteneses, Shem's wife Sedeqetelebab and Ham's wife Na'eltema'uk into the ark. God had told Noah to build a big door in the side of the ark."

"God said, 'but I will establish my covenant with you. And you will enter the ark, you and your sons and your wife and your sons' wives with you. You are to take every kind of food that is eaten and store it away as food for you and for them.'

"The Lord then said to Noah, 'Go into the ark, you and your whole family, because I have found you righteous in this generation. Take with you seven of every clean animal, a male and its mate, and two of every kind of unclean animal, a male and its mate, and also seven of every kind of bird, male and its mate, to keep their various kinds alive throughout the earth. Seven days from now I will send rain on the earth for forty days and forty nights, and I will wipe from the face of the earth every living creature I have made.' "

"Noah and his sons and his wife and his son's wives entered the ark to escape the waters of the flood. Pairs of clean and unclean animals, of birds and of all creatures that move along the ground, male and female, came to Noah and entered the ark, as God had commanded Noah. And after seven days the floodwaters came on the earth."

"In the six hundredth year of Noah's life, on the seventeenth day of the second month--on that very day all the springs of the great deep burst forth, and the floodgates of the heavens were opened. And rain fell on the earth forty days and forty nights."

"The waters rose and increased greatly on the earth, and the ark floated on the surface of the water. The waters rose and covered the mountains to a depth of more than twenty-seven arm lengths. Every living thing on the face of the earth died. Only Noah was left, and those with him."

"The waters flooded the earth for one hundred and fifty days." Jacob told the people, "This story is longer than I intended. I will finish the story next time. We need to get to bed now as tomorrow will be a long day."

CHAPTER 4

——— CONFRONTATION ———

Jacob had reached the hill country of Gilead just a little back of Mizpah. As they were setting up camp, one of Ater's scouts came to him and said, "There is a large group of men in a camp about two hands of time behind us. They are dressed like Jacob and his men."

Ater told the scout to quietly get the men ready to march. Have them take clay jars and torches with them. "Tell them to be ready as soon as they have eaten," he said.

Ater told Jacob, "I'm giving my men night training. We will be back before dawn." He ate a hurried supper, and then bade them good-by. As soon as he arrived in his camp his men were ready to go. They took off at a fast trot and reached Laban's camp in one hand's time. Ater told his men to make a circle around the camp about a stone's throw from it. They were to light the torches and put them in the jars, concealing the light.

Ater approached the camp. "Halloo the camp," Ater called out. Laban and two men came to meet Ater.

"Who are you and why do you disturb the camp at this hour," Laban demanded.

"I am Ater, formerly captain of the guard for the king of the Hittites, now protector of Jacob's camp. Why are you following Jacob?" Ater answered him.

Hearing this, Laban was more conciliatory when he answered Ater. "I am Laban, Jacob's father-in-law. I want to kiss my daughters and grandchildren goodbye and to wish them god speed on their trip," Laban answered quickly.

"I will let Jacob know that you are here. I will suggest that we wait for you. You were in danger of being killed if you had not answered as you did." Ater gave a wolf call and his men broke their jars and the men in the camp could see that they were surrounded. Ater continued, "My men could have entered your camp and before you knew we were there, half would have been killed. The rest would have been killed before they could have armed themselves. Keep that in mind when you talk to Jacob tomorrow." Ater gave another wolf call, and just as suddenly as the lights appeared, they were extinguished. Without a sound, Ater and his men left.

Later that night God sent an angel to Laban in a dream. The angel warned Laban. "You have been warned. When you speak to Jacob tomorrow, you are not to say anything either good or bad to him!" The angel left Laban bewildered.

At breakfast, Ater told Jacob what happened with Laban the previous night. Jacob said, "We will wait here for Laban to reach us. Then we will see what he really wants. I want you and your men to be very conspicuous in my camp, in full battle dress, when Laban gets here."

Laban moved his camp closer to Jacob's. Then he came to talk to Jacob. "Why did you leave without letting me know you were leaving? As your employer I had a right to know you were leaving. You deceived me and stole my daughters and grandchildren away from me. I would have sent you on your way with a feast, music and dancing. You would have left with joy and singing. We would have played the pipes and tambourines for you. You didn't even allow me to kiss my daughters and grandchildren goodbye. I thought I had it in my power to harm you but last night the God of Abraham and the fear of your father Isaac came to me in a dream and warned me not to say anything good or bad to you. I know you left because you longed to see your home again. But why did you steal my gods?"

Jacob was angry with Laban for accusing him of stealing the idols. "I didn't steal your gods! I heard your sons talking about killing me and taking my flocks and herds so I left quickly. I didn't want them to know I was leaving. If they had killed me as they were planning, you would have taken my wives and my property by force. Search my camp and if you find your gods with anyone, that person shall not live and you may have your gods again."

Laban started in Jacob's tent, and then he went to Leah's tent. He searched Bilhah's tent, then Zilpah's tent. Last of all he went into Rachel's tent. Rachel was sitting on her camel's saddle. She had hidden the idols in her camel's saddle. Laban searched everything in the tent, and then he came to Rachel. Rachel said to Laban, "Father, please do not be angry with your daughter for not standing when you came into my tent, I'm having my moon time."

While Laban was conducting his searches, Jacob had told Naphish, Laban's oldest relative to take men and search all the other tents and supplies.

When Laban came out of Rachel's tent, Jacob told him, "I have sent Naphish and our relatives to search the other tents and all the supplies. They have found nothing." Jacob became angry with Laban and scolded him severely. "What crime have I committed? If you or anyone with you has found anything of yours here with me, show it, so that all our relatives may see it. You hunted me down like an escaped thief! You have searched all my stuff! What have you found that belongs to you. Nothing! Let our relatives judge between us. In the twenty years that I worked for you, your sheep and goats did not miscarry. When a wild animal killed one of your sheep or goats, I took one of my own to replace it. I never ate any of your sheep or goats. You made me pay for anything that was stolen from your flocks or herds. I froze by night and was hot by day. It was so cold sleep fled from my eyes. For twenty years I worked for you. You changed my wages ten times. I worked seven years for Rachel and you gave me Leah. I worked seven more years for Rachel. The last six years I worked for the flocks and herds. You kept cheating me at every turn. It was my God that kept you from taking everything I have. If it weren't for my God, you would have sent me away empty-handed. Last night He came to you to let you know that He protects me."

Laban answered, "All the family you have are my daughters and their children. The flocks and herds you have were mine. What can I do against you? Let us make a covenant of peace that will serve as a witness between us." Then they ate the noon meal.

Jacob sent a young man to the cattle to get a young bull, two young rams and two young male goats. When he returned with the animals, Jacob had them butchered and cut in half. The two halves were laid on the ground about a pace apart. Jacob and Laban walked between the two halves to seal the covenant. This was a sacred covenant of blood that indicated that both parties were expecting God to do to them what was done to these animals if they broke this covenant. Jacob took a stone and set it up as a memorial stone. He told his relatives to gather stones and make a great heap. Laban call the heap 'Jegar Shadutha', which in his language means a witness heap. Jacob called the heap 'Galeed' that means a witness heap in Aramaic.

Laban said to Jacob, "We have made a covenant of blood and have set this heap as a witness between you and me and here is the pillar you also set up. Let them be a witness that you will not go beyond them to do me harm and I will not go beyond them to do you harm. May the God of our fathers, Abraham and Nahor, be a judge between us?"

Jacob had reserved the right shoulders, the kidneys and their fat along with the hides and entrails to sacrifice to the God of Abraham and the fear of his father Isaac. A large fire was built to make the burned offering to God.

The animals were prepared for the covenant meal. Jacob and all his relatives ate the covenant meal. Early next morning Laban kissed his daughters and grandchildren. After Laban blessed them with long lives and many flocks and herds, he and his party left.

Jacob broke camp and continued the journey. As he was going along some angels of God met him. When Jacob saw them he exclaimed, "This is the camp of God." He named the place 'Mahanaim'. When he reached the Jabbok River he sent messengers to find Esau. "You are to give Esau this message." "Jacob says, 'I am you servant, our father Isaac sent me to our relatives in Aram. I have been there twenty years. God has given me four wives, eleven sons and a daughter. God has also given me many sheep, goats, camels and donkeys. This message is sent to you, my Lord, that I may find favor in your sight.'"

In a few days the messengers returned to Jacob and told him, "We found your brother Esau. He seemed glad that you are coming home. He is coming to meet you with four hundred men."

This message caused great fear and distress in Jacob. He wondered why Esau was bringing four hundred men. Perhaps, thought Jacob, he is planning on revenge because I cheated him out of the birthright and the blessing. Maybe I should divide my camp into two camps. If Esau attacks one, the other may escape. Jacob planned to send Leah and Zilpah and their children along with half his servants and half of his flocks and herds across the Jabbok River. He was planning to tell his herdsmen and shepherds to go toward the setting sun after they got across the river. He was thinking that Esau would come upon them first. Rachel, Bilhah and their children along with the rest of the servants, flocks and herds were to be sent after the first group were across the river. He was planning to tell those shepherds and herdsmen to go toward the rising sun after they got across the river. He would tell each group to keep traveling until sundown. He hoped to put some distance between the two groups.

Jacob prayed for safety from Esau. Jacob prayed, "Oh God of my grandfather Abraham, fear of my father Isaac. You came to me in Haran and told me to return to Canaan. I do not deserve all the kindness you have shown me but I thank you for it. You promised that if I would return to my home and to my relatives that you would protect me and cause me to prosper. When I left home I had only my staff. You have shown me much more kindness and prosperity than I deserved. Oh God, I am unworthy of your graciousness. Now my brother Esau is coming to meet me with an army of four hundred of his men. I am afraid he will attack me and take my wives and children and all the flocks and herds, You said You would protect me and that my descendants would be as numerous as the sand of the sea, I now ask for that protection. Amen." Jacob sent his herds and flocks across the Jabbok River.

Jacob stayed on the side of the river opposite the flocks and herds. It seemed to Jacob that God told him to send Esau a gift of one out of every ten of his animals. He decided not to send his flocks and herds the way he had planned. He made another plan. Jacob called Oohdal to him and gave Oohdal these instructions. "You are to take one from every ten animals and put them in flocks and herds by themselves and send them to Esau. Take two hundred ewes, twenty rams, two hundred she goats and twenty male goats, thirty female camels with their young, forty cows, ten bulls, twenty female donkeys and ten male donkeys and put them in flocks and herds by themselves. Leave at least one hand of time between each flock and herd.

You are to give this message to all the shepherds and herdsmen. When they meet my brother Esau and he asks 'Who owns all these animals?' "They are to say 'these are a gift from your servant Jacob, sent to his Lord Esau and he is coming behind us.'"

Jacob thought surely these gifts will help Esau forget his anger so he sent the gifts ahead while he stayed in a camp by himself. Jacob was left alone and a man wrestled with him until daybreak when the man saw that He could not defeat him. He struck Jacob's hip as they wrestled and dislocated his hip socket. Then He said to Jacob, "Let me go, for it is daybreak."

But Jacob said, "I will not let you go unless you bless me."

"What is your name?" the man asked.

"Jacob," he replied.

"Your name will no longer be Jacob," he said. "It will be Israel because you have wrestled with God and with men and have prevailed."

Then Jacob said to him, "Please tell me your name."

But he answered, "Why do you ask my name?" And He blessed him there.

God blessed him, "be fruitful and multiply, a nation and a company of nations will come from you, and kings shall come out of your loins, and the land I gave to Abraham and Issac, I give it to you and to your descendants after you." Then God left Jacob. Jacob set up a pillar of stone at that place and poured a drink offering on the stone. Then he poured oil on the stone and called it Peniel.

The sun was rising above the Jabbok as Israel crossed over. He was limping due to his hip being out of joint. He soon reached his camp and told them of his experience the previous night. He explained that his name was now Israel and he would not be called Jacob any longer. He said, "Because the angel of God put my hip out of its socket, my descendants are never to eat of the tendon attached to the socket of the hip!"

Israel sent one-tenth of his animals to Esau but he was still afraid of him so he made an additional plan.

The sun was almost three hands past its highest when Israel saw Esau coming with his army. He put Zilpah and her children just behind him, and then came Bilhah and her children; behind them were Leah and her children. Rachel and Joseph were the last in line. Israel ran to meet Esau.

As he ran, he bowed to the ground seven times. Esau ran to meet Israel and when they met, Esau kissed Israel and fell on his neck, embracing Israel. Esau looked up and saw the women and children and asked Israel, "Who do these people belong to?"

Israel answered, "God has been very good to me and has given me these children."

Zilpah and Bilhah and their children came to Esau and bowed to him. Leah and her children came next and Rachel and Joseph were the last to be introduced to Esau.

"Why did you send all those droves ahead of you?" Esau asked.

"I sent them to find favor in your eyes, my Lord," Israel replied.

"You didn't need to do that, I have plenty. Keep the animals," Esau told Israel.

Israel said, "Last night I wrestled with an angel from God. He told me to give you one out of every ten of my animals. Please accept them as the gift God has told me to give you. He also changed my name to Israel."

Esau agreed to accept the gifts since God had told Israel to give them to him. Esau said to Israel, "Let us be on our way and I will accompany you."

"The children and the animals with young must not be driven hard or I will lose some of the young." Israel told Esau. "Please, my Lord, go on ahead of us and I will come to you in Sier."

"I will leave some of my men to help you," Esau answered.

"You do not need to leave any of your men," Israel said. "Now that I have seen your face and you smiled on me, that is enough."

Esau left and returned to Seir. Israel did not go to Sier. Instead he went down the Jabbok River. The evening of the first day he stopped early to give the animals more time to eat. As the women were preparing the evening meal Judah asked his father to continue the story of Noah.

After the meal, Israel began, "We stopped last time with Noah and the ark floating on the surface of the water for 150 days, now the springs of the deep and the floodgates of heavens had been closed and the rain stopped. The water receded steadily from the earth. At the end of another 150 days the water had gone down, and on the seventeenth day of the seventh month the ark came to rest on one of the mountains of the Ararat range. The waters continued to recede until the tenth month, and on the first day of the tenth month the tops of the mountains became visible."

"After forty days, Noah opened one of the windows he had made in the ark and sent out a raven, but it kept flying back and forth until the waters receded from the surface of the earth. Then he sent out a dove to see if the waters had receded from the surface of the ground. But the dove could find no place to set its feet because there was water over all the surface of the earth, so it returned to Noah in the ark. He reached out his hand and took the dove and brought it back to himself in the ark. He waited seven more days and again sent out the dove from the ark. When the dove returned to him in the evening, there in its beak was a freshly plucked olive leaf! Then Noah knew the water had receded from the earth. He waited seven more days and sent the dove out again, but this time it did not return to him."

"By the first day of the first month of Noah's six hundred and first year, the water dried up from the earth. Noah then removed the coverings from the ark and saw that the surface of the ground was dry. By the twenty-seventh day of the second month the earth was completely dry."

"Then God said to Noah," 'Come out of the ark, you and your wife and your sons and their wives. Bring out every kind of living creature that is with you, the birds, the animals, and all the creatures that move along the ground, so that they can multiply on the earth and be fruitful and increase in numbers upon it.'"

"Noah came out of the Ark, together with his sons and his wife and his sons' wives. All the animals and all the creatures that move along the ground and all the birds, everything that moves on the earth, came out of the ark, one kind after another."

"Then Noah built an altar to the Lord and taking some of the clean animals and clean birds, he sacrificed burnt offerings on it. The Lord smelled the pleasing aroma and said to Noah," 'Never again will I curse the ground because of people, even though every inclination of their hearts are evil from childhood. And never again will I destroy all living creatures as I have done. As long as the earth endures, seedtime and harvest, cold and heat, summer and winter, day and night will never cease. I have put a rainbow in the sky to remind you and Me of this promise.'

"Then God blessed Noah and his sons saying to them," 'Be fruitful and increase in number and fill the earth. The fear and dread of you will fall upon all the beasts of the earth and all the birds of the air, upon every creature that moves along the ground, and upon all the fish of the seas, they are given into your hands. Everything that lives and moves will be food for you. Just as I have given you the green plants, I now give you everything.'

Israel interrupted his story to remind everyone that now God had changed his original command that only plants could be eaten and allowed us to eat animal, birds and fish as well. We do not have to be vegetarians as God has allowed us to eat meat.

Israel continued his story of Noah how God said, 'but you must not eat meat that has its lifeblood still in it. And for your lifeblood I will surely demand and accounting. I will demand an accounting from every animal. And from each man also I will demand an accounting for the life of his fellow man. Whoever sheds the blood of man, by man's laws shall his blood be shed, for in His image has God made us'."

Israel sent everyone to their tents telling them, "Tomorrow we will reach our destination. We will build our homes there."

The next day they came to a field with much grass not very far from the Jabbok River. There he made a place for himself and all his servants. He built shelters for his animals and called the place 'Succoth', which means shelters.

That evening Israel told them about Abraham. "Terah lived in Ur of the Chaldeans. Terah became the father of Abram, Nahor and Haran. Haran became the father of Lot, but Haran died in Ur of the Chaldeans. Abram married Sarai and Nahor married Milcah, one of Haran's daughters. Sarai was barren and had no children. Terah took his son, his son's wife Sarai, and his grandson Lot and Lot's wife Zillah and left for Canaan, but when they reached Haran they stayed there. Terah died there at the age of 205."

"The Lord said to Abram, 'leave your father's household and go to the land I will show you.' God promised to make Abram into a great nation. He told Abram, 'you will be a blessing, and I will bless those who bless you, and whoever curses you I will curse.' Abram left Haran and went to Canaan. He took all his possessions and the people he had accumulated in Haran along with Sarai, Lot and Zillah and traveled toward Canaan. Abram was 75 when he left Paddan-Aram for Canaan. He traveled a different route that we took. He went past Halab. Abram had a herd of white cows that his servants milked. He gave some of the milk to the people of Halab. The people of Halab called him "Habbash Shubba", which means "He milked ashen colored cows". After he left Halab he stayed farther towards the setting sun than we did. He traveled through Babylon, as far as the great tree of Moreh at Shechem. While he was there, God made a covenant with him. God told him, 'to your offspring I will give this land.' Abram built an alter to the God who had appeared to him. From there he went toward the hills toward the rising sun of Bethel. He also built an alter there and called upon the name of the Lord. Then Abram set out toward the Negev."

"There was a famine in the land, and Abram went down into Egypt to live there because the famine was so bad. Before he entered Egypt he told Sarai, 'I know what a beautiful woman you are. When the Egyptians see you, they will say, this is his wife. Then they will kill me and let you live. Say that you are my sister so that I will be treated well for your sake and my life will be spared because of you.' Pharaoh's officials told Pharaoh how beautiful Sarai was and he took her as one of his wives. Pharaoh treated Abram well for her sake. Abram acquired sheep and cattle, male and female donkeys, menservants and maidservants and camels."

"God inflicted serious diseases on Pharaoh and his household. Pharaoh summoned Abram and asked him why he had told them that Sarai was his sister when she was his wife. He gave Sarai back to Abram and told his people the reason, and they sent him on his way with everything he had acquired."

"When he got back to the Negev with his wife his possessions, Lot and Zillah went with him. Abraham had become very wealthy in livestock and in silver and gold. From the Negev he went back to Bethel and called on the name of the Lord."

"Lot came to Abram and told him that the land could not support both their herds and flocks. The herdsmen of Abram and the herdsmen of Lot quarreled over pasture and water. Abram told Lot, 'let's not have any quarreling between you and me, for we are brothers. Let us part company, if you go towards Hittite, I will go towards Egypt. If you go towards Egypt I will go towards Hittite. Lot chose the plain of Jordan and moved toward the rising sun until he lived in Sodom.

"Kedorlaemer king of Elam and several other kings attacked the cities of the plain and captured them. They took the people, Including Lot and his family captive. One of the men escaped and reported this to

Abram. Abram and his friends, Asher, Eshcol and Mamre, and their armies defeated Kedorlaemer and his armies. On the way from the victory, Melchizedek King of Salem came out to meet him. He was a priest of God Most High and he blessed Abram saying 'Blessed be Abram by the God Most High, Creator of Heaven and earth. Blessed by God Most High who delivered your enemies into your hands.' Then Abram gave him a tenth of all the spoils he had taken."

"When Abram was ninety nine years old. The Lord appeared to him and said, 'I am El Shaddai, walk before me and be blameless. I will confirm My covenant between Me and you and will greatly increase your numbers.'"

"Abram fell face down, and God said to him, 'As for Me, this is My covenant with you. You will be the father of many nations. No longer will you be called Abram; your name will be Abraham for I have made you the father of many nations.' God told Abraham that the sign of this covenant would be that all males must be circumcised when they are eight days old."

"God told Abraham that he had changed his wife's name from Sarai to Sarah because she would have a son. Fourteen years earlier Sarai had given her maid Hagar to Abram as his concubine. She had a son named Ishmael. Abraham asked God to bless Ishmael. God told Abraham that Ishmael would become a mighty nation, but that his covenant would be with Isaac. Abraham had all the males in his house circumcised, including Ishmael."

After some time God tested Abraham by telling him to sacrifice his son Isaac. Abraham and Issac went to a mountain for the sacrifice. After the wood was put in order, Abraham laid Isaac on the alter as a sacrifice. Just as he was about to deliver the fatal strike with the knife God told him to withhold your hand. Abraham looked up and saw a ram caught in the brush. He sacrificed the ram instead of Isaac. Then Abraham and Isaac returned to the servants and went to Beersheba.

"Sarah died at the age of 127. Abraham wept and mourned over Sarah for a month. Then he spoke to the Hittites in the village gate. He asked them to sell him a place to bury his dead. Ephron the Hittite said he would sell Abraham the field and cave at Machpelah for four hundred shekels of silver. Abraham weighed out the shekels for him and the field, the cave and all the trees became Abraham's property. Then He buried his wife Sarah there.

"Later took another wife, named Keturah and had 6 sons by here. Before he died at the age of 175, he gave gifts to Keturah's sons and sent them away."

Israel told everyone to soon get to bed since they would start their new lives tomorrow.

He told Oohdal to have the herdsmen start to build permanent shelters for the herds. Oohdal asked for some of the people to come and help with building. Israel gave him twenty more men and women to help build the shelters. The shepherds were to build sheepcotes that were big enough to hold three hundred sheep or goats. Israel drove a stake in the ground and tied a rope to it. He tied a sharpened stick to the rope and used that to mark out big circles for the bases of the sheep pens. Rocks were placed around the circle. Another ring of rocks was placed about one step outside the first ring. The space between the rings of rocks was filled with small rocks and dirt. Another layer of large rocks was placed on top of the first rings and closer together. The space between this layer of large rocks was also filled. This procedure was continued until the walls were as high as Israel. Thorny brush was placed on top to keep both two and four legged predators out. Twelve sheepcotes were built.

Walls of rock were made for the shelters for herds. A long wall nine paces long was built as a back wall. End walls two paces long were built at right angles to the back wall. These walls were the same height as the back wall where they joined together. The fronts of these walls were the height of the back wall less one forearm. Men cut long straight trees and put then from one side wall to walls in the middle. There were three paces from each end wall to the middle walls and two paces between each of the three middle walls. On top of the trees, a layer of rushes from the Jabbok River was placed to hold the brush and mud that was put on top. The shelters would hold the cattle, camels and donkeys during the winter rainy season. During the summer men would cut grass and store it to feed the animals during the rainy seasons. Ten shelters were made for the herds. The shepherds sought a place with lots of good pasturage and plenty of still water.

Asher, who was two months from being three, asked Israel. "Father, why do they want to find still water?"

"Sheep cannot drink from running water; their mouths are shaped so that running water goes through it and they cannot drink" Israel told Asher. "If the shepherds cannot find still water, we will have to dig cistern or wells to water them."

"Thank you Father," Asher replied. The shepherds looked for good pastures for the animals. They found good pasture near the Jabbok so they didn't have to dig wells.

Israel went to Ater's camp. "You did a very good job of protecting me." Israel told Ater. Here are five gold rings, which is more than our agreement. You earned them. Here are twenty-five silver rings for your men. You have an excellent army."

"Had an excellent army," Ater said. "Half of my men want to take up shepherding. They feel that with wives and families now, they would rather find another line of work. With the plunder we took from the raiders, including the sheep, donkeys and camels they think that their new families would be happier if they settled down. Some of them wanted me to ask if they could stay with you for a while so you could teach them how to be good shepherds."

"I'd be happy to help them get started," Israel replied.

"You have been very generous with us," Ater said.

"If it hadn't been for you and your men I would have lost at least an entire herd of camels. You were worth every ring I gave you," Israel assured him.

Ater replied, "I thank you and I will tell the men who want to become shepherds to meet with you in the morning."

Shortly after breakfast, nine of Ater's men and Mibsam came to see Jacob. Mibsam started the conversation, "Master I would like to become a shepherd like you. I have enough rings saved to buy ten ewes and a ram. You said you would allow anyone to leave if they wanted to go after we reached Canaan. I would like to join with these other men to start our own flocks. Would you sell me ten ewes for two gold rings, fifteen silver rings and 40 bronze rings?"

"Yes," Israel replied to Mibsam. "That is a little less than what I would get at the market, but I will accept that from you for ten ewes."

One of the other nine men said, "We each have ten sheep and a camel and an donkey from our portion of the plunder. We intend to put them all together and work as a team. We intend to stay together for three or four years. Then we will divide the sheep equally."

"That is a very good idea," Israel replied. "If you want, I will train you as shepherds. This land is big enough for hundreds of flocks. This is a land flowing with milk and honey. The grass and plants and shrubs will provide all the food you need for your animals and a lot for your families to eat. Grapes grow in abundance along the Jabbok River. I have seen grape clusters so big that it would take two strong men to carry them. Wheat and barley will grow strong with big heads. Figs so ripe they almost fall into your mouth can be found in their season. Dates are so sweet they seem to melt in your mouth. Pomegranates will break apart easily and are full of seed with much juice. Bees make hives in the clefts in the rocks and in hollow trees. We can harvest honey during the month Chislev. You will find everything you need in this land. This is the land that the one true God promised to Abraham and his descendants. I will give each of you a shepherd's bag with all you will need to get started. You know how to use a sling but did you know that when a sheep wanders away from the flock you can startle the sheep by dropping a rock on the far side of it and it will return to the flock. I will show you how to make a pipe from two reeds. Playing the pipe calms the sheep."

The shepherd's bag was made of a dried goatskin with the legs tied together to form a bag. A rope was tied from the hind legs to the front legs so it could be carried over the shoulder. A stout stick about the length of the arm with a knob on the end could be used as a weapon. They would need a longer stick with a hook on the end to retrieve sheep that got in the water or mud. Since the shepherd would be gone all day, his wife could put food in the bag for him.

"You may stay close to my flocks for the years you are together. If you will work for me I will give you each five bronze rings for twelve moons work."

Zibeon, who seemed to be the leader of the soldiers, ask? "What kind of work will you want us to do?"

Israel answered, "Your skill as soldiers will help protect my property. Also I want to plant wheat and barley. I will give you some land so you can plant wheat and barley for your families. I will let you use my oxen and plows to cover your seeds. Since you will have one flock, all of you will not be needed to tend the sheep all the time. For a ram each, I will give you and your families food to eat and other supplies you will need to get started."

Lotan, another of the soldiers said, "But we don't have rams to give you."

"I know you don't have the rams now but you will next year." Israel continued, "You see, about half of your ewes will have two or three lambs next lambing season. You can figure that you will have about one and a half lambs for each ewe. That means that together you will have around 150 lambs next lambing season. That will probably mean 75 ewes and 75 rams. If you learn to take care of your sheep, they will take care of you. In six years you should each have a flock of around one hundred ewes."

"I will provide for your families for a year." Israel explained, "At next shearing time when you shear your one hundred sheep, you should get around a silver ring for each fleece. With the ten silver rings each of you will get, you will be able to provide for your family for the next year. The following year you will probably have around a hundred and seventy sheep to shear. Besides the money you get for the fleeces you can sell at least sixty five yearling rams to the meat market for about three silver rings each. From the third year on, you will not have to worry about taking care of your families."

Ithran, another soldier, said, "Israel, I tried to talk Ater out of taking the job of protecting you but now I am very happy that he took the job. Then I didn't know what the future held for me. I thought I would be a soldier until I got killed. Now I have a wife, two boys and a girl in my tent. My future looks much better now."

Israel said, "I have a learned Egyptian as one of my servants, Jurrad is his name. I suggest that you discuss how you will split the work and the profits and how you will schedule who tends the sheep. After you decide all these things, find Jurrad and he will draw up an agreement for you to sign. That way each will know what is expected of him and what he can expect from the others."

Mibsam said, "Israel, the reason I asked to come to work for you was that the men of Haran said you would treat your workers fairly. I thought I was lucky when you hired me. Now I know just how lucky I am!"

The ten men left talking about what Israel had told them. Ater and ten men came to Jacob. Ater told Israel. "Seventeen of my men have left to become shepherds or farmers in this area. Two of the men I trained as soldiers would like to go with me, if that is alright with you."

"That's fine with me," Israel answered. "Now that I am home and settled I won't need as many men. I will give them their wages and they can take the property they have accumulated and go with my blessings."

"We will leave first thing tomorrow morning," Ater told Israel. "I don't know what we are going to do with the sheep we have."

Israel suggested, "Perhaps the nine that are staying would trade their camels for your sheep. You can lead the extra camels to a large town and sell them for money and split the money among the men."

One of the soldiers spoke up, "I think that is a good idea. How many sheep should we give for a camel?"

"Since you have no use for the sheep, you can be generous. A camel is worth eight or nine sheep. You could give ten sheep for a camel. Each of you would have over five gold rings when you sell the camels."

"Wow! One of the young soldiers exclaimed, "I have never had five gold rings. Now I have my share of the plunder and will get five more gold rings. I feel like I'm rich."

Next morning Mibsam came to Israel. "Lord, the nine soldiers traded their camels for ten more sheep. They have twenty sheep each and I have only ten. I still have one gold ring, twelve silver rings and eighteen brass rings. Would you sell me ten ewes for that amount?"

"You were a good worker, except for the training at first", Israel replied. "Yes I will let you have ten ewes for that amount. Since you are single, you won't need any rings."

"I'm single now but one of your hired servants and I have became betrothed. We have talked about asking your permission to get married," Mibsam replied.

"She won't need my permission. I told everyone that they might leave after we got to Canaan. If she chooses to leave, then you won't need my permission. I will give you my blessing. I will also give you the ten year old ewes as a wedding present. Take her to Leah so that Leah can help her plan and get ready for the wedding."

"Thank you very much," Mibsam said. "I can't wait to tell her the good news!" With that he left to find Adah.

CHAPTER 5

——— A WEDDING ———

Israel told Leah about the wedding. Leah was glad to have an occasion for a celebration. Leah called all the women and told them that Mibsam and Adah would soon be married. When Adah heard that Israel had approved the marriage, she was very glad. Leah asked when she wanted to be married. Adah answered, "as soon as we can!"

Leah responded, "We have to weave a wedding canopy for you and Mibsam to sit under. You will need more curtains for Mibsam's tent. The women will be glad to help you weave the canopy and curtains as their wedding present for you and Mibsam.

Leah took Adah aside and told her, "There are other things to consider. We want to have the wedding about half a moon after your moon time. That way the chances of you conceiving during the wedding week will be better and the women need time to make gifts for you."

Adah said, "I have just finished my moon time. Do you think we could be married in half a moon?"

"I don't see why not," Leah replied. "That will be during the time of the new moon. Getting married during a new moon gives your marriage a special blessing."

"You and Israel have been very kind to Mibsam and me. Mibsam told me that Jacob is giving us ten ewes as a wedding present so we will have the same number of ewes as the others," Adah told Leah. Then she hurried to find Mibsam and tell him that Leah had agreed on a wedding date.

Leah went to Israel and told him what the woman had decided. She said, "I need several men to drive the stakes for ground weaving looms. They want to get married when the moon is full. That is about half a moon time away. We need to get started weaving today.

"Let's build two standing looms", Israel said. "We are going to stay here for some time. I will send men to the woods to cut the small trees to make the frame and beams. I think we can have two looms made by noon tomorrow. We will make them waist high so the women will not have to kneel to weave."

"That would be great," Leah replied. "It is so much easier to weave standing up at a loom than squatting at a ground loom."

Israel told five men to take axes and find some trees to make posts for the looms. Leah packed a goatskin full of barley cakes for them to eat. The men took five bronze axes and left. Jacob sent ten boys to bring back the posts as soon as they were cut. In a little over two hands time, the boys returned with the eight posts. Israel sent the boys back to help the men bring the rest of the poles. The men and boys were back after the evening meal had been eaten. They brought more than enough poles to make the two looms.

Next morning, Israel had eight men peel and smooth the posts. He had eight more men dig the holes for the posts. The posts were tall enough so that poles could be lashed to them about as high as the women's waist. Israel selected two poles that were about as thick as two of his fingers. He took these poles to the carpenter with instructions to cut the poles to a length that would be four times the length of his arm from the elbow to the fingertips plus the width of two hands. The poles were to be cut down on two sides to the thickness of one finger's width. The poles were to extend six fingers past both sides of the loom. The ends of the poles would be turned to raise and lower the woof strings. This is called the heddle that raises half the woof strings and, when turned over, the other half. After smoothing the pole, Jerah cut notches on the top and bottom about one fourth of the way through and about two fingers apart. Within one hand's time the holes had been completed and the poles smoothed.

When the looms were finished, Israel called Leah over to inspect them. She was pleased with the size and construction but she told Israel they were not finished. "You need to have the men cut four more poles about the size of two fingers width. When they get back with them, have the carpenter lash them to the end posts.

Israel sent four men with axes back to the woods to get the poles. The men returned very quickly. They told Israel that they had trimmed the tops of the trees that had been cut earlier. Israel had them peel and smooth the poles. By the time the poles were ready the carpenter was there to lash them to the posts. Israel, Leah and many of the women came to look at the looms. All the women were very happy to have looms they could use to make new tent panels and curtains. Leah thought that it would be better to let the looms dry until the next morning.

After breakfast the next day Leah selected two of the best weavers and their daughters. They got the shuttles and a pile of yarn made from goat hair. Goat hair was used because it was porous enough to let air through in the summer, but when it got wet it would swell and become watertight. Tents made of goat hair did not leak.

The women and their daughters had done a lot of weaving before so they fell into a routine. They tied the strings to the poles at one end and let them drop down on the other end and tied them to rocks to keep the woof strings tight. The mother would pass the shuttle to the daughter. When the daughter got the shuttle past the last woof string on her side, the mother would turn the heddle half a turn. The daughter would pass the shuttle back to her mother. As soon as her mother got the shuttle past the last woof string on her side, the daughter would turn the heddle half a turn. Back and forth, back and forth, back and forth the shuttle went. After ten or so complete throws of the shuttle, the women would tighten the warp by pressing a board called 'the bow' against what had been woven. This process was repeated hundreds of time for a panel or a tent curtain.

Since these weavings were to be a wedding present, Leah had the weavers changed every two hands of time so the present would be from everyone.

One of the men that had helped cut the trees came to Israel and said, "Master Israel, we saw a large patch of wild flax growing by the grove of trees we cut. Three of the soldiers said they know how to make rope. If you need more rope while we are here, we could cut and dry the flax and they could make ropes."

That is a very good idea," Israel responded. "Tell those three soldiers to come see me."

Three men came to Israel early the next day. "I am Madai, and these are my two cousins, Togarmah and Kittim. When we were younger we worked for our uncle, the oldest of three brothers. He made ropes that were longer and stronger than others."

Israel asked them, "Where did you live?"

Madai answered, "Your servants lived in a small village along the Euphrates River. We had a ropewalk all along the docks the fishing boats used. The ropewalk we had was over two hundred paces long. We seldom made ropes that long but we could do it."

Israel was impressed. "You have really made ropes that long?" He asked.

"Yes," Madai told Israel. We can make ropes that long for you if you want us to."

"We don't need ropes that long but we do need new ropes. There is a patch of wild flax down by the trees. Do you think you can make rope from it?"

"The rope will not be as strong as rope made from the flax we grew back home," Madai replied. "But we can make strong ropes from that flax. It will take at least a moon's time to get the flax ready to prepare for rope making."

"Why does it take that long to start making rope once the flax has been cut?" Israel asked.

Togarmah, who knew the most about this process, explained to Israel, "The flax must lay and dry and have dew fall on it for a least a moon's time so that the skin and the pulp inside will rot. Then we must break the flax and that will take at least half a moon time. Then we must run a shard knife down the broken flax to remove most of the straw. If you will have Tubal the flint knappers make twenty shard knives that would be very helpful. After that we have to draw the flax through boards with nails driven in them to remove the rest of the straw. We will need three sets of blocks with nails in them. Each block will have many more nails than the previous one."

"I see that making ropes is much harder than I thought." Israel said. "I will get Tubal to make the knives you need if you will tell him what you want. If any other men can help, just tell me what you need for them to do."

Togarmah answered, "If the carpenter can make the breaking machines and the carding blocks, that will be very helpful."

"I will get him right on it," Israel said. "If you will explain what you want him to make, I'm sure he can build it."

"I don't think there is a rush. First we must cut the flax, and that will take several days. Then it has to dry for a turning of the moon so we won't need the machines for a while."

Israel took the men to Jerah. "A patch of flax had been found, he said. These men know how to make ropes and can make new ropes for us. I want you to make the machines they need," Israel instructed Jerah "We will also need ten more sickles for cutting the flax."

Togarmah started to tell Jerah how to make a breaking machine when Jerah interrupted him, "I made several breaking machines when I was a servant of a rope maker along the Euphrates River," Jerah said. Israel told them to work out the details and then he left. Jerah and the three men were in an animated discussion of life on the Euphrates River as he left.

After lunch, the three men came to Israel and told him, "Jerah asked us to go to the woods and find ten curved branches to make the sickles. He gave us this old one so we would know what kind of branch he wanted. He also asked us to go to the stream to find some flint rocks." They took two bronze axes and went to the woods. As they left Kittim was saying, "I don't understand what Jerah meant when he said that if we can't find any branches like this to just get straight branches and he would bend them to shape."

"I don't either," Madai replied. "But that man has been a carpenter for many years. I believe he can do anything with wood." They kept up a friendly conversation while they were looking for the right branches. They were back in two hands time with several curved and straight branches. Jerah selected the curved ones he could use. He told them. "To curve a straight branch into the shape for a sickle, the branch had to be kept in boiling water for three or four hands of time. The wood becomes softer and can be shaped by tying it around a jar and letting it dry for several days."

Jerah called Tubal, and told him to take the flint nodules that the men had brought and knap one hundred knives for sickles. "They also need twenty shard knives," he told Tubal. "Do you know what a shard knife look like?"

"Yes," Tubal answered. "I have made shard knives before. They are square blades just like a drill bit, with a notch in the middle. The notch needs to be dulled just a little to keep the men from removing the fibers from the flax."

Oohdal came to Israel to tell him that many of the she goats had young. Israel told Oohdal to pasture some of the goats with kids close to the camp as soon as they could be milked. Three days later the goats were brought to a pasture close enough that the women could see them. The women were happy to be able to milk the goats. With the milk they could make leben, butter, and cheese, besides having fresh milk to drink. Oohdal told Israel that some of the camels and cows had young. "Do you want me to send some of them to you?"

"That is a good idea," Israel answered. "Some of the men would rather have camel's milk, some prefer cow's milk. There is plenty of pasturage here so bring some of each."

Soon tripods had sprung up all over camp. Many of the women had hung a goatskin filled with milk to a tripod. They let it sour for two days. They and their daughters would twist the milk filled goatskin to churn butter. Once the butter had been churned, it was taken from the milk and boiled. After boiling, the butter was put in small goatskin bags. In the summer heat it would melt into oil. In the winter it would taste like candy when honey was put into it. Soon many shallow bowls of milk with leavening stirred in were covered with a cloth and set out for a day or two to make leben. This allowed the milk to sour and curdle so that they could scoop out the curds and drink the whey. Israel told his boys, "Leben will make a healthy man feel better and it will make a sick man well." So he and his boys took bread and scooped the curds out to eat.

The women were getting ready for the marriage. Leah mentioned to Jerah that she wanted to be able to weave a strip three times as long as the length of the loom. After thinking for two days, Jerah came up with an idea he thought would work. He asked Leah to come to the loom while he explained his plan. "If I cut the lashing and put the poles on the outside of the posts and replace the lashing with pegs above and below the pole, the women could roll the woven material onto the pole by twisting it,"

Jerah told Leah. Leah thought for a short time, trying to visualize the new arrangement. Then she told Jerah, "Yes, I think I understand how that would work. We can make panels or curtains as long as we want. How long do you think it will take you to put the pegs in place of the lashings?"

"I can have it done in about one hands time." Jerah said. "I will go get my bow drill and while I'm there I will make the pegs we need."

While he was gone Leah, explained the new procedure to the women. They were excited to know that they could make longer panels and curtains.

Jerah had brought three other men, two bow drills and some rope. They tied the rope to the ends to the pole and put it on the outside of the posts. Two men pulled on the ropes so that tensions could be maintained on the woof. Jerah started drilling with the bow drill. The drill bit was a sharp piece of flint that had been knapped square on the bottom. It was attached to a shaft about two hands long and thicker than his thumb. The drill was shaped like a bow with a leather strap between the ends. The strap was wrapped around the shaft of the drill so that when Jerah pulled the bow back and forth the bit spun one way and than the other. He held a short board, with a hole part way through, on top of the bit to hold it steady. The hole was drilled in a very short time. Jerah took the peg and drove it into the hole. His helper was a little slower but soon both pegs were in place. The rope was loosened and the pole holding the woof did not sag. Jerah and his helper soon had the top pegs in place.

Leah told the weavers to cut the end of the woof and tie lengths of yarn to each piece. Then they stretched the woof and retied it. The women were soon back to weaving.

Next morning when the women tried to roll the woven part onto the pole they had a very difficult time. Leah called Jerah and asked him to make it easier to roll. Jerah drilled holes in each end of the pole and drove a stick through each hole. The women could use the sticks for leverage.

Israel thought everything was going fine. The women were ready for the marriage five days before the wedding.

Three days before the wedding Leah had several women bake barley loaves to be used to make beer. Israel had brought twelve large jars of wine with him when he left Haran.

The day of the wedding Israel called for all unnecessary work to stop until after the wedding. The long panel had been completed and was put up as a canopy for the couple to sit under during the wedding feast.

The day of the wedding Mibsam was dressed in the finest clothing available in the camp. In theory he was to be a king that day. Tedan, a worker of bronze, had fashioned a crown from a copper sheet. He had made it to fit Mibsam's head. At the top of the points he had left holes to attach shiny stones. The women had scented his clothing with frankincense and spices. His tunic was tied with a multi-colored silk belt. One of the leather workers had made him a pair of sandals with animals carved on them. The sandals were very carefully laced so that the lacings were equally spaced. The way he was dressed with a cloak flowing around him gave him the appearance of graceful bearing. For this day the shepherd would be a king!

Adah had to undergo a lot of bathing and being rubbed with palm oil to make her as glossy and shining as possible. Her hair was fixed with flowers and jewelry entwined into it. Many women loaned her their finest jewelry and many gold and silver rings. Her veil had gold rings sewn onto it along with some jewels that Leah and Rachel had loaned her. This was her day! She would always remember how fine she looked and how wonderfully she was dressed.

As dark was approaching, Mibsam led the wedding party to the tent were Adah lived. It was the custom for the bride's parents or other relatives to bless her before she left. Since she did not have any relatives there, Israel gave the blessing "We praise you, El Shaddai, our God, maker of Heaven and of earth, creator of joy and gladness, of friends and lovers, of love and kinship. O God may these always be heard in this camp, the voices of loving couples and the joy of children playing. We ask all these blessings on the marriage of Mibsam and Adah grant them many sons in their tent and let their children possess the gate of those that do not like them. May they live a long, prosperous and happy life, Amen."

Everyone in the wedding procession going to Adah's tent had to carry a light and wear a wedding garment. The light was a bowl filled with olive oil with a piece of flack twine as a wick. If they did not have a light, they could not join the parade. In this case a wedding garment was a clean tunic or cloak.

Normally the bride's relatives and friends escorted the bride and groom. Adah didn't have any relatives so her friends and their husbands escorted her. Several of the men beat drums and many shepherds played their pipes. People danced all along the way. It was a very grand parade. Some people were not able to go to Adah's tent so they joined the parade along the way to the wedding feast.

Israel had a young bull, three yearling male goats, and three young rams butchered and roasted. Leah had the women make mounds of wheat and barley bread, many large bowls of lentil stew, bowls of parched grain, and a salad made with orach leaves, onions, black radishes, dandelion leaves, leaf chicory and endives, with a sauce made of olive oil heated with dill, saffron and thyme. Leah had one of the women weave loose baskets to use as strainers to strain the husks and other scraps from the beer. The feast was ready for the bride and groom.

Arrival at the groom's house was the most important moment of the wedding festivities. Several older women took Adah into Mibsam's tent and tied up her hair and placed a veil over her face. Custom required well-to-do women never to show their face in public after they were married. This custom did not apply to slaves and servants. After her face was covered by the veil, Adah was led out of the tent and Leah led her around Mibsam three times. Then Adah was taken to her place beside Mibsam under the canopy. Mibsam and Adah sat side by side while Israel gave the benediction. "May El Shaddai, the one true God, bless you and keep you. May your sheep never miscarry. May you live long and have many sons. May your life together be long and filled with much joy. May your days be warm and your nights pleasant. May you both live to see your children's, children. Amen." At the end of the benediction he handed a mug of wine to Mibsam. Mibsam took a drink and handed it back. Israel gave the mug to Adah. She took a drink and handed the mug back. He them tried to explain some of the problems and joys they would have as a married couple. He talked for half a finger of time. Then he gave Mibsam and Adah the cup a second time. He told everyone there, "Children of the bridal chamber, you may now eat, drink and celebrate this marriage."

As soon as Israel announced that they could eat, everyone sat around the platters of food; first the men, then the boys, then the women and finally the girls. As Israel was the host it was his task to see that everyone had a good time. He constantly went through the gathering to see that mugs and horns were filled with beer or wine. The women put the meat in shallow bowls and placed the bowls and stacks of bread on the hides that were scattered around the area. Besides the meat and bread there were bowls of salad and charred grain. Everyone sitting on a hide ate from the same bowl by tearing a piece of bread and folding it to scoop up some meat or salad. Leah brought food and beer to Adah. The celebration lasted until early morning. His friends escorted Mibsam to his tent after the meal ended. Her friends had taken Adah to the tent a little earlier. They were not involved in the rest of the celebration. The festivities lasted for one phase of the moon. The entire moon cycle was called the days of marriage. The first moon time of the marriage was sweet as honey so they called it the "honey-moon."

Mibsam and Adah were not to do any unnecessary work for one phase of the moon. They would not be assigned any routine tasks for that moon cycle.

The nine soldiers asked Israel for permission to plow a small patch of ground for a garden. Israel gave them permission and allowed them to use his oxen and plows. A large patch of ground was plowed for Israel's family. Leah, Zilpah and Bilhah and their children planted beans, lintels, muskmelons, leeks and onions.

Mibsam and Adah finished their moon's cycle of living together and not working. When Adah went to talk to her friends, they teased her, "Well Adah, how did you like staying in the tent and doing nothing?" The word 'nothing' was pronounced in such a way that the women knew the insinuation. Adah blushed and all the women laughed. Adah joined in the laughter. She was happy with her husband and happy to be able to gather with the other women. She was also happy to be able to get back to being useful.

The barley and wheat would be planted after the former rains had loosened the soil. Pulling weeds and hoeing the garden were tasks required of the children. The Jabbok River was one hands time from the gardens. After the rainy season, boys of six or seven had to go to the river at least twice a day with buckets made of goat skins to bring water to the gardens. Levi, Dan and Gad did the weeding and hoeing. Judah, Naphtali and Asher carried water. Israel had Joseph being taught by Jurrad so he did not have to carry water. Every time Gad or Dan saw Joseph they would taunt him, "Father's favorite is too good to carry water. All he can do is sit with the women and study."

Joseph was studying math, logic, the Egyptian, Hittite, Sumerian and Canaanite languages, poetry, history and literature. He and Jurrad sat on blocks of wood that had been placed under a tree. He studied with Jurrad from after breakfast until the sun was at its highest. Joseph took his lessons and studied by himself in the afternoon. He really hated to learn the Egyptian language, and history. Several time he complained to Jurrad, "Why do I have to learn this dumb Egyptian language? I am going to be a shepherd like my father. I need to know more about sheep than Egypt." Jurrad would reply, "Master Joseph, we don't know what we need know for the future. We need to learn all we can about many things."

Israel was looking for a place to plant his wheat and barley crops when four shepherdesses passed by with the sheep. "Marnar," he called to the oldest girl.

"Yes Master Israel," she answered.

"Those sheep should have been sheared two moons ago. Take them to their pen and I will talk to your fathers." Israel instructed. Israel went to the area where the soldiers and Mibsam lived. When they saw him coming with the sheep, they came to meet him.

"Why have you brought our sheep back to the pen?" Madai asked. "You told us to take the sheep to the pasture early."

Israel told the men, "It is two moons past the time most sheep are sheared. The longer it is before we finish, the less the buyer will pay you. I'll get fourteen pairs of shears so we can all start shearing. I will send one of my men back to camp to get a cart and a team of oxen to pull it." Israel went back to his camp to get three of his servants who knew how to shear sheep.

Israel and his three servants soon returned. Israel gathered the ten new shepherds to him near the pen. He selected a sheep and brought it out.

"Israel took the sheep and held it so it couldn't get away. "See how this sheep is trying to get away," Israel said. "Now watch what happens when I turn it on its back." Saying this he turned the sheep over. As soon as the sheep was turned over, it stopped fighting. "She is asleep, we call this stage sulking. She can't figure out what is happening so she goes to sleep. When a sheep is in sulk, you can roll it over so you can shear it without any kicking or wiggling," Israel said. "A shearer can shear twelve to fifteen sheep in a hand's time."

Israel pulled the ewe to a position where it was sitting on its rump. "Some shearers like to start by trimming the hind legs first but I like to start making a long cut down the belly like this." Israel then clipped a strip from the head to the tail. He was careful not to cut her teats since she had two lambs and was lactating. He made two cuts down her belly. He said, "As you see, I have her head between my legs so I can roll her around a little with my feet. Notice how I stretch her skin tight with my left hand so I can shear her very close." Israel made several more passes down her belly. Then he rolled her to the left and starting at her forehead cut a strip down her side and onto her right flank. He sheared the hind leg at this time, and then made several more passes down her side. Israel rolled her the other way and sheared that side. Next he sat her on her rump and sheared her back. After her back was sheared, he rolled her forward and sheared her rear end and tail.

"Do you think you can shear a sheep now or do you want to watch some more?" Israel asked.

They all wanted to watch more sheep being sheared. The three servants and Israel each got another sheep and started shearing. Two or three men gathered by each shearer to watch. Epher, who was the fastest but not the cleanest shearer, said "I have heard of a man who claimed he could shear three hundred sheep a day. I have sheared over two hundred but it was a long hard day. On a good day I can shear close to two hundred sheep."

As he was talking, he was quickly shearing a sheep. "Slow down," Mibsam told him. "We are trying to learn and you are going so fast we can't see what you are doing."

Epher finished that sheep and got another one. "I'll go much slower on this one. I just wanted you to see how quickly a good shearer can shear a sheep." Saying that, he went slowly and told them what he was doing at every point. He had the men feel along the shearing strip and pull the skin taut. After he had sheared three more sheep, he decided that it was time to let them try.

Madai was the first to try. He took the shears and turned a sheep over. When it went to sleep, he let the sheep roll onto its feet. The sheep jumped up and tried to run away. Madai caught it and turned it over again. This time he held it against his legs so it couldn't get away. He made a few tentative cuts with the shears.

"That first cut is the hardest," Epher told him. "Just keep cutting slowly all the way down her belly and when you get close to her teats, feel them out with your left hand so you don't cut them."

It took Madai two fingers' time to shear that sheep. He was proud of himself when he finished. The other men were just as slow and were just as proud when they finished their first sheep.

Fourteen men started shearing. They had two hundred sheep to shear. Israel and the men he brought with him could shear forty sheep each hand of time. With the ten new shearers helping, they were shearing over 75 sheep every hand of time. When there were only twenty sheep left, Israel told the men with him to stop working. "Let the new shepherds finish up, they need to practice.

CHAPTER 6

TIRZAH

The cart arrived before they finished shearing. Israel had his men load the fleeces onto the cart. When all the sheep were sheared and the fleeces loaded, Israel told them, "You should start for the market as soon as you can get ready. The sun will set in about three hands time. If you go in this direction, Israel pointed in a direction that was between back and left, you will reach Tirzah tomorrow afternoon. When the buyer asks what you want for your fleeces, tell him you want one silver ring and three or four bronze rings. He will probably tell you your fleeces are old and not worth that much. Then he will tell you what he will pay. When he tells you this, you say 'these are very good fleeces. We will not take less than one silver ring and two bronze rings. Argue with him until you get close to one silver ring for each fleece. While you are in town, you may want to buy what you will need for the next year and get something nice for your wives."

The ten men left and headed for the Jordan River. They reached the Jordan River before sundown so they decided to cross it and camp on the other side. They traveled two fingers time before settling down for the night. They were up before sunup and were on their way by the time the sun was cresting the eastern horizon. The cart was loaded with fleeces so the men had to walk. By noon they saw Tirzah on the horizon. In Tirzah they made their way to the sheep area. The buyers saw the cart loaded with fleeces and one came to make an offer. He looked at the fleeces and offered five bronze rings each. Togarmah just looked at him and continued on. The next buyer asked, "What do you want for the fleeces?" Two more fleece buyers had come to the cart by the time Madai answered, "You don't get many fleeces this time of the year. We want one silver ring and five bronze rings each." The three buyers talked quietly among themselves. Then one said, "You are correct about us not getting fleeces this time of the year. Sheep sheared this late do not produce good wool. We will give you eight bronze rings."

"You may be right about the quality of wool from late sheared sheep. But this wool is of a good quality. We will sell them for one silver ring and three bronze rings each," Madai replied.

Another buyer looked shocked and told them," You are trying to take food from our children's mouths. Your fleeces are not worth that much. One silver ring is all I can give you."

Kittim turned to the other men and said, "I told you we should have gone to another town with our fleeces. We can go home and go to Penuel or Adam to sell these fine fleeces." He took hold of the lead rope and turned the oxen as though to leave.

"Wait, wait, wait, and please don't leave! I'll give you a silver ring and a bronze ring for each fleece. How many do you have?" The buyer asked.

The nine men looked at each other. Then Togarmah said, "You are taking food from our children's mouths but we will take your offer. We have two hundred fleeces so that will be two hundred and twenty silver rings or twenty gold rings and twenty silver rings for all the fleeces."

The buyers went to their stalls and came back with the amount they had agreed on. Once the cart was unloaded, the men decided to walk around and see if there was anything they needed. They stopped at a stall that sold material and bought fabrics of several colors and patterns so that their wives could have a new tunic. One of them remarked about how thirsty he was as they were passing a tavern. They went in and ordered beer. The beer came in a large jug with long straws. The owner told them that she served many Egyptian soldiers and they liked to drink their beer this way. The bottom of the straws had been inserted into bronze strainers to keep the barley husks and other impurities from being swallowed. After two jugs of beer, they decided to start for home. They got the cart and left Tirzah two hands time before sunset. They made a cold camp that night and left before sunup the next day. They saw their camp about two hands time before sunset.

One of the boys saw the cart coming and ran to tell everyone else. All of their wives and children came out to meet them. Israel came over to their camp. The men told him how they had bargained and the price they got. Israel congratulated them.

Israel said to them, "Now that you are rich, I don't suppose you will want to keep working for me."

Kittim answered for all of them, "I think working for you has many advantages. We have learned much from you, and I think there is still much we need to learn but I wonder why you have been so kind to us."

Israel answered, "That is an easy question to answer. We are but one family. I think that in the future I may need ten friendly families to help me or my descendants."

"Yes," Madai replied. "I can see where having friends can be to your advantage. We may need the friend of a large family later on."

"Tomorrow let us make a covenant of friendship," Israel said, "vowing that we will never become enemies and that there will always be friendship between us. Your boys may marry my girls and my boys may marry your girls." All the men agreed that it would be a great thing to have a covenant with Israel. It was agreed that a feast would seal the covenant. This would be a covenant of salt. Salt was for purification and to preserve meat. Therefore a covenant in salt was made committing those making the covenant would be pure and preserve the agreement. They ate the covenant meal in the evening. A bowl of salt was put on the table between the men making the agreement. Each man took a little of the salt and sprinkled on his food to show that he accepted this covenant. Israel also provided wine and beer for the festivities.

It was time for the goats to be sheared. Shearing goats was very different than shearing sheep. Goats are smarter. If one was turned upside down, it would fight to get back on its feet. The goats were put into a pen and not allowed to eat until they were being sheared. The goats would climb onto the milking platform and be fed to keep them distracted while being sheared. The platform had a pole on each side. The feed was put in a box on the end of the platform for the goat to eat. When the goat began to feed, a curved branch was slid down the poles to keep the goat from removing its head.

Shearing started with the hind legs, then very carefully around the teats or scrotum. If the teats or scrotum was nicked, the shearer would pour olive oil on the cut. Then the shearer would start at the belly and shear up to the backbone, first on one side and then on the other side. The head was not sheared but the neck and face was sheared. Shearing started with the young goats because the fleece of young a goat is worth more than the fleece of older goats. Once the fleece was cut off it was rolled and tied and placed in a cart. It took a little longer to shear a goat than it took to shear a sheep. The shearing took over four days to complete.

Israel told Leah to have the women take enough goat fleeces to make panels for their tents. The women didn't need much goat hair since they had good tents. Israel decided to take half the fleeces to Tirzah and half to a town toward Egypt named Adam. Leah asked if she and some of the wives could go with him. She said the wheat and barley they had purchased was almost gone. She wanted to buy more since they had arrived too late to plant barley and wheat last year.

Half the goat fleeces were loaded on three carts. They left for Tirzah early the next morning. They hurried the oxen along with goads. Israel had the goads made sharp enough to get the oxen's attention but not sharp enough to puncture the skin. They traveled until after the sun had set before they could see the town lights. A cold, quick supper of barley bread was eaten while the tents were put up by firelight.

The fleece buyers were delighted to see three carts loaded with goat fleeces. Prices are way down on goat fleeces they told Israel. Before Israel asked what they offered he told them, "This is just half of my fleeces. We live just as close to Adam as we do to Tirzah. I am taking half to each town to see where I get the best price. Whoever gives me the best price will get my fleeces as long as we are in this area. I also have over two thousand sheep that I will shear next year."

The buyers walked a little way from the carts and talked quietly among themselves. Israel couldn't hear what they were saying but he knew they were discussing the total package of goat and sheep fleeces.

One of the buyers said, "The price is way down, and we have to store the fleeces until a caravan comes through here. A caravan came through Tirzah less than a moon ago. We may have to wait for at least three moons before we can sell these fleeces. A caravan may be coming through Tirzah about then on its way to the eastern countries. They pay about one silver ring for a goat fleece. We will look at the fleeces and if you promise to bring your sheep fleeces to us, we will give you a silver ring and two brass rings for the young fleeces and one silver ring for the others."

Israel answered, "If the merchants in Adam do not give me more for the other half, I promise to bring my fleeces here."

One buyer told Israel, "What you don't know is that the fleece buyers in Adam bring their fleeces here to sell. We give them less than we are offering you."

The carts were driven into the sheds and the buyer's servants unloaded the fleeces. As the fleeces were being unloaded, the buyer would point to specific places to place different fleeces. They were grading the fleeces and were pleased to see so many fleeces from young goats.

"We counted three hundred and five fleeces from young goats and thirteen hundred and seventy five others," the lead buyer said. "That will be 163 gold rings, seven silver rings and five bronze rings." After he said that he produced a bag and started to count the rings into Israel's hand.

Israel asked, "Could I have thirty-five bronze rings and thirty silver rings with the rest in gold rings? We have some shopping to do and I would rather have bronze and silver rings to pay the small shopkeepers. We need half of a cartload of wheat and a cart and a half of barley. The women want to do some shopping."

"There is not that much wheat and barley left in all of Tirzah," the buyers told Israel. "The only person who would have that much extra wheat and barley would be a rich man who lives in Edom. His name is Job. He is one of the richest men in this whole area. He said his God gave him the fortune. He has several hundred yokes of wheat and barley planted each year."

"I know him," Israel replied. "He was a young man when my grandfather, Abraham, was his friend. He was my father's friend also. I think he is younger than my father."

One of the buyers told Israel. "You said you took one day to get here from the Jabbok River. Job lives four or five days towards Egypt from the Jabbok River."

"We didn't harvest any grain before we left Haran up in the land of the Hittites. What little grain we had and what we purchased at Halab is almost gone. We will purchase what your town can spare. Then we must go see Job."

"Do you have a wine merchant and an olive oil merchant here?" Israel asked.

"Yes we have a fine wine maker and merchant. He will take your grapes and turn them into a fine wine. He charges one goat skin full of wine for each ten he makes. You have to provide the grapes. Large grapes grow abundantly along the Jabbok River. The olive oil merchant has a very large press. He will turn your olives into oil for the same price of one goat skin full for each ten he makes." One of the merchants told him. "If you want us to, we will introduce you to both of them."

The fleece buyers went to the grain merchants and explained to them that if they gave Israel a good price he would do business with the town as long as he was in this area. They took Israel to the wine maker and the olive oil merchant and introduced him to them. Israel talked with them for a short time. The wine maker told him that the grapes were ripening now.

Israel asked, "How many goat skins of wine do you get from a cart load of grapes?"

"If they are good, ripe grapes, I can get over sixty skins full of wine from a cartload. You can provide the skins or I can charge you for them," the merchant told him.

When the carts pulled into the grain merchant's area, they were ready to bargain. Israel was ready to purchase all they would sell him at the low price they offered. He got a half a cartload of wheat and almost a cartload of barley. The women walked through the shopping areas buying things they needed for their tents. They bought bronze pots, knives and ladles. Leah saw some small boards with many bronze nails driven through them. She knew they were used to card wool and goat hair before twisting it into yarn. She bought twelve sets. When the women were through shopping, Israel took them to the tavern for some beer. He purchased enough small pitchers so that two people could share each pitcher. After they finished the beer, they loaded into the carts and started home.

On the way back to camp Israel began figuring how long they had been gone from Haran and when the grapes and figs would be ripe. He told Leah, "We left Haran after I had sheared my sheep. That was in the month of Ziv. We traveled during the month of Sivan. We have been at

Succoth since the month of Tammuz. We are now midway through the month of Ab. The grapes, olives and early figs should be starting to ripen now. The dates won't get ripe until in the month of Elul. As soon as we pick the grapes and figs, we will pick olives. The early figs are the largest and sweetest. After we cross the Jordan River, we will go upstream for two hands of time to see if we can find grapes and a grove of fig trees."

They reached the Jordan River two hands' of time before sunset. They crossed the river at a shallow place where the trees had been removed so people and carts could cross. While they were traveling, four of the women began grinding barley so they could make bread for supper. They built a fire and soon the rocks were heated enough to bake the bread. The women rubbed mutton fat on the rocks so the bread wouldn't stick. One of the men found some short sticks. He carved one end thin and flat so the women could use them to turn the cakes. After supper they sat around the campfire talking. They talked for several hands of time. Finally Israel said, "We should get to bed so we can get started early tomorrow."

Before sunup the women were grinding grain for breakfast. They didn't have time to grind the grain very small so they cooked the cracked grain. They ate the boiled grain by tearing bread into small pieces and folding it to scoop up the boiled grain. After a quick breakfast they were on their way again. Israel turned the oxen upstream.

Leah asked, "How do you know the grapes, figs and olives are starting to get ripe?"

Israel answered, "I lived in this area for 77 years before I went to Haran. Figs, grapes and olives always ripened in the month of Ab. I think it is too early in the month for many figs to be ripe. When we get back to Succoth, we will wait two hands of days. Then we will bring as many people as can be spared to gather figs. We will wait half a moon's cycle and come again for the main harvest. We will dry most of the figs to eat during the cold months."

They followed the Jordan River but had to travel some distance from it. The jungle on both sides of the Jordan River was so dense that people couldn't easily walk there. Leopards, lions, tigers, panthers, and bears lived in the thickets.

They traveled two hands of time before they saw a large grove of trees with long slender leaves that were green on the front and silvery on the back. When they got closer, Rachel was amazed to see a tree that looked like someone had drilled large holes all over the trunk. It was gnarled and very old. Israel told them that olive trees lived for hundreds or even thousands of years. There was another old tree that looked like two large trunks had been twisted around each other. A little farther and they saw a large grove of fig trees. Israel had been right. The figs were just beginning to ripen. They were able to find enough to eat but not enough to take any back to camp.

The camp was glad to learn that a grove of figs had been found. Everyone would be able to eat their fill and have cartloads to dry for winter. Israel had told them that wild figs were not as large as the ones farmers raised but they would be just as sweet.

Some of the older boys had been fishing in the Jabbok River. They found many grape vines growing in the trees. They cut down a bunch of grapes and tied it to a pole so two of them could carry it back to camp. Israel told everyone to be ready to pick grapes the next day. They left early next morning with three carts. It took less than two hands of time to reach the grapes. Some of the grapes were high in the trees. Young men and older boys would climb up, cut a bunch loose and lower it with small ropes to people below. There were many bunches low enough to be picked from the ground or from the carts. The grapes were large and ripe. By three hands of time after the noon lunch the carts were as full as Israel thought they should be. He and two men started for Tirzah. Leah had packed some goat meat and barley bread for them to eat on the way. The sooner they got the grapes to the wine maker the better the wine would be. They drove until it got too dark to see. They ate a cold supper and went to sleep under the carts. Next day they took the grapes to the wine maker. He told Israel to send one hundred and eighty goat skins for the wine. He said the wine would be ready in a moon's time.

When they got back to camp, Israel loaded the goat fleeces to take them to Adam to sell. He planned to continue on toward Egypt into the land of Edom and find Job. Israel called Oohdal and told him that he and his family were going to Edom to buy wheat and barley from Job. Israel said to Oohdal, "You are in charge of the camp while I am gone. In half a moon cycle I want you to take everyone that can be spared to a fig grove we found and pick three cartloads of figs. The men who drove the carts to Tirzah know where to find the grove. When you get back, have the children and older boys spread them out to dry. We will be gone at least half a moon cycle."

Israel had four camels saddled with the slings attached to the saddles for his wives. The goat fleeces were loaded onto three carts. Five camels were loaded with grain and supplies for the trip. Israel would drive the first cart. Reuben would drive the second cart and Simeon would drive the third cart. Early next morning they ate a quick breakfast of leftover boiled cracked grain and were on their way. They reached Adam before the sun set. Camp was set up and everyone sat around the fire and talked.

Next morning Israel sold his fleeces. The best price he could get was nine bronze rings per fleece. That worked out to ninety gold rings. Israel had brought fifty gold and one hundred silver rings, along with a bag of bronze rings to buy supplies and the wheat and barley. He had asked the merchants if they knew Job. They did not know him but they knew of him. They were able to give fair directions to his house. They said it would take about four days to reach his house.

Four days later, about four hands of time after sunup, Israel looked up and saw men coming quickly on camels. The men reached Israel much quicker than he thought possible. The men circled around the carts. The leader approached and said to Israel, "Welcome to the humble house of Job. He requests that you and your party will be his guest tonight. May I tell my master who will be visiting?"

"Yes," Israel replied. "Tell him that Israel, who was named Jacob by his father, has come to see if he could buy grain. The grandson of his friend Abraham and the son of his friend Isaac has come to visit him. I and my family have traveled five days to see if I could buy some wheat and barley."

The leader of the men called one of the men to him. "Did you hear what this man told me?" He asked.

The man said that he had heard and that he would take the message to his master. Then he rode off toward the house.

Israel asked the man, "How did you get here so fast? You covered a distance of three hands time in less than one hands time."

"These are swift Arabian camels, called 'deloul' camels. They travel three times as fast as your camels. The legs are longer and slimmer and they don't carry as much fat. They are harder to ride. We must wear strong leather belts around our chest and stomach. They have a movement that one must get used to before riding very far. My master, Job, has a herd of three hundred of these animals. He sells them to the Bedouins who live toward the sunrise. They are very fond of them. But this is enough talk. Let's get you and your family to Job."

In two hands of time Israel saw a man riding towards them on a white mule. He was dressed richly in a silk robe and a bright purple turban with a gold crescent fastened to it. The mule also had a gold crescent on its forehead.

Israel jumped from the cart and ran to meet Job. Israel bowed down seven times to Job. Job picked Israel up and said, "It is not right for one man to bow to another. Bow only to God."

They saluted each other with a kiss and then Job asked about Isaac. "The pilgrimage of my father, your servant, has been long and hard. He has seen one hundred and fifty seven years, but he is still in good health," Israel answered.

They continued talking about people they both knew until they reached Job's house. As they entered the house a man a little younger than Israel came to meet them.

"This is my steward, Abida. He is also a grandson of Abraham. He is the fourth son of Midian, the fourth son of Abraham by his second wife, Keturah." Israel and Abida greeted each other with a kiss and began talking.

"I met your father, Midian, when I was a young man," Israel began. "Is he well?"

"Yes, he is well and very prosperous. Our grandfather was generous with Ketruah's sons. He gave them gifts of a hundred sheep, a hundred goats and fifty gold rings each. By using the skill as a shepherd that Abraham taught them they have all done very well. When I left home ten years ago, my father was a wealthy man. I got tired of herding sheep and goats and set out to make my fortune. I became a guest of Job. When he learned that I was Abraham's grandson, he hired me. I have been working for him since. How have you been?"

Israel told Abida, "Our stories are similar. I left my father's house and went to Haran. There I met my mother's brother, Laban. I worked for seven years for my first wife and seven more for my second wife. God has been very good to me. I now have four wives, eleven sons and a daughter. I have many sheep and goats, a herd of camels and twenty-four yoke of oxen. We left Haran just after shearing time and didn't bring much wheat and barley with us. I heard that Job had grain to sell so I came from my home to see if he would sell me some."

Job entered the conversation, "I will give the grandson of my friend all the wheat and barley he wants without cost."

Israel answered, "That is very generous of you but you know my grandfather often said 'do not accept a large gift as that will make you indebted to the giver.' I came prepared to pay the current price."

Job smiled and said, "Let's not talk business now. I have had a fatted calf made ready and it is roasting now. My wife and her servants are preparing a banquet for us. It is not often I get to celebrate with two of my friend's grandsons. Abida, have the servants show our guests to the rooms that have been prepared for them. After you have rested, I will send servants to your room with a change of clothing for each of you. The servants will wash your feet as soon as you get to your rooms. Until then I pray you enjoy your rest."

Rooms had been prepared for Israel and his family, a room for each of his wives, a small room for Dinah and a large room for the eleven boys. There were soft mats on the floor stuffed with sheep wool for each person. Some servants came in and washed the feet of all the travelers. They lay down and napped for three hands of time as was the custom of the Edomites. When they awoke, there was a change of clothes for everyone. Refreshed and with clean clothes, they awaited the summons to come to the evening meal. The meal was served on a table with chairs for everyone. The fatted calf had been roasted with mustard seed crushed in vinegar, mint and marjoram. There were many varieties of food that they had never eaten before. The wheat bread had been made with yeast and baked in a large brick oven in loaves instead of flat cakes. There was a salad of garden rocket, leaf chicory, black radishes and wild lettuce with a dressing of hot oil flavored with cumin, caraway seeds and garlic. Almonds had been roasted, ground and mixed with honey. Several bowls of cows' butter were on the table. Cattails grew in a lake toward the sunrise. Cattail roots and young stems had been baked in the oven with garlic, cumin, saffron and thyme. Wine and beer had been put in jars and lowered into a deep well so it was cold. Everything was delicious. Job's wife, Uzit, Israel's wives and the girls ate in a separate room.

The boys really liked the sweetened almond paste. They would tear a piece of bread, dip it in the melted butter, and then spread almond paste on the bread. Job warned them, "Be careful not to eat too much of the almond paste. It may upset your stomach if you are not used to eating such rich sweet food."

Talk was lively and everyone was in a festive mood. Gad said, "This food is so good I want to eat more, but I'm stuffed."

Job smiled and said, "You can." He clapped his hands and some servants came in with small bowls of a brownish liquid along with some leaf chicory. Job instructed them, "This is a special sauce that was brought from a country far past India. Dip a green leaf into it, eat the leaf and you will be hungry again."

Gad and Dan were the first to try the sauce. Almost as soon as they had eaten one of the leaves dipped in the liquid, they were hungry again. All the boys ate a leaf with sauce on it. Then they started eating more bread dipped into the butter and spread with almond paste.

Job clapped his hands and dancing men and women came in to do an acrobatic dance. After the dance, musicians and singers came to entertain them. The boys had never had such an exciting evening.

Israel said to Job, "This has been a wonderful evening, but if you don't mind, I think we had better go to sleep."

Job answered, "Please forgive me. I didn't mean to keep you so late after you had traveled all this way. You must be very tired. The servants will take a lamp and show you to your rooms."

That night wives were up trying to soothe the boys. They had stomach aches from eating too much almond paste. Next morning they were fine.

After a good breakfast, Job showed Israel and the boys around his house and barns. When they came to the camel pen, Job asked if anyone would like to ride one of the swift Arabian camels. Reuben and Simeon said they would like to ride. Job had the boys put wide leather belts tight around their chests and stomachs. He explained that the gait of these camels was different than regular camels. The belts would keep the boys from getting sick. Two of the swift Arabian camels were saddled and led out and made to kneel. When the boys got on, the camels got up so fast that they were almost thrown off. Job pointed out a bunch of trees some distance away. Israel said it would take a camel three fingers of time to get there and back. The swift camels were there and back in less than one finger's time. Israel was amazed at the speed of those camels.

The boys were shaken but very excited. Reuben's face was red with the excitement "Wow," he exclaimed! "I have never gone so fast! The wind blew through my hair so hard I thought it would blow off!"

Simeon was just as excited when he said, "I didn't know anything could go so fast. The ground was a blur as we passed over it. We came to the trees so quickly I thought that magic was bringing them to us!"

Gad and Dan decided they didn't want to ride that fast. When they got back to the house, Reuben and Simeon told everyone about the ride. They told how the wind had stung their eyes and how fast the ground passed under them.

Next morning Job told Israel, I sell wheat and barley to caravans going to Egypt. They buy it in sacks they call 'khar'. Each khar holds over two and a half Ephah of grain. I charge one silver ring and three brass rings for each khar of wheat and six brass rings for each khar of barley. After Israel agreed to that price, Job had his servants load as many khar of wheat on one cart and barley on the other two carts as each cart would hold. Israel counted out the rings Job had calculated. They started for home that morning

Israel kissed Job goodbye. Job told them, "God speed on your journey home. You are a very lucky man to have so many strong boys and such a lovely daughter. May our God keep you well until we meet again." The trip took five days.

CHAPTER 7

— PICKING FIGS —

When the moon had gone through half of the moon cycle after Israel had left to see Job, Oohdal told everyone that the next morning they would pick figs. The pickers reached the fig trees in two hands of time. Everyone started picking bunches of figs as fast as they could.

Figs grow low and in bunch on a tree that has soft leaves and no thorns. When the figs become ripe, the bunches drop a little. Figs were picked by raising the bunch up to loosen it from the branch. When the sun was directly overhead, Oohdal called a halt. One of the carts was almost full. Everyone took a large bunch of figs and a few cakes of barley bread and went to the stream for a drink. The rest period was about as long as it takes the sun to move down one hand. With much frivolity they went back to picking. When the sun had dropped another four hands of time, Oohdal said it was time to start back. He congratulated everyone on the amount of figs they had picked. The carts were almost full to the top. With the carts loaded and everyone tired from picking, the trip back took three hands of time. Oohdal told them it was too late to spread the figs. In the morning while the women were grinding barley grain for bread for the day, the children and older boys would spread the figs. Extra tent panels were spread all around the campsite. The children and older boys carried several bunches of figs at a time and put them on the panels. Soon there were figs drying everywhere. Every three days the figs had to be turned. The children didn't mind turning them since they could eat a few.

Israel and his family got back two days after the figs were picked. Israel was surprised to see how many figs had been picked.

He sent Reuben and Simeon to Tirzah with 180 goat skin bags to get the wine. The wine merchant would keep his share and put the rest into the goat skin bags. The young men hitched the oxen to carts early the next morning and returned two days later with 162 skins of wine.

One clear morning Israel called everyone to the center of the camp and announced. Today we are going to pick ripe and green olives. We will be gone all day so pack some lunch and be ready as soon as you can." The young men and older boys climbed the trees and beat the branches. Everyone picked up the olives that fell. By the time the sun was one hand from setting they started back to camp with two carts loaded with olives. Israel took Reuben and Simeon with him to Tirzah to get the olives pressed into oil. The merchant told him he thought the two cart loads would make about one hundred skins of oil. He would keep the oil in his vats until Israel brought the skins. The oil would be ready in two hands of days.

The summer passed quickly. Every morning the sound of grinding barley was heard all over the camp. Reuben and Simeon went to Tirzah and returned with 90 skins of oil. The children had been turning the figs for over a moon cycle. They were dried enough to be stored.

The dates had become ripe along the Jabbok River. Israel sent a cart with thirty people to pick the dates. Some were eaten but most were allowed to dry in the sun to be eaten during the rainy seasons.

Togarmah reported to Israel that the flax was ready for scuthing. He asked Israel for men to help him prepare the flax to make the ropes. Israel sent seventeen men to help with the scuthing. The men pulled shard knives down the length of the stalk of flax to remove some of the straw. If they were not careful, some of the fibers would be removed. This was inevitable but the men tried to remove as few fibers as possible.

Breaking the stalks was the next procedure. Jerah had made three breaking machines. Each was a large limb that had been smoothed across the top and down one side with legs pegged at an angle to the underneath side so it would stand as a platform. A board was pegged beside this limb so that when it was pulled down it just missed the platform. Men sat by the breaking machines and took a handful of flax to break. They put it on the platform, spread it evenly and pulled the board down breaking the stalks. The flax was moved about the width of two fingers between breaks. Each handful was broken as many times as needed to break the entire stalk.

Heckling was the final process before twisting the fibers into string. Blocks of wood the length and width of a hand had nails driven through them. There were three sets of heckling blocks for each man. The first had only ten bronze nails in each row across and five rows down the block. This set of blocks started the process of removing the remaining straw and started aligning the fibers. The next set had more nails and removed more straw and did more aligning. The last set had one more row of nails than the second block and completed the process of removing the straw and aligning the fibers for twisting into twine.

The women and older girls took fibers to twist them into twine. Each woman or girl took a basket of fibers to spin. They picked up a handful of fibers and started twisting it into twine. When the twine was long enough, they turned so that the fibers came over their left shoulder when they had a small amount twisted they attached it to a spindle. The spinal was a straight piece of a branch with a rock or wooden weight on the end to keep the fibers twisting into twine.

The women and girls worked for days making the twine. With so many people working, they made a lot of twine to be used to make rope. Togarmah was pleased to see so much twine. He put a heavy branch into the ground for a post. He pegged a board with three hooks onto the post. He tied three strands of twine onto each hook. He put another post twenty paces from the first post. The rope would grow shorter as the twine was twisted into rope. Kittim stood by this post and played out the twines which were twisted once around the post to allow for the rope to grow shorter. By twisting the twine around the post it wouldn't slip as easily. This held the new rope tight but allowed it to be lengthened as needed.

Madai twisted the board the twines were hooked to. Togarmah controlled the tightness of the twists with two small boards he had nailed together to form a cross. He held the small boards between the strands of twine moving slowly back toward Kittim. As he moved back, the twisting of the board made the rope take shape. From the bottom the handle was raised up the side of the rising sun and then down the side of the setting sun, so the rope would have the right twist. As the rope grew longer the twines grew shorter. Kittim allowed the twine to slide around the post enough to make up for the difference in length.

When they quit for the day, they had made three ropes each twenty paces long. Israel was glad to have three new ropes. Israel told them that after they had made ten ropes for him they should make as many as they could and take them into town to sell. They could earn money making ropes of such good quality.

As the weather started to cool, Israel said, "It will soon be time for the early rains."

Rachel asked, "How do you know the early rains are about to start?"

"Do you see that the birds are gathering in large flocks? When the birds gather like that it means that summer is over. The birds are about to go south and the rains are about to start. When we plant wheat or barley, we must cover it quickly or the birds will come and eat it."

He told Oohdal to go with him to the level field where he wanted to plant wheat and barley. When they arrived, Israel took sticks and shoved one in the ground. He walked directly toward the rising sun for three hundred paces and placed another stick in the ground. He walked at a right angle to that stake for eight hundred paces and placed the third stick. He walked toward the setting sun until he was in line with the first stake to plant the last stake. He told Oohdal to have the shepherds build a temporary fence around the area defined by the stakes and to bring enough sheep into the enclosed area to crop the grass down to the ground. The sheep were to stay until they could no longer find anything to eat. Then the shepherds could take the sheep back to their normal pastures.

Israel said, "I will have wheat and barley planted here after the early rains have softened the ground."

Oohdal and the shepherds brought several hundred sheep into the area to graze while the fence was being built. The sheep couldn't find anything to eat after half a moon cycle. Oohdal asked Israel to see if the area was clean enough. Israel said, "You and the shepherds did a good job. Take them back to their pasture. I can tell that the rains will begin in a few days."

Israel was right. Three days later, in the month of Ethanim, the rains began. The goat hair and camel hair tents and panels were porous enough to let air through when dry but as soon as rain landed on them, the fibers swelled and the tents became water tight.

After it rained for a fourth of a moon cycle, the rains stopped for a few days. Israel was waiting and ready for the break. Israel called some of the men to come to the large piece of ground to plant wheat and barley. Oxen were brought to the camp to pull the plows. Twenty four pairs of oxen and a cartload of wheat were taken to the field.

Israel had a large bag full of wheat over his shoulder hanging on his left side. As he walked the length of the field, he scattered the seeds with his right hand. The seeds covered an area as wide as the plows would cover. Plowing was to cover the seeds not to loosen the soil.

The plows had bronze points on them to better penetrate the ground. The plowman had to keep a steady upward pressure on the handle to keep the plow in the ground. If the plowman looked back, the plow could come out of the ground and flip over onto its side. If that happened, it took about one finger of time to get the plow back to the place where it left the ground. All the other plowmen had to wait until the plowman was ready to start again. When this happened, the birds came and ate many of the seeds.

It took the plowmen half a day to plow from one end of the field to the other. Boys brought a lunch of barley bread, leben and drink to the men at noon. While the men ate lunch, the boys took the animals to graze and carried leather buckets of water for them to drink. The men and animals rested for the time it took the sun to move one hands width across the sky. They hitched the oxen and plowed back to the other end of the field. There they unhitched the plows and took the animals back to the pasture near camp. They planted twenty four yokes of land every day. A yoke of land was the amount two oxen could plow in a day. Israel wanted to have the land planted before the former rains started falling again. The wheat was planted in eight days. As they started planting the barley, the rains began again. They had completed planting by the middle of the month of Bul. Half a moon after they finished planting, the heavy rains started in the month of Kisley. During the first part of the month of Tebeth the ewes had their lambs. The shepherds had to stay in the field day and night. If a ewe did not clean the new lamb's nostrils right, the lamb would suffocate and die. The shepherds had to check each newborn lame as soon as it was born to be sure it had been cleaned right. If it had not been cleaned enough, the shepherd had to clean the mucus from its nose.

In Shebat the winter rains came. It rained hard at times and at other times it poured. Everyone tried to stay inside during the heavy rains. During the summer grass had been cut, dried and stored in the shelters. This year the animals were fed dried grass and some barley along with what they could find to graze in the pastures. Next year the cattle would be fed barley mixed with threshings.

Around the middle of the month of Adar there was a clear bright winter day. Israel put on a heavy cloak with a leather belt around his waist and went to the center of the camp. He called out in a loud voice, "There is an almond grove about a walk of three fingers time toward the rising sun. The almond trees should be in bloom. I'm going to look at them. Does anyone want to go with me?" He waited about two fingers time and almost everyone was ready to go. They walked slowly and talked cheerfully. The rains had been so heavy that they had gone outside only when necessary. They had walked three fingers of time when they saw a lovely sight. The whites and light pinks of the almond trees could be seen for a long distance. They continued walking as a group until they reached the grove. Everyone went their own way in search of what they thought was the prettiest tree. After wandering around the grove of almond trees for about a hand of time, the group reassembled and walked back to camp. On the walk back Rachel said, "The trees with the pink blooms are the prettiest."

Israel told her, "the pink trees are pretty but the almonds on those trees are bitter and not fit to eat." They all agreed the walk to the almond grove was worth it. Getting out on a clear bright winter day was an added treat.

Everyone was very happy to see the month of Adar come to an end. That was normally the end of the heavy rains and the beginning of the latter rains. This year the heavy rains held on for half a turning of the moon. Then spring hit quickly. In the month of Ziv the sun came out bright and warm on most days and dried up the land. The rivers and streams were soon crossable. Flowers bloomed and the barley harvest began. It took almost a moon's time to harvest the barley.

Shearing time came as soon as the barley was harvested. Israel's sheep had over three thousands lambs. In two years, when today's lambs were ready to breed, his flock would be more than three thousand five hundred ewes that could bear lambs. The ewes of the flocks of the ten men who were staying near Israel's camp had 306 lambs. They were pleased with the increase and told Israel they appreciated the help and knowledge he had given them. Each of the ten men had sheared a few sheep last year so they did their own shearing this year.

Israel had two thousand ewes and almost three hundred rams to shear. Besides Israel, there were four other shepherds that could shear well. Together the five of them could shear over six hundred sheep a day. They finished in four days. Israel had the fleeces stored in the shelters.

During barley harvest the wheat was in the "fereet" stage. The kernels had left the milk stage and had started to get harder. At this stage the wheat was harvested to eat raw or parched and stored. People grabbed a handful of wheat, rubbed the husks off and ate it. Reapers cut handfuls to be carried to camp where women and older girls rubbed the husks off in their hands. This was hard tedious work.

The women liked to go to the pastures and pick flowers to make their tents smell better after the wet winter. During the rainy season the panels on the tents had not been raised. The tents had begun to have a bad odor. Raising the side panels was a real treat. The wind blew through and cleared out the odors. They picked many bouquets of the small red pheasant's eye, the yellow chain bulge, the deep pinks of wild leeks and the purple of wild onions. They also dug the tubers of the wild leeks and onions to use in cooking. The children splashed in the puddles and got scolded for getting their feet muddy and their tunics dirty. It was a happy time for everyone. The shepherds were delighted to see the goat grass blooming as they knew that would mean more food for the goats. The camel grass and the desert cotton were also in bloom.

The barley had been harvested. The sheep and the goats had been sheared. Israel checked the wheat every day. This time of the year was extremely busy for them. During the first of the month of Sivan, the wheat harvest began.

Jerah had made twenty sickles for the harvest season. He had taken stout oak branches and heated them in boiling water for five hands of time. Then he tied them around large jars and shaped them with a handle and a curved area for the cutting surface. He cut a slit in the curved area and used glue made from boiled hoofs and bones to secure sharp pieces of flint onto the sickles.

Harvest time was a festive time. Leah had the women make a lot of beer for the harvesters so they could celebrate each evening. The wheat had ripened and twenty men started cutting it with the sickles. These men would grab a handful of stalks and cut it with a sawing motion to remove the stalks about three hands below the head. The cut stalks were dropped behind the worker. Women, men and older children would follow the reapers and pick up armfuls to tie them into bundles by wrapping a few strands around the bundle and twisting the cut ends under the strands. These sheaths were tied onto the donkeys and camels with rope. When loaded, the animals carried a stack of wheat almost as tall as they were to the threshing floor.

The threshing floor was a flat, round space about ten paces across that oxen had walked around and around until it was smooth and packed hard. Leah had the women sweep the threshing floor to remove the dust and small rocks. The wheat was unloaded and spread evenly. Oxen were driven around and around over the wheat until the kernels were separated from the husks. This was an efficient way to thresh grain. The grain was the heaviest and fell through the straw which was called threshings. The threshings were next and on top were the husks. The threshing continued all day. In the evening the wind increased a little and the winnowing began. Men and women took a winnowing fork, called a fan, and threw the grain, husks and threshing up into the air in the direction the wind was blowing. The grain fell first, the threshings next and the husks fell last or further from the person doing the throwing. The threshings had been broken into small pieces by the hooves of the oxen. The threshings were saved to be mixed with barley and fed to the animals in the winter time.

After the grain was winnowed, it had to be sifted. Women and girls took a flat basket, put several handfuls of grain in it and shook it vigorously. The grain went to the bottom of the basket and the chaff was blown away. The small rocks and tares had to be picked out by hand. The shaking, blowing and picking were repeated until the grain was cleaned. Tent panels were laid out so the grain could be piled to dry.

This was a time of celebration. Food was plentiful and beer was available. Children were allowed to eat all they wanted. Music and dancing were allowed until late. The men danced in one area and the women danced in another. The wheat kept piling up on each panel. As a panel was filled, another was put down. The harvest festivities continued for a full turning of the moon.

With the wheat harvest over, Israel thought it was time to go back to Tirzah and sell his fleeces. Israel saved three hundred fleeces for the women to spin into yarn to be woven into cloth. The two thousand fleeces filled ten carts. With the fleeces stacked high above the sides, they were lashed down so they wouldn't fall off. Israel allowed anyone who was not needed in camp to go with them to Tirzah.

The ten shepherds had twenty fleeces each to take to market. Besides the twenty fleeces Togarmah, Madai and Kittim had fifty-four coils of rope. They loaded their fleeces onto donkeys.

Three days later a large group started off in high spirits. The ten shepherds took their wives and children with them. Their fleeces were not as good as Israel's because they did not have experience shearing sheep. The oxen pulling the carts walked slowly so the people had no problem keeping up with them. They crossed the Jordan River about one hands time before sunset. A camp was made on a hill near the river. They had brought barley bread so everyone ate barley bread for supper. They went to their tents before dark and were soon asleep.

They were close to Tirzah late the next afternoon but decided to camp a short distance from the town. News of their arrival had reached the merchants of Tirzah. The wool merchants came out to their camp to see the fleeces. They were surprised to see two donkeys loaded with good quality rope. They tried to get Israel to sell them but he told them he would bring the fleeces and ropes into town mid morning.

Next morning Leah, Zilpah, Rachel, Bilhah and about twenty other women went into town to look at the merchandise in all the stalls. Israel and the ten men took their fleeces and ropes to the market to sell. Israel negotiated the price for all two thousand two hundred fleeces. He accepted the fourth offer of, one silver and five bronze rings for each fleece. The merchants had to cooperate to come up with the three hundred gold rings and three hundred silver rings. Each of the ten shepherds received two gold rings and ten silver rings for their fleeces.

Togarmah, Madai and Kittim didn't think the merchants offered them enough for their ropes. They found an empty space and sold the rope themselves. They sold all the ropes within four hands of time. They had received sixty six silver rings for the fifty four ropes.

After selling the ropes, the three found the other seven shepherds in a tavern. They and their wives joined them. Each bought a mug of beer for himself and one for his wife. After they drank their beer, they went shopping. This was the first time nine of the wives had been to a town since they were kidnapped several years before. They were very excited about being able to buy things they wanted. The men were generous. The women bought cloth to make new tunics for their children. Some of the children needed new sandals or belts. The men allowed the women to buy whatever they needed. In the end most of the ten shepherds had each spent their two gold rings. Happy with their purchases and their newfound wealth, they bought some roasted goat and wheat bread and went back to camp.

Leah and Zilpah bought sandals and belts for their boys. Leah also bought some cloth to make new tunics for three of her boys, and some pretty material for a tunic for Dinah.

Rachel and Bilhah looked at jewelry and fancy cloth. Rachel bought some dark brown material to make a new tunic for Joseph. Israel and Leah bought a hind leg of a roasted young ox along with many cakes of barley bread. Everyone was back at the temporary camp long before dark. The roasted ox was sliced and cut into small pieces and put into bowls. The bread was placed on panels placed around the camp where the people could sit and eat. After Israel gave thanks to God for the fleeces, they ate and talked and sang until after dark.

As was Israel's habit, he woke everyone at dawn. They soon were loaded and on their way. They reached the Jordan River just before sundown and crossed so they could camp on the side toward Succoth. They build a fire and the people that were wet from crossing stood close to get their cloaks and tunics dry. They were up early the next morning and reached camp around two hands of time after noon.

The main crop of figs, grapes and olives came on in the middle of Ab. Israel took five carts to the fig grove. The weather was warm so they slept under the trees. The five carts were loaded in two days. When they got back to camp the children spread the figs so they could dry.

Israel sent Oohdal with fifty of the servants to gather olives while he took 75 servants to pick grapes. He sent the grapes and the olives to Tirzah for processing.

Half-way through the month of Elul one of the helpers came running into camp. He told Israel that a group of Bedouins had attacked the herd he and the herdsman were keeping. The Bedouins killed the herdsman as he was trying to protect the herd. The camels scattered and the raiders made off with about half the herd.

Israel called ten men to go with him. They went to where the camels had been scattered. They searched for the camels that were left. It took them four hands time to gather all the camels. Israel left two men to watch the camels until he could send another herdsman and helper.

Israel called most of the shepherds and herdsmen together in a few days. "I am greatly troubled by the loss of my camels. I think we are too close to the desert. I think we will move toward the sunset for a few days" The men agreed and added that the pasture was drying up. It was getting harder to find good pasture for the flocks and herds.

Israel told the entire camp that they were moving toward the sunset. He told the shepherds to start moving the flocks toward the Jordan River. Word was sent to the herders of the camels, donkeys, and cattle to start moving the herds to the Jordan River. The goat herders would follow the sheep. The camp was packed and ready to go four days later. Israel went to the ten men that had been working with him to tell them goodbye.

"If you want to, you can make a plow and plant barley and wheat in the field I had cleared. You don't have enough help to plant it all but plant as much as you can. Take some flax twine and weave it into panels about one pace long and as wide as the loom. Have your wives sew the panels into a bag. When you harvest your crops, keep what you will need and bag up the rest and take it to Tirzah to sell when you take your fleeces and ropes. If everyone works hard you should have many gold rings to divide. I am sorry to leave you. You have all been my friends. May God grant you peace and prosperity in the future." After he told them this, he kissed each one." Israel sent four carts with Reuben, Simeon and two servants to get the wine and olive oil. They got the wine and olive oil and hurried to catch up to the rest of Israel's camp.

The carts rolled out soon after he returned. They made it to the Jordan River by sundown. The sheep, goats and other animals were pastured close to the river. "We will make camp on this side tonight. Tomorrow we will try to get the animals across the Jordan," Israel said.

The river was low and they found a shallow place to ford the river. The herders were quick to get the cattle, camels, donkeys and goats across the Jordan. The shepherd of the first flock called his sheep. "Tadahoo, Tadahoo, Tadahoo," as he waded into the river. The sheep that were nearest followed him. The sheep that were further away hesitated to enter the water but as the shepherd kept calling and getting farther away most jumped in and followed. Some of the yearlings and lambs would not get into the water. Israel told men to pick them up and put them in the river. As soon as they were put in the water they started following their shepherd. It took almost half of the day to get two thousand ewes, the rams, and all the lambs across the river.

They ate a quick lunch and were on the way by the time the sun had moved about three hands' past noon.

Traveling with young animals was very slow. Three days later they crossed a line of high hills. As he looked down from the top of the hills, Israel saw a large flat valley without any one living in it. There was a large town at the edge of the valley. The shepherds and the herdsmen moved their animals into the pasture they thought best for the animals. The goats liked the hillsides because they liked to browse on the leaves and twigs. Israel knew that the town was Shechem.

CHAPTER 8

— SHECHEM —

Early the morning after they had arrived at Shechem Israel had two camels brought to the camp. Israel's camel was saddled and a large gold crescent was on its forehead with a gold chain around the neck. Leah's camel had two poles attached to the boards of its saddle and another attached to the pommel of the saddle. A rope net slung between the two lower poles. Rugs were on top of the rope net with cushions on the rugs. As Israel and Leah were about to get on the camels, Judah asked Israel, "Why do you have to get someone's permission to stay here. You didn't need permission at Succoth?"

Israel explained to Judah, "There was no king at Succoth. We did not need to get permission. We are in king Hamor's area. We need to get his permission. I will pay him to have his army protect us."

The ride to Shechem didn't take very long. When Israel entered the city gate, he saw that it was made of cedar, three fingers thick with carvings of animals. He asked for directions to Hamor's palace. The palace was at the end of the street. The street had markets on both sides.

Israel rode up to the guard and asked the steward to announce him to the king. The steward told Israel the king was expecting him. The king's steward escorted Israel and Leah to king Hamor.

When Israel approached the king, he bowed seven times to the king. "I am Israel; I was named Jacob by my father Isaac. God changed my name to Israel."

The king replied, "Isaac I know. Jacob his son I have heard of. Why do you want to see me?"

"I have moved my flocks and herds to the land just beyond the hills," Israel answered. "I have come to ask your permission to stay there. I would like to purchase the land where I am camped."

Hamor asked Israel how many sheep and herds he had. Israel told Hamor, "I have around 3000 sheep and 2700 goats. I also have cattle, camels and donkeys. I have come to ask for your protection should it be needed."

Hamor answered Israel, "I will sell you all the land in the valley for one hundred silver rings. You can have the protection of my army for 50 rams every year."

"Agreed," Israel said. "I will send fifty yearling rams to you tomorrow."

Israel pulled out a bag of silver rings and counted out one hundred for Hamor.

Hamor asked if Israel wanted to trade in his city. Israel told him that his family and servants would like to trade with the merchants in his city.

Hamor's steward took Leah to the queen's apartment to meet with her. The queen was happy to meet someone who could be a friend. The queen called her ladies-in-waiting and took Leah for a tour of the city. Israel had given Leah five gold rings and ten silver rings. He said she could buy anything she wanted but to be sure to buy a good present for the queen. Leah bought the queen a heavy silver bracelet with decorations carved in it for one gold ring.

The king had the steward bring his son. When the lad arrived, the king told Israel, "This is my son, Shechem. He is fourteen. He was born the day I became king so I named him for the city." The king's son and the steward took Israel on a tour of the market place.

When they came to the merchants that buy sheep and goat fleeces, the steward told the merchants that Israel had over three thousand sheep and nearly three thousand goats. The merchants all saluted Israel with a kiss. The steward took Israel back to the palace for lunch.

The queen and Leah arrived at the same time. The queen and Leah had lunch with the ladies in waiting on a patio lined with trees. The talk was lively and cheery. Their food was roasted gazelle, flavored with cumin, caraway seeds and garlic and a salad of leaf chicory, endive and wild lettuce served with a sauce of olive oil flavored with garlic and caraway seeds. A bowl of goat cheese was a side dish. The wine was mild and sweet.

Israel and the king ate in the royal dining hall. The king said he had known Israel was coming so he had a fat calf roasted and flavored with garlic, onion juice and caraway seeds. The salad was the same as the ladies were served. Slices of cheese made from sheep's milk were a side dish. The wine was chilled. After a leisurely meal, Israel excused himself by telling King Hamor that he had to get back to his camp to get the sheep and goats and other animals to pasture. On the way back Leah told Israel, "I liked the queen. She is a no nonsense lady. She runs the castle very well."

When Israel returned to his tent, he set up an altar and called it, 'El Elhoe Israel', God, the God of Israel.

Oohdal took fifty yearling rams to Shechem the next day. He looked at all the booths in the market place. He sat in the city gate talking to the city elders for a long time. He told the elders that Israel intended to build some shelters for his livestock on the land he had purchased. They would probably need skilled workers for the project. The elders told Oohdal that they would provide the laborers for one bronze ring per week for each worker. They talked of many things. After Oohdal left the, elders felt good about the prospects of having such a rich leader living so near. They knew that his family would need many supplies.

Israel had his servants dig four cisterns in the valley. Each cistern was three paces across and one pace deep. The cisterns would fill with water during the rainy season.

Israel started building shelters for his cattle, oxen and camels. He hired fifteen laborers from Shechem. He also bought the timber and other supplies from the merchants in Shechem. This was the beginning of a prosperous relationship between Hamor and Israel. Israel knew they had more figs than they could eat so he took a cartload to market. He set the price of two bunches for a bronze ring. Rueben and Simeon stayed in town to sell the figs in the market place. They sold all of the figs in six days for a total of 75 silver rings.

Israel knew that the former rains would start soon so he had sheep brought to eat the grass from the area he planned to plant. He was checking the plows when Mibsam and Adah came to him.

"Master Israel," Mibsam began. "Adah and I would like to have our jobs back. We miss you and our friends."

"I'm glad to have you back," Israel said as he kissed Mibsam. "What about your sheep?"

"I have hired one of Kittim's boys to be my shepherd," Mibsam told Israel. My flock is pastured toward the rising sun from your flocks."

You served under a captain Seggre for five years and became a corporal. You were trained even more under Captain Ater and he considered you as the sergeant of my army. We are alone here with just the poorly trained army of king Hamor to protect us. I will pay you one silver ring a year to be the captain of my army. You were trained by the best. I will give you the men Ater trained and others to make fifty men. You are to continue training them. They will work five days and train two."

"That is such a generous offer that I could not refuse," Mibsam replied. "When do I start?"

"As soon as you and Adah get settled," Israel told him.

"We are already settled in a camp by our sheep. We can move into your camp tomorrow," Mibsam replied.

Leah was very glad to see Adah. Adah said to Leah, "I am with child. You were right to say that getting married under a full moon was lucky."

Leah went to Israel, "I have weaned Zebulon. Mibsam and Adah are back. We need to have a celebration to announce the weaning of Zebulon and to welcome Mibsam and Adah home."

"I think you are right," Israel said. It is about half a moon until the former rains start. We need to have the celebration before then."

Leah called the women together and told them to get ready to celebrate the weaning of Zebulon and to welcome Mibsam and Adah. They decided that the celebration should be in six days. Israel sent Reuben to Shechem to invite Hamor, his family and friends to the celebration. When Reuben returned, he told Israel that many from Shechem would come. Israel thought as many as 100 people would be coming to the celebration from Shechem. He had two young bulls, five yearling rams and ten yearling goats brought to the camp to be prepared for the celebration. The women baked hundreds of loaves of bread and made two hundred jars of beer.

Israel called Mibsam and asked if he could get the fifty men into a formation to welcome king Hamor.

"I have had the men practicing a welcoming ceremony for the king," Mibsam replied. "It is a ceremony used by Captain Ater's friend while I was in his command on the Euphrates River. The men already knew how to ride camels in formation," Captain Mibsam told Israel.

The day of the celebration Reuben went back to Shechem and told Hamor the celebration would began that evening. When he returned, he told Israel that Hamor was coming with his army.

The two young bulls, three rams and seven he goats were roasted. The rest were boiled. The meat was cut into small chunks and put in bowls.

A little before dusk the guests arrived. King Hamor led the procession with Shechem at his side. Behind him came his army of twenty-five soldiers led by an African. The queen and her party were next and then came some merchants and their families.

When the King was about one finger's time from the camp, fifty men on camels came riding as fast as the camels would run. They were yelling a war cry and swinging swords. They charged right towards King Hamor. When they were close they separated into two columns about six paces apart. The Camels were made to face in and kneel. The men dismounted and stood at attention with their right hand held to their left shoulder. Mibsam walked to the king and saluted him and said, "This guard is in your honor, King Hamor."

The king returned the salute and began to walk toward Israel and the party.

Israel met King Hamor with a bow. The king introduced his party, "Schechem you already know," he said. "The black man is named Oregabeme, but we just call him Reggy. Most people have trouble pronouncing his name."

Israel motioned for Mibsam to come to them. The king told Mibsam he was very impressed with the honor formation his soldiers had preformed.

Israel told the king, "I am fortunate to have such a skilled soldier as Mibsam as captain of my army. He was trained by one of the greatest soldiers in the Hittite army. Now he is training my army."

The queen was shown to Leah's tent Rachel, Bilhah and Zilpah were there. Leah introduced the wives and all their children to the queen. The queen remarked that they were fortunate to have so many boys. Before the meal was served, Israel called for everyone's attention. Holding up

Zebulon, he said, "this is my youngest child, this celebration is to tell everyone that he has passed from being a baby to being a boy." Everyone cheered.

Roast lamb with a hot mint sauce flavored with dill, cumin and mustard seeds was the main entrée. A salad of fresh picked mint, rue, fleabane, chives, wild onions and coleroot was served with seasoned hot olive oil that had been heated with caraway seeds, garlic and sweetened with dates for a dressing. Chard mixed with lentils and flat beans were used as side dishes. Boiled dandelion greens and artichokes were also served. The choicest pieces of meat and the tenderest vegetables were taken to Leah's tent. Wine and beer that had been strained twice were served.

The soldiers sat on mats that had been placed end to end so they could all sit together. Captain Reggy told of his childhood in Africa. He said he was a Shilluk and had been captured by some Egyptians. After he served at menial tasks while his loyalty was being tested, he was put in the army as a soldier that carried bundles of sharp staves to be put in rows in front of the archers to protect them from a charge. The staves were driven into the ground at an angle so that the horses or men would be impaled on them if they charged.

Reggy and Mibsam told of past wars they had fought. Reggy told about the time he was fighting Egyptians at his home village when he was captured and taken to Egypt. A captain bought him to train to become a warrior. He told about many battles along the border of Egypt. The Pharaoh brought his army into Canaan. There was a terrific battle along the Great Sea. During the battle, Reggy was hit on the head and knocked unconscious. When the battle was over they left him for dead. When he woke up the army had moved on. He wandered around until he came to Shechem. King Hamor heard that he was a great warrior and hired him as his captain.

Mibsam told about life along the Euphrates River and the battles he had fought. He explained to Reggy and his men about Israel hiring Ater, the great Hittite Warrior, and his army. He and the men told about training under Ater and the fight with the Bedouin raiders. They told about the three brothers and their clan that wanted a blood feud. They explained how Ater and two of his men had killed the three leaders so the others were convinced to return to their camps and forget the feud. The talk of battles and training continued until very late. Mibsam had posted four guards around the perimeter of the camp to protect the king. This was a needless precaution but the king liked the security.

The queen and the ladies talked almost as long as the men and soldiers. Breakfast was eaten late the next morning. After a light lunch the king and his group left for Shechem.

The former rains started four days later. After the rain had fallen for five days, Israel and his servants planted the barley and wheat. Even though the barley and wheat were planted at the same time, barley ripens sooner than wheat so it is harvested first.

The rainy season set in with a vengeance for a little over a moon's time. Shechem was located in the hills that were east of the mountains, north of Mt. Gerizim and south of Mt. Ebal, so the wind from the great sea blew the rain fast and furious. Lambing season came during the first of the month of Tebeth. Everyone was happy when the winter rains stopped and the latter rains began. The end of the latter rains started the busy period.

The barley harvest started soon after the latter rains ended. Israel was pleased with the amount of barley they harvested. He knew he had enough for his camp and several cart loads to sell in Shechem. Shearing began as soon as the barley was harvested. It took half a moon to shear all the sheep and goats. Wheat harvest was started while the sheep were being sheared and because of the heavy rains the wheat grew tall and had large heads. There was more wheat as needed so Israel would have some to sell.

Israel's sheep had 4519 lambs; his goats had 2507 kids. The camels had twenty-three foals, the cattle had sixteen calves and the donkeys had thirty-two foals.

After harvest was over, Israel loaded 3000 sheep fleeces on carts and took them to Shechem. The merchants were very glad to see so many fleeces. They haggled for almost half a day before Israel agreed to a price of one silver ring for the good fleeces and eight brass rings for the lesser quality fleeces. Each fleece was checked as it was unloaded. The merchants accepted 2832 fleeces as good and 168 as being of a lesser quality.

The next day Israel sent 150 young rams to Shechem, fifty were pay for protection by his army. The 100 were taken to the market. Israel received two silver rings for each ram.

Three weeks later Israel took 2500 goat fleeces to the market. After much haggling, he got one silver ring each.

With the 250 gold rings, Israel went to a goldsmith and had two plates made of thirty gold rings each. These would be attached to the head dresses of both Leah and Rachel. Next he went to the silversmith and had two plates made of thirty silver rings each for the head dresses for Bilhah and Zilpah. The law of the land said that if a man divorced his wife she was entitled to take the clothes she wore. That meant that if Israel divorced any of them they could take the head dresses with the gold or silver plates. Israel was a leader and he wanted his wives to dress appropriately. The wives were very excited to receive the plates for their head dresses. Leah said to Israel, "We need to go to town and get material worthy of the plates you have given us."

Israel replied to her, "I am going to take a cartload of wheat to market in four days. Anyone who wants to go may go with me." He gave Leah ten gold rings and said, "Buy the material and whatever the other wives need."

Israel loaded a cart with wheat and started to Shechem. He had taken two baskets which held two ephah each. The baskets would be used to measure the wheat for sale. Two of the men that went to market with them would measure the wheat. As soon as they arrived in Shechem, Leah and the other three wives went to pay their respects to the queen. The queen was glad to have the company. She ordered wine and raisin cakes brought for them. After they visited for two hands of time the wives asked permission to go shopping.

Israel found an empty area in the market and started selling the wheat. He sold it for five bronze rings for a basketful. When a customer bought a measure of wheat, one of the men would put enough wheat in the basket to fill it. Then he would shake the basket vigorously to settle the wheat. After settling the wheat, he would pat it down and make an indentation in the middle. Then he would put handfuls of wheat into the indentation until it was full and running over. Israel had told them to give a good measure, shaken down and running over.

When the sun was overhead, Leah and several other men and women got to the market where Israel was selling wheat. Rachel said she was hungry. Israel took them all to the food section of the market and bought them meals of roast lamb. After lunch the women went shopping again.

Israel sent two men back to the market to relieve the two men who had been selling wheat. When the two men who had been selling wheat returned, they told Israel they had sold over half the wheat. They gave Israel a sack with silver and bronze rings. The sun was two hands from going down when they sold the last of the wheat and started back to camp. The women at the camp had prepared the evening meal for them so they ate as soon as they arrived.

Three days later Israel sent two cartloads of barley and another cartload of wheat to market. He sent six men besides the men leading the oxen to town. He told them to sell the barley for three bronze rings a basketful, and the wheat for five bronze rings. They left early in the morning and planned to start back two hands time before sunset.

The men returned after sunset. They had sold all the wheat but not much of the barley. Everyone said the price was too high and wouldn't buy it. Israel sent the barley back the next day and said they were to sell it for two baskets for five bronze rings. The men were back to camp one hand of time before sunset. They had sold out.

Israel saw that the animals needed a better water supply. He sent 20 men to dig two wells in the area. The area Israel purchased from King Hamor was forward and a little toward Hittite from Shechem. One of the wells was called Jacob's well near Sychar.

Oohdal came to ask Israel what he wanted to do with the young born to the camels, cattle and donkeys. Israel answered, "Save all the females and five of the best males. Send the rest of the males to the market in Shechem." Six days later Israel sent Reuben and Simeon, and several helpers with the 2250 rams, 1250 goats, eleven donkey foals, six young camels and three calves. They reached Shechem as the markets were opening. A caravan was going through Shechem. The caravan owner gave ten gold rings for each young camel. The donkeys' foals sold quickly for one silver ring each. The calves brought four silver and five bronze rings each. A butcher wanted to pay one silver ring and seven bronze rings each for 150 rams but Reuben wouldn't sell them so cheaply. After bargaining for two hands of time, the butcher took 140 rams of his choice for two silver rings each. The butcher also bought 200 goats for one silver ring and four bronze rings each. The rest of the day they sold lambs and goats to many different customers. At the end of the day they had sold 728 lambs and 543 goats, besides the camels, calves and donkeys. When the market closed, they had taken in 60 gold rings for the camels, 1456 silver rings for the lambs, 543 silver rings for the goats, 33 silver rings for the donkeys and thirteen silver and five bronze rings for the three calves. Late in the afternoon Mibsam and four soldiers came to the market.

Mibsam told Reuben that Israel had sent them to take most of the money back to him. Israel would allow Mibsam, Reuben, Simeon and the four soldiers to have a good meal and a mug of beer before they started back. Reuben was very glad to be rid of all the money. After paying for the meals and beer, he gladly gave the bag of money to Mibsam. Mibsam shook the bag and said, "You fellows sold a lot of animals and it seems you got a good price for them. We will come back tomorrow about the same time. See you then."

Reuben decided to rent space in the market to keep the sheep and goats for the night. He paid five bronze rings for the sheep and goats to have pens to stay in and guards to keep them safe. Once the sheep and goats were taken care of, Reuben and Simeon decided to go to a tavern and get something to drink. Taverns were operated by prostitutes. The women tried to ply their trade with Reuben and Simeon but the young men didn't know what the women were suggesting. They went to the pens where the sheep were kept and slept. Next day they were selling again, but the sales were slow and much bargaining was required to get a fair price. Reuben and Simeon were getting tired of selling.

Reuben had kept ten silver and ten bronze rings to make change. Sales remained slow the next day. By evening they had sold only 283 lambs and 143 goats. They had to come down a few bronze rings to sell them. Mibsam and the soldiers came for the money. As they were eating, Mibsam look at the bag of rings and said, "I see you didn't sell as many today, did you?"

"No," Reuben answered. "Sales are slow and we have to talk long and hard to make any sale. We even had to lower our price a few bronze rings."

"Israel told me to tell you that each day will be harder and you will sell less but you are to keep selling until he tells you to come back to camp."

Simeon complained that the sales were so slow that he thought they should take the lambs and goats back to the camp. Reuben told him that their father told them to stay and sell until he told them to come back.

The next day they sold 99 lambs and 48 goats. Mibsam did not come back until two days later when the sun was about half way down the western sky. He brought several shepherds and herders with him.

"Israel said it was time to bring the rest of the sheep and goats home. He said you two are probably ready to leave," Mibsam told them.

"We are!" Reuben said. "We have sold very little yesterday and none today. We have 1440 lambs and 516 goats left."

"I have brought a camel for each of you to ride. The shepherds and herders will take the animals," Mibsam told them. "I am to leave four soldiers to help and to guard the men and animals. We will ride on ahead of them as soon as you are ready to leave."

"I will tell the man who runs the market that we are leaving and see if I owe him anything. After that we can leave," Reuben said.

As Reuben was going to check with the person running the market, the shepherds and herders were moving the animals out of the market. When Reuben and Simeon got home, Israel kissed them and said, "You men did a fine job. I'm proud of you. You sold more than I thought you would. After you rest a day I will give each of you ten silver rings. You may go back to Shechem and buy whatever you want."

Reuben said, "Thank you father, I am glad that you thought we did a good job. Your praise is worth more than the ten silver rings. I do need a new leather belt and I would like to have a fancier knife. Thank you father."

Simeon was also pleased with his father's praise. He said, "Thank you, father. I appreciate your praise and the ten silver rings. But what are you going to do with the lambs and goats we brought back?'

Israel answered, "In a moon and a half, the figs, grapes and olives will be ripe. We are going to visit our friends that are living at Succoth and while we are there we will take the lambs and kids to the markets in Tirzah and Adam. While we are waiting, Reuben and Dan will take a flock of 240 of the lambs to pasture. Simeon and Gad will take another 240 of the lambs. I will have four good shepherds take the rest. They can take Levi and Judah to help them."

The lambs were split into six flocks the next day and taken several hands of time from the main camp. Reuben and Simeon were proud that their father trusted them with a flock. Israel had given each of them two helpers.

The young goats were split into two herds of 258 each and two herders and helpers were sent to take care of them.

When Israel thought the figs would be ripe, he sent the six shepherds and two goat herders toward Tirzah with the lambs and young goats. Two days later he started toward Tirzah with everyone that wasn't needed to care for the animals that were remaining in the pastures. He left twenty people to care for the camp. The rest started out with five carts. The supplies and tents were carried in the carts. Leah and Rachel rode in carts with the small children. Without the lambs and goats to slow them down, they reached Tirzah half a day before the animals. Israel went to the market to talk to the merchants.

The merchants were happy to see Israel. Israel told the merchants he was bringing 1440 lambs and 516 young goats. They said they probably couldn't buy that many but when they saw them they would decide how many they could use.

Israel set up camp outside of town. Israel took his wives and children into town to the food area. After the meal they walked through the markets. The ever practical Leah looked for things the women would need to make their work easier. She also looked at sandals, belts and cloth. She didn't buy much as the items in Shechem were of a better quality and didn't cost as much.

Rachel looked at jewelry and fancy cloth. The children were excited just to wander around the market and watch the bargaining and haggling. This was the first time some of the younger children had been in a market. Israel allowed the children to buy some sugared dates.

The following day Israel took 400 lambs and 200 goats to the market to sell. He told Reuben and Simeon to watch and learn. The merchants said they would give one silver ring and five bronze rings for each lamb. Israel told them they were trying to cheat him out of his eyeballs. They laughed and came up one bronze ring. Israel still couldn't believe they were so mistaken as to offer such a little amount for such fine fat lambs. The haggling went on for the entire morning, in the end Israel got 610 silver rings for the 400 lambs and 200 silver rings for the goats. After the bargaining, he asked Reuben and Simeon what they had learned.

Reuben said, "I learned that you have to have a bottom price you will accept and to keep discussing the price until you get it.

Simeon said, "I see you have to be really hard and not come down from your lowest price even if it takes all day to get that price."

Israel asked, "Do you think you could stay and bargain like that?" Both young men said they didn't think they could.

Next day Israel took 319 sheep and 157 goats to Tirzah. He had Gad and Dan stay and try to sell them. It took them three days to sell 226 sheep and 121 goats. They got one silver ring for the sheep and seven bronze rings for the goats. Israel would take the rest to Adam and Adullam. He wouldn't get as much for the sheep and goats but he would be rid of them.

They camped in the fig grove that night and left early the next day to visit their friends. When they arrived, they were startled to see that all their friends were looking very sad. Israel asked why?

One of the men told them they had come at a very bad time. A group of twenty-five Bedouins had raided their camp. The leader had taken one of ten sheep from each family. Several of the girls had rings in their noses. The Bedouin leader told them that when they returned after selling the sheep, they would take the girls with them as brides for their boys. The Bedouins had been raiding villages and shepherds' camps for fourteen days and had many sheep. They started from Jabesh-Gilead and had taken one out of every ten sheep from each flock they saw. They also put rings in the noses of many girls and single women along the way. They were taking the sheep to Adam to sell them. The leader said they would be back in ten or twelve days and they had left six days earlier.

Mibsam had been listening to the conversation. He spoke up, "I have fifty trained soldiers, and twenty men trained in either slinging stones or shooting a bow. With the nine of you that makes 79 men to teach those Bedouins a lesson they will never forget." Mibsam sent five of his soldiers to scout the area and see which way the raiders had gone. Most likely they would return the same way. The five were to select several places for an ambush before returning to camp. About half a day from Succoth the raiders had taken a road that led through a valley with steep hills on both sides. After Mibsam looked at the area he thought that would be the place to attack the raiders. He chose 45 men to go with him. Nine men with less training were to be runners and bring supplies. When they arrived in the valley Mibsam sent six men ahead to be watch for the raiders. Two men would work as a team. Each team would be two hands of time ahead of the previous team. Wolf song would carry farther than a man could walk in two hands of time. After the raiders passed, each team of soldiers would sing the wolf song and then follow them. When Mibsam challenged the raiders, the six men were to come behind to prevent any from escaping and to start the attack.

Mibsam and the men with him would just wait until they heard the wolf song from the closest pair. Then they would deploy eighteen soldiers on each side of the valley. Mibsam and two of the soldiers from Succoth would stand in the road to confront the raiders. They arrived at the valley eight days after the raiders had taken the sheep and left. Mibsam and Kittim inspected the sides of the valley and decided where to place the men. Each man would have on his brown cloak and would sit behind a rock, tree or shrub to be almost unseen by the raiders until they stood up and began to advance. Eleven days after the raiders had left their camp, when the sun was four hands high, they heard the wolf call. The men deployed to their places. Mibsam, Kittim and Zibeon sat in the center of the road with their brown cloaks over them. They tried to look like three rocks in the road.

The leader's second in command rode up to the leader and said, "Today I have heard a wolf song every two hands of time. Do you think it could be dangerous?"

The leader responded, "Who would dare attack twenty five armed and dangerous fighters like us? Don't be afraid. We can handle anyone who would dare attack us. We have fought and won many battles."

When the raiders were half a finger's time from Mibsam the second in command rode up to the leader again and said. "Look at those three big rocks in the road. I do not remember them."

"You have never been on this road before," the leader said "except when we drove the sheep to market. Of course things will look different coming this way." The raiders continued on their way with the leader in front and the rest following in columns of twos. The shepherds they had forced to take the sheep to Adam were walking behind. As they approached to within twenty paces of the rocks, the rocks stood up.

The leader yelled, "Who are you that would dare stand in my way?"

Mibsam answered, "I am Mibsam, Captain of Lord Israel's army. Who are you?"

The leader answered, "I am Abdul the Magnificent. I am leader of these twenty-four brave fighting warriors."

Mibsam told him, "To me you are Abdul the insignificant, an insignificant drop of spit on the tongue of a dead dog."

"That insult will cost you and your friends their lives!" the leader yelled.

It was the custom for men to ride camels with the saddle behind the hump and to guide them with a long pole. They were good for transportation but useless in battle. Abdul yelled and all his men dismounted from their camels. Mibsam gave a wolf call and the men stood up and started forward.

Mibsam yelled to the raiders, "My soldiers and I are going to kill all of you! If anyone doesn't want to die, drop your weapons and walk to one of my men!" One young man, the last in line, walked to the soldier nearest him. He told the soldier, "I, my mother and my sister were kidnapped by these men three moons earlier. I do not want to fight for them."

"You have proven your words, sit in the shade of that tree and Captain Mibsam will talk to you after the battle," the soldier commanded.

Seeing the soldiers beside them, Abdul yelled, "Attack!" The raiders made the mistake of charging toward the solders. The first barrage of stones and arrows killed all but six of the raiders. As soon as they reached the soldiers they were engaged in a sword fight with one of the soldiers. They were no match for a trained soldier. In a very few minutes all the raiders had been killed or wounded.

Abdul and two men had walked up to Mibsam, Kittim and Zibeon with swords drawn. Abdul had a method he had used to defeat many men. Being bigger than most, he would hold his sword straight out in front and charge his opponent like a raging bull. The opponent would normally take a step back, giving Abdul the advantage. He tried that on Mibsam, but Mibsam had defended against that move. Mibsam knocked the sword to the side with his shield and pushed his shield into Abdul's face very hard. This knocked Abdul back. Abdul started swinging his sword very vigorously at Mibsam. Every swing was met with the shield or the sword. In two minucts Abdul was showing that he was not up to a long fight. He dropped his sword just a little. Mibsam knocked it aside and with a quick flick of his sword he put out Abdul's right eye. This enraged Abdul and he started swinging his sword harder trying to get past Mibsam's guard. It didn't take long for Abdul to run out of breath. When his sword dropped a little again, Mibsam pushed it aside and put out Abdul's left eye. The other two raiders were tiring rapidly. When Kittim saw that Abdul was out of action, he used Captain Ater's favorite stroke. His opponent was gasping for breath and had opened his mouth to get more air. Kittim thrust his sword into the open mouth and out the back of the neck. Zibeon struck his opponent on the side of the neck cutting the artery and then just stood there and watched him bleed to death.

Abdul had tired himself out and was standing cursing. Mibsam got behind him and with one stroke he severed both of the tendons on the back of Abdul's ankles. Now Abdul could neither see nor walk. Mibsam pushed Abdul. Abdul tried to take a step and catch himself but he couldn't control his feet and he fell. One of the soldiers grabbed the sword from Abdul's hand. Mibsam told four of the soldiers to strip his clothes off. Abdul fought but without eyes he couldn't see what they were doing.

When they had taken all his clothes off, Mibsam spoke to Abdul, "You can neither see nor walk. I'm going to let you lay there and think about all the people you have robbed, all the girls and women you have raped, all the shepherds you have killed and all the sheep you have stolen. Yours will be a slow painful death. I'm not from this country. Do you think the hot sun, the vultures or the jackals will get you first?"

CHAPTER 9

—————— NEW MEMBERS ——————

As they were ready to leave, Mibsam called the lad who had not fought. "What is your name and why did you not fight?" he asked.

"My name is Kenet, my mother, sister, and I was kidnapped by Abdul and his men about three moons ago. They raped my sister and mother and took us to their camp. I was told that if I wanted my sister and mother to live I would have to ride with them. I have seen them kill men and women, boys and girls just for the fun of seeing them die. They were horrible people and I'm glad you killed them all!" the man replied.

"Can you show us the way to their camp?" Mibsam asked.

"Yes," Kenet answered. "I will be happy to show you their camp if you free my mother and sister."

The men who had been forced to drive the sheep to market walked up to Mibsam.

"What are you going to do with us?" one asked.

"Nothing," Mibsam answered. "I will take the bag of rings from Abdul's camel and pay you for the sheep he stole. Then you may go on home. How much did they get for each sheep?"

"Abdul forced them to pay two silver rings for each sheep," One of the men said. "We each had twenty sheep taken."

Mibsam went to Abdul's camel, took the bag of money and gave each man four gold rings. "We are going back to our camp to get supplies and then we will go free all the people Abdul kidnapped," Mibsam told them.

Several of the men told Mibsam that Abdul's men had been taking girls and women from their camps for years. Most wanted to go with Mibsam to Abdul's camp but Mibsam told them that their families needed them. The shepherds were so angry with the raiders that some picked up sticks and began to beat on the bodies. One shepherd was crying and beating on one body very hard and shouting. "You tied me up and raped my wife and daughter before my eyes. I'm glad you are dead! I wish I could have killed you!" He beat on the body until he was too tired to hit it again.

Mibsam and the army left the area to go back to Succoth. They rode the camels or ran at a slow ground eating trot that brought them to Succoth after sunset that day. There was much joy in the camp. The mothers and girls were really happy that the girls would not have to go with the raiders. Israel had the women prepare a great feast. They ate, drank beer and talked until nearly midnight.

The women built a fire and put a large clay pot on to heat. They wanted to boil the raiders' clothes to kill lice or other vermin that might be in them.

Mibsam introduced Kenet to Israel. Kenet told his story and then added, "I will be very happy to lead your army to their camp. Captain Mibsam has promised to free my mother and my sister."

Israel told him, "We will not only free them and everyone else who is there, we will also see that they get a share of the tents, supplies, and anything else that is in the camp. How long do you think it will take us to reach their camp?"

Kenet told him it would take at least seven days and the last three days would be through the desert where there wasn't water. There was a wadi about half a day's ride from the edge of the desert where the raiders filled their water bags before crossing the hot dry sands. "I think there will be several wadies along the way so we can keep our water bags filled until we reach the last wadi."

"Take three camels with you to carry extra water," Israel told Mibsam. "Do you think you can be ready by two hands of time after sunup tomorrow morning?"

"My men are eager to go," Mibsam replied. "We could leave tonight if you wanted us to go so soon."

"What are your plans?" Israel asked.

"Twenty-five of us will put on the cloaks and turbans worn by the raiders. We will attack at sunup, coming in from the sunrise. The men without robes and turbans will surround the camp to keep anyone from escaping. After we get to the middle of the camp we will tell them who we are and that we have killed the men who went raiding. If any man attempts to resist us, we will kill him."

"May the God of my grandfather, Abraham, and the fear of my father, Isaac, go with you and protect you. You may leave in the morning as soon as you are ready," Israel told all the men.

They made good time, and by noon the fourth day they were at the wadi Kenet had told them about. They filled the water bags and the camels were watered. They camped at the edge of the desert that night. One of the men remarked that they should sleep well since this would be the last grass they would see for six or seven days.

The trip across the desert was uneventful. Kenet knew the landmarks and led them directly to the raiders' camp. By evening of the third day they were in between two sand dunes. Kenet said, "Here is where we should stay tonight. If we top this dune, the people in the camp will be able to see us."

Mibsam sent scouts out to see the camp and the surrounding area. When they returned, they told Mibsam that the camp was an oasis with many trees. A pool was in the center of the oasis. Large sand dunes were on the sides toward Egypt and Hittite but toward the rising sun there was a valley which would allow the soldiers to ride into the camp almost unnoticed.

The sun was two fingers high in the morning sky when twenty-five men came riding into camp from the rising sun. No one paid any attention to them at first. When they reached the middle of the camp, an older man came running to them. When he was a short way from them, he shouted, "Did you have a good raid, my son?" Then taking a closer look he shouted, "You're not my son! Where is my son?"

He pulled his sword and came running at Mibsam. Mibsam jumped from the rear of his camel and met the charge. The old man swung his sword at Mibsam who deflected it with his shield. Then with a quick swing of his sword he cut the man's throat, nearly severing the head from the body.

The men also jumped from their camels and drew their swords. Everyone was watching. Mibsam called for everyone to come stand in front of him. They came and stood quietly. There were three older men who seemed to have a hard time walking, four older boys, forty women, sixteen girls, and some children.

Mibsam said, "I am Mibsam, captain of this army. We have killed all the men who raided our friends' camp and stole their sheep. We are here to free all those who were kidnapped and are here against their will. You will bring all swords, knives, bows and arrows and slings here and put them in a pile."

Kenet ran to his mother and told her, "These men are here to free us. We can go home!"

Mibsam said, "You have heard what Kenet has said. That is true, but you will not go empty handed. You may take the tent you lived in and anything in it that you want. If you will show me where the leader kept his gold, I will give every woman two gold rings for every year she were here."

The three older men came to Mibsam and asked, "My Lord, what is to become of us?"

Mibsam answered, "I do not know. That depends on you. If you have family you may go to them. If you do not, you may go where you chose. I will give you some gold rings so that you may live."

A woman came to Mibsam, "I am Sudun, I was Abdul's woman. What will you do to me?"

Mibsam replied, "You will be treated like the other women. You may keep any gold or jewelry that Abdul has given you. With the gold rings I will give you, you can go anywhere you choose and live at ease for the rest of your life."

"Why are you being so kind to us?" one woman asked.

Mibsam told her, "The leader I work for is rich. He serves the God who created the world. That God requires him to be kind to people less fortunate than he. He has enough without taking anything from this camp. The only thing we will take is a little for the men with me. Those who want to may go into their tents and weep for their dead. Those who want to may join us in a celebration of their freedom."

One woman came to Mibsam and said, "That one," pointing to an older boy, "has a knife hidden in his cloak. He is Abdul's son and is just as mean and wicked as his father."

Mibsam called the boy to him, "Give me the knife!" Mibsam told him.

"I will not," the boy yelled. He pulled the knife and ran toward Mibsam. Mibsam caught the boy's arm and twisted it until the knife dropped.

Mibsam had two of his soldiers take the boy's clothing off down to his breech clout and tie him to a tree.

Mibsam came over to him. "Your father was a vile, evil, wicked man. I put out his eyes and cut the tendons on the back of his ankles so he couldn't see or walk. I left him that way so he could think about all the evil he had done in his life. When we left, the vultures were overhead and the jackals were in the hills. You should think about all the evil he did before you decide to walk down his path."

Most of the women were very happy to be going home. Just being free and going home was enough but Captain Mibsam had said he would give them gold rings and they could take the tent they lived in and all their possessions.

Sudun was very unhappy. As Abdul's wife she had lorded it over the other women for so long and so hard that they hated her. Mibsam could tell something was troubling her. He called her to him and asked, "What is troubling you?"

She replied, "All the other women hate me. As soon as they can they will kill me and my son."

"Let us go into your tent so the others can't hear us," Mibsam said.

Once in the tent Mibsam told her, "I thought that was the problem. Here is a knife. I will have two camels saddled with water bags on them. While the celebration is going on, cut your son loose. I will tell my soldiers to let you pass. Show me where Abdul kept his money bags. I will give you two gold rings for each year you were here."

"You are very kind and generous, my Lord," She replied. She removed a pile of baskets and dug into the sand. She pulled out three large bags of gold and silver rings.

Mibsam asked her, "how many years have you been with Abdul?'

"I'm not sure, I can't count. I was brought here two years before my son was born. He is fourteen now."

Mibsam counted out 30 gold rings. "What do you want to take with you when you leave?" he asked. "Pack what you can in four baskets and my men will tie them on the camels."

Mibsam left her tent and told the women to get the food started for the festival. Five goats were quickly skinned and put on a fire to roast for the evening meal. Jugs of beer and wine were brought to the pool to cool. A fingers time before the sun set the food was ready and the drinks chilled. Abdul's wife came to Mibsam and asked permission to take some food and water to Barabdul, her son.

Mibsam talked roughly to her, "You may take some food and water to him but do not attempt to release him. If you try, my men will shoot both of you with arrows."

They were surrounded by blackness; it was the dark of the moon. Mibsam looked at the tree and noticed that the boy was not there. One of the soldiers came and told him that the woman and the boy had left safely.

Next morning there was quite a stir about Abdul's wife and son not being in camp. But when Mibsam called all the women and started giving them the gold rings he had promised, they forgot about the missing woman. They began breaking camp and packing for the trip. Mibsam allowed them to use the camels to carry the tents and supplies. About noon everything that the women wanted to take was loaded on the camels. The soldiers piled everything else into a big pile and set it on fire. Two of the soldiers were goat herders so Mibsam had them herd the goats.

On the evening of the fourth day the group reached the edge of the desert. One of the three men told Mibsam that his family lived a little toward Hittite and that the other two would go with him. All three men left with the gold rings Mibsam had given them. Mibsam told the women, "We are going toward Egypt. Anyone who wants to go that way may travel with us until you reach your camp."

Two of the women and six of the children said they were going toward Hittite. They took their belongings, loaded them on camels and departed. Most said that their camps and villages were toward Egypt so they would travel with the soldiers.

When the sun was four hands high, they came to a small unnamed village of twelve tents. As they walked down the dirt road towards the village twenty armed men came to meet them. Before anyone could say anything, three of the women ran forward shouting "We are free; we are free!"

The people in the village recognized them and began asking questions all at once. "How did you get free?" "Who are these soldiers?" Where did you get those camels?" With everyone shouting questions, no one could be understood.

Mibsam raised his hands for silence. "I am Mibsam, Captain of Israel's, army. We came---"

A man shouted, "I have heard of Israel. He built Succoth. Then he moved to a town toward the setting sun from there. What are you doing in this area?"

Mibsam continued, "We came to gather figs in a grove near Succoth. We arrived early and went to Succoth to visit our friends until the figs got ripe. The families at Succoth had been raided by the same raiders that took your sheep. We ambushed and killed all the raiders except one. He led us to the raiders' camp and we freed all the people in the camp. We are now on our way back to Succoth."

The village leader came to Mibsam, "my Lord, you have done us a great favor in freeing our women. Please spend the night with us so we can show our gratitude by having a festival in your honor."

"I wish we could stay for your festival. We have over 100 people left in our group. Your village would make itself poor to feed that many. We would like to get back to Succoth so we can help pick the figs and return to our homes in Shechem. We will be on our way with your blessings. Have the festival to welcome home the women that have been freed."

"You go with our blessing and thanks," the leader responded.

The sun was about to set when the group came to the tents of four shepherds. One of the shepherds ran to meet them. He was one that had been compelled to go with the raiders. As he ran up he shouted, "Greeting Mibsam, I see you have freed those kidnapped by the raiders." Two of the women and three children came forward. It was a joyous reunion. The shepherd told Mibsam, "We don't have much but all we have is yours. Even that is too little for all you have done for us. Allow me to roast some sheep and goats for your soldiers."

"We will eat with you but I insist on providing the goats for the meal," Mibsam replied. "Where can we set up our camp?"

Pointing to a small rise of ground, the leader said, "Just over that rise is a small spring. You may set up camp there. By the time you have set up your camp, the meal should be ready."

When they returned to the shepherds' camp, everyone was talking about how kind Mibsam and the soldiers had been to the women they had freed. They were amazed that the women were given two gold rings for ever year of their captivity, a camel and anything they wanted that had been theirs at Abdul's camp. During the meal the women were talking about a calamity that had befallen one of the families in the camp. Lions had attacked and killed the husband and most of his flock. The wife was struggling to maintain her household and keep the few sheep that was left.

When Mibsam heard her story he asked the leader, "What can be done to help her?"

The leader answered, "I don't see what could help her. Her children are not old enough to help her."

"Here are ten gold rings for her," Mibsam said. "Two of the boys that came home are old enough to work together and shepherd a small flock. Have her pay them a good wage and buy more sheep."

The leader was amazed at the generosity. Mibsam told him, "This is Abdul's blood money. I know Israel would want me to do good with this money that was gotten by stealing and raiding."

The meal was eaten quickly so that the travelers could get a good night's rest. The camp got up at sunup. They were packed and ready to leave in one hands time. As they were leaving the entire village came to bid them Godspeed. They shouted blessings and good wishes as long as they could see the travelers.

They experienced the same thing at all the villages and shepherd encampments they passed. They first met with hostility. Then when one or more of the women told the men what had happened, they were treated as heroes.

Shortly after noon of the fifth day they reached Succoth. Mibsam had given a long wolf song when he was about one hand's time from the camp. The people at Succoth came to meet them. The wives were happy to have their husbands home safe and sound. The wives and children walked with their husbands, the soldiers told their families about the battle, embellishing their parts in the encounter.

Israel and the shepherds had taken the lambs and goats to Adam and Adullam and sold them. He didn't get much for them but he was rid of them.

When they got to Succoth, Kenet and his mother and sister were still with them. Seven other women and eleven children were still with them. Mibsam took them to Israel. He explained that they did not have a home. Kenet told Israel that the raiders had destroyed their village when they captured them and had killed his father so they did not have a home to go to. The six other women said that also happened to their homes and that they wanted to live with Israel and the great Captain Mibsam. Israel told them they could live with his people. He told the women that he would hire them as servants for five bronze rings a year.

A festival was quickly made. Food, drink and talk were enjoyed throughout the evening. Several of the women from the camp came to the seven women who had been freed. The women explained to the newcomers, "we had been kidnapped by raiders and Israel freed us and gave us a safe place to live. We have found husbands and have been accepted as equals." Hearing this, the freed women were happy to be in a camp that would not hold their misfortune against them.

The story of the battle and the freeing of the women was told and retold. When someone mentioned that Mibsam had been very generous with the gold he had taken from Abdul, everyone looked at Israel to see what he would say about Mibsam giving so many gold rings away.

Israel said," I'm glad you put that evil money to a good use. That was blood money. Money received for doing evil. I would not have any of it in with my money. God will not bless money gotten by evil means, nor will he bless any treasure with that kind of money in it. If I put any of that money with mine, God would not bless my money or me. If you have any left, share it with the soldiers that went with you. Give the young man, Kenet his share."

His speech made the soldiers very happy. Mibsam kept twelve gold rings, gave six to each of the soldiers and still had a few left. He gave the rest to Leah, asking her to buy something for each of the freed women when she got to town.

The figs were ripe and some had been picked and were drying on mats all around camp. Next day everyone went to the fig grove and made short work of completing the task.

The following day was spent in packing and saying goodbye. Israel thought they had enough wine and olive oil so he didn't want to take time to pick any more. Early on the fourth day after the soldiers returned, the camp was traveling again. Everyone was glad to be going back to Shechem.

The trip back to Shechem was uneventful. In their eagerness they started early and traveled late. On the third day they arrived at home. When they got home, Deborah, Rebeckah's nurse, was there. She had been living with Esau, but he was talking about moving to Edom and she wanted to stay in Canaan. She was over 100 years old.

Everyone had a story to tell to the ones who had stayed to maintain the camp and keep the flocks and herds. The season had passed quickly and Israel was expecting the former rains to start at any time.

The rains started earlier than expected. Soon after the wheat and barley were planted, the winter set in with a vengeance. The rain was heavy and the wind from the Great Sea blew almost continuously. Israel's sheep had 4509 lambs. It was a happy day when the latter rains began to soften and became much warmer. Due to the heavy winter rains, the wheat and barley grew much bigger than was expected.

CHAPTER 10

—— LEAVING SHECHEM ——

The barley harvest was over and shearing the sheep and goats was half finished, Mibsam came to Israel and told him that Captain Reggy was coming to see him.

Captain Reggy came with his army of twenty-five men. "I have come from King Hamor," Reggy began. "His brother, King Homan, has received a letter from the outlaw chief, Nodal, demanding 1000 sheep and 250 gold rings yearly as tribute. If that amount is not paid, they will sack the town. King Hamor sent me to ask you for help. Will you send twenty-five of your soldiers under Captain Mibsam to help us?"

"I would like to send some men with you but we are in the middle of shearing and cannot afford to let any go," Israel answered,

"I need to get started right away," Reggy told Israel. "The travel time will be four or five days. Nodal's letter gave King Homan one turning of the moon to get the tribute ready. If we leave now, we should have three days to set up our defenses."

"May the one true God grant you safety and success," Israel blessed Reggy. Reggy said his goodbyes and he and his men departed.

One turning of the moon had past: the wheat harvest was over. Israel sent the four oldest sons of Leah with 400 sheep to the left for two days time to find better pasture for them.

Israel and a servant took two cart loads of fleeces to Shechem. Diana asked permission to go to Shechem with him. Leah didn't want her to go but Diana said, "Mother, I am fourteen years old! I am a young woman and capable of taking care of myself!" After much discussion Dinah was allowed to go with a twenty-one year old woman named Maritia to accompany her. While they were in Shechem, they went to the palace to visit the queen.

The queen was glad to see them. They were invited to have the noon meal with the royal family. The prince, Shechem, and two of his friends were there. Shechem was very attentive to Dinah. After the meal the young people went into the yard to play. They played a game where someone would roll a circle past the others. The rest would try to throw a stick through the circle. Dinah threw a stick so hard that she lost her balance. Shechem picked her up and held her tenderly. Dinah had emotions she had never had before. Shechem had intense emotions also. He told his two friends, "Get Maritia's attention and take her some place so that I can be alone with Dinah."

The friends asked Maritia to go with them to see the fast camels that the king had just bought. They said they would stop for a mug of cold beer on the way. Maritia looked at Dinah for approval but her attention was on prince Shechem. As soon as they were alone, the prince put his arms around her and kissed her. He told her, "I have had my heart set on marrying you from the first time I saw you. Come into the palace with me." He took Dinah by the hand and led her into the palace. He didn't go to the main part of the palace. He led her into his bedroom. "I want you for my wife," he told her.

Dinah said, "You will have to ask my father."

Shechem replied," I can't wait that long, come lay with me."

"Oh no!" Dinah told him. "Ladies do not lay with men until after they are married!"

Shechem had moved her until she was close to his bed. With a quick shove he pushed her onto the bed and got on top of her. Before she knew what was happening, he raped her.

"Now you will have to marry me. You are defiled and no other man will want you," Shechem explained to her.

Dinah ran into the garden yelling for Maritia. The two friends and Maritia were coming into the garden. Dinah grabbed Maritia's hand and said. "Come, we must leave right now." She tore her clothes and put dust on her head.

They ran to the market. Israel realized that almost all of the men had gone with Reggy. The ones who had not gone with Reggy were in the fields with their animals. No one was there to buy the fleeces. When he saw Dinah, he asked, "Did Prince Shechem lay with you?"

"Yes. He pushed me onto his bed and did a terrible thing to me!" Dinah told him.

Israel and the servant took the lead ropes of the oxen and started home. He sent one of his servants to find his sons and tell them to come home immediately. When he got home, he sent five servants to watch the sheep so his sons could get home sooner.

His sons got home four days later. Israel told them what had happened. As they were discussing the situation, King Hamor and Prince Shechem came into the camp.

Hamor said, "My son has his heart set on marrying your daughter. Please give your permission for them to marry. Intermarry with us, give us your daughters and take our daughters for your sons. You can settle among us. The land is open to you. Live with us, trade with us, and buy property in our land."

Then Shechem said to Dinah's father and brothers. "Let me find favor in your eyes, and I will give you whatever you ask. Make the price for the bride and the gift I am to bring as great as you like, and I'll pay whatever you ask. Only give me the girl as my wife."

Because their sister had been defiled, Jacob's sons replied deceitfully as they spoke to Shechem and his father. Reuben said to them, "we cannot do such a thing. We cannot give our sister to a man who is not circumcised. That would be a disgrace to us. We will give our consent to you on one condition only; that you become like us by circumcising all your males. Then we will give you our daughters and take your daughters for ourselves. We will settle among you and become one people with you. But if you will not agree to be circumcised, we will take our sister and go."

The proposal seemed good to Hamor and his son Shechem. The young man lost no time in agreeing to what they said because he was delighted with Jacob's daughter. Dinah was to live in the palace in a separate room until after the wedding.

Hamor and his son went to the gate of the city to speak to their fellow townsmen. "These men are friendly toward us," they said. "Let them live in our land and trade in it. The land has plenty of room for them. We can marry their daughters and they can marry ours. But the men will consent to live with us as one people only on the condition that all our males be circumcised as they themselves are. Won't their livestock, their property and all their other possessions become ours? So let us give our consent to them and they will settle among us."

The few men who were there agreed with Hamor and his son and were to be circumcised in half a turning of the moon.

Israel sent the servant who did the circumcising for his camp to Shechem. Hamor, Shechem, and the few men who were still there were circumcised. Three days later when the men were too sore to move Simeon and Levi took their swords and killed Hamor, Shechem, and the men still in Shechem. The rest of Dinah's brothers came after them and looted the town. They took all the women and children captive. The goods were loaded on carts and taken also. They rounded up all the flocks and herds they could find. The sons of Israel were proud of what they had done.

When they returned to camp, Israel was appalled! "What is this you have done? You have made me and my family a stink in the nostrils of the Canaanites and Perizzites and all the peoples living in this land. They will come together and kill us! You are no better than the raiders Captain Mibsam killed!"

Reuben answered very angrily, "They disgraced our sister. Shechem treated her like a harlot. Such a vile disgrace could not go unpunished! We did what needed to be done!"

When they tried to take Dinah from Hamor's palace, she was too embarrassed to leave. "I will not leave until I am married," she told them. Israel said she could not be married to an uncircumcised man. After much discussion, they decided that she would have a marriage of convenience to one of her brothers. Again after much discussion, Simeon was selected. She went back to Israel's camp and the wedding was held. Israel gave her a tent of her own. The marriage was never consummated.

That night God came to Israel in a dream. God told Israel, "Go to the place where I met you when you were fleeing from your brother Esau. You are to build an altar there, and sacrifice seven year old rams without a blemish. Then I will forgive your sons and keep you safe. As soon as he got up the next morning Israel told the entire camp to get rid of their foreign gods, purify themselves, bathe, and put on clean clothes. "Do this today" Israel commanded. "Tomorrow we will get ready to move to a new camp." His servants gave him the idols of their false gods and the earrings they wore in honor of their gods and Israel buried them under a tree.

"God came to me in a dream last night and told me to go to Bethel. That is a place where I met God when I was fleeing from Esau on my way to visit Laban. God came to me in my distress and comforted me there. He is the God who created the earth and everything in it. When He met me there he said, 'I am El Shaddai. I will make a nation and many nations from your loins. Kings will be your descendants. The land I gave to your grandfather, Abraham, and to your father, Isaac, I now give to you and your descendants.'"

That day everyone cleansed themselves, washed their clothes and prayed to God for forgiveness and a safe journey. Next morning Israel sent a servant to tell all the shepherds and herdsmen to start the animals toward Egypt. The camp was going to travel two days toward Egypt. Israel would come to them in about seven days.

On the fifth day after they had purified themselves, they started on their journey.

About noon the second day of the trip, Captain Mibsam came running to Israel. "An army of men are riding this way. I don't know who they are. They are too far away to identify. I will set up a defense and we will intercept them." Mibsam informed Israel.

Israel replied, "I knew the local people would pursue and kill me. Do what you can to protect us."

Mibsam gave a series of short wolf calls. All the soldiers stopped what they were doing and rallied around Mibsam. He put them in lines of twenty-five men abreast and started marching toward the approaching army. Mibsam was in the lead. When the army got closer, it looked like the leader was hurt and barely able to keep in the saddle. As they got closer, they saw that most of the army was leaning heavily in the saddle. Mibsam soon recognized Captain Reggy as the leader. He told his men to stand easy while he went forward to talk to Reggy.

When Mibsam got beside Reggy, Reggy said, "Captain Mibsam, I salute you." Then he fell from the saddle. Mibsam caught him and lay him on the ground. The second man came forward. He saluted Mibsam and said, "Captain Mibsam, we have just gotten back from the battle. We found Shechem looted and all the women and children gone. We are not in shape to go searching for them. We would like to recover for a while. Then we will try to find our families."

Mibsam was at a loss as to what to tell the man. He called his men and told them to help the wounded soldiers. They were to take them to Israel. He sent a runner to tell Israel the situation. When Israel heard the report from the runner, he told them to make camp. He told the captive women to set up tents and start cooking meals. Then he started walking toward the approaching men. When he got to them, Captain Reggy was able to sit up and talk. He told Israel that they had won the battle but almost every one of his men had been wounded.

Israel told him, "You and your men are welcome in our camp as victorious warriors. When you get to our camp you will be in for a great surprise."

When Reggy and his men were helped into the camp, they were shocked to see their wives and children there.

Israel told them what had happened and why. He said, "My sons have disgraced me. Tomorrow I will attempt to set it right." He told their wives to help their husbands to their tents and to tend to their wounds and feed them.

The men were feeling better the next morning. Most of them could walk without help. Israel called a meeting of all the people in the camp. After they had all assembled he said," As you know I did not approve of what my sons did at Shechem. I will now try to make it right. Captain Reggy, come here."

Captain Reggy walked as erectly as he could. When he got to Israel, he was commanded to kneel. Not knowing what to expect, he knelt. Israel pulled a sword and tapped Reggy on both shoulders three times. Israel said, "Reggy you knelt before me as a captain, I now raise you to be the King of Shechem. Arise King Reggy." When Reggy arose, Israel took the crown that King Hamor had worn and placed it on Reggy's head. Everyone cheered. All the people from Shechem shouted "Hail King Reggy, Hail King Reggy."

Israel told Reggy, "I give you all the women and children, all the carts loaded with the things from Shechem and all the livestock my boys took."

Reggy was amazed and pleased. He said, "I knew you to be an honest and generous man. I never expected you to be this generous. I accept your gift and I thank you. I would like to make a covenant of friendship with you.

"I accept your covenant of friendship," Israel said. Israel called for a two years old bull and four young male goats to be brought from his herds. They were dressed and cut in half. The halves were laid on the ground about one pace apart. To seal the covenant, both Israel and Reggy walked between the halves of the animals. They roasted the meat as part of the covenant meal that evening. The rest was offered to God as a burnt offering.

Israel came to King Reggy after breakfast and said, "My herds and flocks are well ahead of us. We need to catch them before they get too far. With your approval, I will leave ten of my soldiers to assist you in any way you need. They may stay until you get back to Shechem."

Reggy thanked Israel for leaving the ten able soldiers to help him. With that Israel's camp started on toward Bethel.

CHAPTER 11

———— BETHEL AND BEYOND ————

Two days later Deborah died. Israel sent a runner to tell Esau and invite him to her burial. Esau arrived with his family the next day. Esau and Israel buried Deborah under an oak tree. Israel called it Allon Bacuth, which means 'the Oak of weeping'. Esau suggested they have a feast to celebrate her life. Israel had two male calves and five male goats butchered and roasted. Before they ate, Israel spoke of Deborah. "She was like her namesake. She was as sweet as a honey 'bee'. She was kind to everyone. When Esau and I were children, she took care of us. She was very kind and loving," Esau said. "She taught us many things. She was loved and admired by everyone in Isaac's family. In fact we considered her to be part of our family. It is with deep sorrow that we bury her today, may El Shaddai have mercy on her." The feast lasted late into the night. Many people had something they wanted to share about how Deborah had affected their lives.

Next morning, Esau told Israel, "These past years you and I have become brothers again. I am happy that we are together again but this area cannot provide pasture for all our flocks and herds. My grandson tells me that there is a land to the right and forward of the Dead Sea. It is a land of rolling hills and few people. You may stay here and I will take my flocks and herds there. Let us keep sending runners to each other's camp so we can share about our fortunes and where the other is living." They said their farewells and Esau and his family left.

Israel's camp reached Bethel early in the evening the second day after burying Deborah. They pitched their tents and started fires for cooking and for protection. Mibsam posted sentries around the perimeter. They were in new country and did not know what to expect from the local people. Israel told the people what had happened when he was on his way to visit Laban twenty-five years earlier. He told them that his God had commanded him to build an altar now and to sacrifice seven one year old rams. If he did that, God would forgive him and his sons. The altar was to be built using natural stones. The stones could not be shaped by any tool. He was to use clay to bind the stones. Israel called the place, El Bethel, the 'God of the House of God'. Israel built the altar one pace long and half a pace wide. He dug a small trench in the middle for the blood to drain away. After the altar was completed, he had fires built on all four sides to help the clay harden. He kept the fires burning for seven days. With the fire and the sun to dry it, the clay became very hard.

On the tenth day he laid a ram on its back on the altar. When a sheep is turned upside down it goes to sleep. While it was lying there, Israel took the flint knife he had made to kill the sacrificial rams and slit its throat. Israel caught most of the blood in a basin. He took the basin of blood and threw some on each side of the altar. He had a large fire started and placed the ram's body on the fire. This was a whole burnt offering to God. Every day for seven days Israel sacrificed one ram to God. At the end of the seven days, Israel called a holy convocation. All the people spent the day fasting and praying for God's forgiveness.

Joseph found some mandrake plants and took them to his mother. Rachel went to Israel and said, "You have to sleep with me tonight. Joseph found some mandrake plants." That night Rachel conceived. During that night Israel told Rachel to make Joseph a new cloak from the material she purchased in Halab. As soon as she knew she was pregnant, she blessed God by saying, "Blessed be the God of Israel who has granted me the removal of the curse of being barren."

While they were at Bethel, Rachel made Joseph a cloak from the silk she had purchased in Halab with long sleeves that reached to his hands. The cloak was long enough to reach his feet. This was a cloak that spoke of privilege. Joseph could not do any work while wearing that cloak. The other boys made fun of Joseph. They said, "Joseph thinks he is a man but his mother treats him like a baby."

When Shechem raped Dinah, she became pregnant and she delivered a boy. Jacob named the boy Shaul. Shaul would be listed with the descendents of Simeon along with Dinah who is called 'that Canaanite woman' since she had Shechem's baby.

After nine months Israel moved his flocks and herds toward Ephrath that is Bethlehem. While they were two days from Ephrath, Rachel went into labor. She had a very hard time with this pregnancy. This was a difficult birth. The midwife told her "You are having another son." Rachel tried to name the boy Ben Oni, 'son of my trouble' with her last breath. Then she died. Israel said his name would be Benjamin, 'son of my right hand'. Rachel was buried on the way to Ephrath. Israel placed a tall stone over the grave. That pillar marked Rachel's tomb. Israel mourned for Rachel for a turning of the moon.

Israel moved and pitched his tent near the watch tower of Eber, called Migdal Eber. There they sheared the sheep and goats. Israel told Oohdal, "I don't know how long we will stay here. I want you and the shepherds to build temporary pens for the sheep and goats and shelters for the other livestock."

Reuben came to Israel and said, "Father, I am twenty one. I would like to have a wife."

Israel asked, "Why do you want a wife? You have your own tent. Have I lacked giving you anything you wanted?'

"Oh no, father," Reuben replied. "But I want to experience the joy of having a wife."

"I was 84 when I married your mother," Israel told him. "You are too young to have a wife. Besides, there aren't any women in this area that are of our family except your sister. Later when you are ready I will send you to your uncle Laban."

Bilhah heard the conversation between Reuben and Israel. She thought to herself, Israel has not preformed the duties of husband to me for years. Maybe I can show Reuben the joy of having a wife without Israel's knowledge.

That evening she took Reuben his favorite meal. She was very attentive to his every want. She brought him a jug of wine. After he drank several mugs of wine, she invited him into her tent. Once in her tent, she told him, "I heard what you told your father about wanting a wife. I would like to show you the comforts a wife can give you. Come lay with me and I will teach you what you need to know about having a wife." Reuben had been thinking the same thing so he accepted her invitation. He left her tent three hands of time later.

Next morning, Reuben was talking to Dan and Gad. He told them he had something to tell them. "Let us go into my tent and I will tell you." When they went into the tent, Dan asked, "What is so secret that you couldn't tell us in the open?"

"Did you ever lay with a woman?" Reuben asked. He explained that he had lain with Bilhah the previous night. He went on to tell them about the pleasure he had in the experience. They talked for a long time about lying with a woman. Joseph was sitting in the shade of Reuben's tent studying his lessons. He didn't pay any attention to their conversation until he heard Reuben say that he had lain with Bilhah.

Joseph didn't know what it meant to lay with a woman. He went to Jurrad to get his work checked. After Jurrad checked the work, Joseph said, "Jurrad, I have something to ask you."

Jurrad answered, "What do you want to know, Master Joseph?"

Joseph asked, "What does it mean to lay with a woman?"

"Why do you want to know about that subject?" Jurrad asked.

"I overheard Reuben talking to Dan and Gad about lying with Bilhah. I wanted to know why he thought it was so much fun." Joseph replied.

"We will get to that lesson quite a bit later, Master Joseph" Jurrad told Joseph.

Jurrad went to Israel and reported the conversation to him. Israel was furious. He called Bilhah to him, "why did you lay with my son Reuben?" Israel asked her.

"You haven't come into my tent for years. I wanted you to lay with me but you wouldn't. I went to Reuben because he looks and acts just like you" Bilhah answered.

"You may continue living with us in your tent but if you ever lay with one of my sons again I'll sell you to a tavern keeper as a prostitute! Do you understand me?" Israel asked her angrily. "Now get out of my tent!"

Esau sent a messenger to Israel to tell him that Isaac was very ill. Israel told Oohdal that he would be in charge while he and the family went to

Mamre, near Kiriath Arbr, also called Hebron. Israel took Leah with him and went to his father. When he got there Isaac was very sick.

Isaac mustered his strength to bless Israel. "Blessed be my son Jacob. God will give you an abundance of sheep, goats and grain. Nations and kings will come from your loins. Those who curse you, God will curse. Those who bless you, God will bless" Isaac blessed Esau also, "You will live far from rich pasture lands. The dew of heaven will not fall pleasantly on your land. In the end you will do very well."

Isaac then declared that Jacob would get the inheritance of the first son. When Esau complained, Isaac reminded him that he had sold his birthright to Jacob. Therefore Jacob would get two thirds of all of Isaac's property.

Two days later Isaac died at the age of 180. He had instructed his sons to bury him in the cave at Machpelah which is near Mamre. Abraham had purchased the field with its cave from Ephron the Hittite for four hundred silver rings. There Abraham had buried Sarah. Abraham was also buried there. Rebeckah had been buried there. Now Isaac was to be buried there.

After Isaac was buried, Esau took Israel to the flocks and herds. "Father has allowed me to get flocks and herds of my own. I Have over 4500 ewes and 2300 female goats. Father has over 6000 sheep and 4500 goats, 30 camels and 45 donkeys. I will have shepherds drive your share to your camp. Father also had three bags of gold rings. Here are two bags for you. Let us make a covenant of blood to bind our brotherhood and friendship.

Israel was amazed at Esau's generosity but he accepted the animals and gold. After they had walked between the halves of the animals, the animals were roasted and the covenant meal was eaten. Israel departed and returned to his camp.

Three days after Israel got back to camp, the animals arrived. A group of 58 men and their families came with them. "We were slaves of Issac. We are now your slaves," one of the older men said.

"Are you the leader of these people?" Israel asked.

"Yes, I am named Hadam. Where do you want us to set up our tents?" Hadam replied.

Israel said in a loud voice so all could hear, "You may set up your tents anywhere you like. I give all my servants whatever they need and pay five brass rings for a year of work to each servant."

"Master I don't think you heard when I said. We are slaves, not servants," Hadam replied.

"Everyone working for me is a servant. The God I serve tells me that no one should own another person. Here you will be servants, doing a servant's work and getting a servant's pay," Israel told them. He went on to ask Hadam, "Do you know the trade or ability of each of your people? If any are good shepherds or herdsmen I will send them out with my shepherds and herdsmen to care for my livestock. You may set up your tents on the side of our camp toward the sunset. If any are married, they may set up their tents as a family. If any do not have tents, we will give tents to them," Israel said."

Hadam dropped to his knees and kissed Israel's feet. Israel raised him up and told him that was not necessary. Israel told them to get fires started and to draw food from the supply tents as needed.

They went away rejoicing that they were no longer slaves but servants. They soon had shabby tents set up. When Leah saw the conditions of their tents and the clothes they were wearing she told the women they could weave new tent panels and she would take, Mordan, Hadam's wife to town to buy cloth for clothes for all of them.

When Leah told Mordan that she would take her to town and let her buy cloth for the women to make clothes for their families, Mordan started to cry. "Mistress Leah, I have never been to a town. I have never bought anything. I have never been given any money."

Leah told her, "I will go with you and you may take some other women. You tell me what you need and I will show you how to bargain for it."

When Mordan told the other women that some could go to town they all wanted to go. They were so loud in their requests that Israel came to see what was causing the uproar. As soon as he approached, the women became very quiet "What were you discussing so loudly?" Israel asked.

Mordan told him that Mistress Leah had said she could go to town and that she could take some of the other women with her. "They have never been to a town and all of them want to go," she said.

"Ok," Israel said. "We'll all go. In two days I am going to take some sheep and goat fleeces to market. Bethlehem is close but Adullam is on the caravan route. Adullam is much larger. It is one of the Royal cities of the

Canaanites. I will get a better price for my fleeces there. Their products will be of a higher quality and will cost less."

They took 3000 sheep and 2500 goat fleeces to Adullam. They also took thirty-four young camels. The trip to Adullam took a little over half a day. They set up a camp outside the city. Israel called all the people together. In a stern voice he said, "I expect my servants to dress well. When you buy anything, I want you to ask yourself, would this be what a leader's servant would wear?"

Leah told Mordan to select ten women to go to the market first. Leah took the eleven women with her to shop. The women were amazed at all the people and all the stalls of things to buy. Leah took them to the cloth merchants' area. The merchants had been told that a person was bringing many women to the market to buy cloth. When Leah and her women reached the area, many merchants were calling to them about the quality of their cloth. All the noise and confusion made the women very nervous. Leah walked around looking at the cloth in over ten shops before stopping at one. Leah told the merchant, "I am going to bring the women from 58 families to buy cloth. These women will pick out the material they want and tell you how much of each kind they want. If I think you are charging too much, we will go to another shop."

Leah told the women to tell the merchant what material they wanted and how much of each color. Mordan told Leah, "Mistress, these women have never had to make a decision. Please advise us on what we should buy."

"What material do you want?" Leah asked her.

Mordan pointed to a bright blue material with a pattern in it. "May I have enough of that lovely material to make a tunic for me?'

Leah told the merchant to show her that material. Mordan ran her hands over it and kept saying, "It is so lovely."

Leah took the material and wrapped it around Mordan to find out how much she would need.

"What do you want for Hadam and your children? I would suggest a more basic color like brown or black for the men and boys and a simple one color cloth for the girls."

"I know you are right, Mistress Leah," Mordan said. She picked out some light brown for her two boys and some dark brown for her husband.

For her girls, she selected a light gray material. The other women went through the same procedure.

After all eleven had made their selections Leah asked the merchant how much all the material would cost. He wrote numbers on a scrap of broken clay pottery. After changing the figures several times he told Leah, "I can let you have all that material for three gold and four silver rings."

Leah looked at all the material and thought he was giving her a fair price so she gave him the rings. The women picked up their cloth. They were so proud of themselves. They had actually gone to a market and picked out material for their families.

Leah started back to the temporary camp to get ten more women. On the way she stopped at a vendor that sold honeyed figs. "Have you ever eaten honeyed figs?" she asked the women. They all shook their heads no. She bought twelve bunches of the figs and they walked away eating.

Israel sold his sheep fleeces for two silver and three bronze rings. He sold the goat fleeces for one silver and six bronze rings each. A caravan was passing through Adullam. They gave Israel nine gold rings for each young camel.

The figs were eaten before they got back to camp. Leah told Mordan to select the next ten women to go with them. She knew that if she selected the women it would change the status of the women according to the order they were selected. Mordan knew the relative status of each of the women. By letting Mordan choose, she was putting Mordan in the position of lead woman for her camp.

Each group went to a different booth to get material. Leah wanted them to get different colors and patterns so they wouldn't all look alike. It took the entire afternoon to get material for all the families. When evening came, Israel took them to the food stalls and bought roast goat and yogurt for all of them.

It was almost dark when they got back to camp. Everyone was too excited to go to bed. Each woman wanted to show everyone else the material she had bought. Israel and Leah thought they had never seen so many happy people. They were happy to have material to make good cloaks and tunics for their families.

Hadam came to Israel and told him that 40 of his men would like to become shepherds "When my ewe lambs are old enough, I will have over

9000 ewes. If I put 150 ewes in each flock I will need 60 shepherds and 60 helpers. I have 30 shepherds and 30 helpers now. Do you think your men would make good shepherds?" Israel inquired.

"Thirty men would make good shepherds. Most were shepherds or helpers for Master Issac," Hadam told Israel.

"Have them meet with my chief Shepherd, Oohdal, in the morning. He will put them with the shepherds. After one turning of the moon he will give those that are qualified flocks of their own." Israel told Hadam. "If any of the boys or girls wants to become shepherds, have them meet with Oohdal and the men."

Israel didn't like the area where he was living. He told the entire camp that they were going to move toward Hittite. They would leave in five days. He liked the pasture around Shechem but he didn't want to go there. He thought there was a good valley half way between Bethel and Shechem. The valley was about four days drive for the animals. No one lived in that valley and it was large enough for all of Israel's animals.

When Oohdal took the new shepherds to be with the other shepherds, he told them to start moving their flocks and herds toward Hittite. Israel had sent Simeon ahead to look at the valley. He would show the shepherds the way.

They arrived in their valley in time to get set up before the former rains started. They planted wheat and barley and settled down for the winter rains. The wind wasn't very strong and the rain not as harsh because they were protected by high hills on the side toward the Great Sea.

During the winter rains, Israel's sheep had over 13,000 lambs. At the end of the latter rains they harvested the barley, sheared the sheep and goats and harvested the wheat. Israel trained some of the shepherds to shear sheep. With 9000 sheep to shear he needed all the shearers he could get.

He took most of the fleeces to Adullam to sell. He got two silver rings for each sheep fleece and one silver and three bronze rings for each goat fleece.

On the way back, Leah asked, "How many winter rains have we seen since we left Haran?"

That was the eleventh winter rain since we have been here. I am now 108 years old. Our boys have grown. Reuben is now 23 years old; Simeon is over 21; Levi is 18; Judah is 17; Issachar is nearly 14 and little Zebulon is 11. Joseph is now a young man of 17 and Benjamin is three. Joseph has learned to speak four languages. He has studied logic and numbers. Jurrad says he can write using Canaanite, Egyptian hieroglyphics and Hittite." Israel explained.

Dan and Gad were given flocks of 200 sheep and 100 goats. Naphtali and Asher and two younger boys went with them as helpers. Three of Hadam's boys were also sent as helpers. They took their flocks to the region around Tappuah. The graze was good and they were close to the town.

One day some of the goats wandered away. Gad and Dan went to look for them. As they were going up a small hill, they heard talking and giggling coming from the other side. When they reached the top they were amazed to see two young women playing in a pool. The women were not wearing anything! Gad and Dan had never seen a nude woman before so they crept as close as they could. They were not as quiet as they thought. One of the women yelled, "Who's there?" The other said, "Look, it's two of the shepherds from over the hill. Come here and join us."

Gad and Dan went to their side of the pool. The first woman told them, "We are priestesses of the goddess Ashtoreth, the goddess of fertility and war and mistress of the lord Ba'al. I am Mulun and this is Dulon. We are purifying ourselves for high worship tonight. Would you like to worship with us?"

"How do you worship?" Dan asked.

"The high priestess says a few words. Then we select our male worshiper and go into our rooms. We undress, and then you get to lay with us. I think you would enjoy worshiping with us." Then the women got out of the water and dried off. They put on light gowns. They came over to the boys and patted them on the cheek.

Gad asked. "Why do you lay with men to worship?"

Dulon answered. "We believe in sympathetic magic, so that if we lay with many men the goddess Ashtoreth will be pleased and tell Ba'al and he will cause the sheep and goats to have more offspring."

"Our temple is in that grove of trees on top of the hill toward the rising sun. You should each bring a lamb to the temple. After we leave, get in this pool and wash," Mulun instructed Gad and Dan

Gad and Dan waded into the pool with their cloaks on. They splashed around until most of the sweat and stain was washed out of their cloaks and tunics. They talked about what Reuben had told them about laying with Bilhah. He had told them it was very enjoyable. As they were walking back to camp, one of the helpers met them to tell them that the goats had returned.

After a supper of parched fereet and the last of their beer, they put the sheep and goats into the pen. The younger boys and helpers lay in the entrance of the pen. Gad and Dan each picked up a lamb and started to the temple in Tappuah. The women were watching for them and came to meet them. "We will put the lambs in that pen," they told the boys. They told the man watching the pen their names. Then taking the boys by the hand they led them into the temple.

The temple was a ring of trees. A large stone had been placed on the side toward the setting sun. Gad noticed a bronze bull with red garnet eyes placed on the back of the stone. The bull statue was about as long as his hand and about as tall as the width of his hand. He knew that this was a representation of Ba'al. The Ba'al of Tappuah was a storm god. He was said to ride on the back of a bull. On the side toward the rising sun a row of sheds had been built. The High Priestess was talking when they arrived. She was holding a newborn baby girl in her hands. "The priestess, Lulan, gave birth to this baby this afternoon. She gives it to our lord Ba'al. There is no higher honor for a woman than to give a baby to Ba'al." She held the baby over her head, and walking around the circle of trees, she implored Ba'al to accept this gift. She made two circles. When she came to the large stone for the second time, she stopped and swinging the baby high over her head she brought its head down on the stone. "Ba'al please accept this baby whose life we have aborted to please you and to allow this priestess to get back to worshipping you by laying with many men." Then she threw the dead baby into a large jar with many other dead babies and baby skeletons.

The priestess and the men with whom they had chosen to worship danced around singing the praises of Ba'al, the lord of rain. "It is Ba'al that gives us the rains that grows our crops and feeds our animals," they chanted as they danced around the circle four times. Then the priestesses began leading the men to their worshiping rooms.

Mulun came to Gad; took his hand and led him to her room. Dulon led Dan to her room. As soon as they reached their rooms, the women dropped their gowns and lay down. "Take off your clothes and lay down with me. I will show you what to do," each woman told her man.

When Gad and Dan returned to camp, the others were asleep. At breakfast they told the younger boys about the worshiping the night before. The young boys listened and paid close attention. Asher asked, "Won't father be very mad if he finds out?"

Dan assured them, "Father will never know. He has so many sheep that he won't miss two small lambs."

Israel called Joseph to him. "Zilpah has baked some bread and made some beer for your brothers. They are tending the sheep back of Tappuah. Take the food to them and let me know how they are getting along."

Joseph left and by noon he had found his brothers. He gave them the food and beer. As they were eating, Naphtali and Asher were off to one side. They thought that Joseph could not hear them. They were talking about how wonderful it would be if they could worship with Mulun and Dulon. They mentioned that their father would never know because he had so many sheep that he wouldn't miss two lambs.

Joseph listened to the two boys long enough to get the whole story. He was back to Israel's camp before sundown. As soon as he returned, he went to his father and reported what he had heard. Israel was furious! He called Oohdal and told him to send two shepherds to relieve Gad and Dan.

Gad and Dan reached Israel's camp before noon the next day. As soon as they arrived Israel called them to him and said, "Gad and Dan, why did you take two of my lambs and go worship Ba'al with his prostitutes? You not only gave my property to Ba'al, the false god of Tappuah. You could have gotten one of them pregnant and then my grandchild would be sacrificed to Ba'al. I will teach you not to do such a terrible thing again."

Four men were standing nearby. At a motion from Israel, they grabbed Dan and Gad and threw them onto the ground face down. They held them there and pulled their tunics up over their backs. Israel had a leather belt. He whipped them each thirty-nine times. When he got through their butts and legs were red and blistered. "If you ever do anything that stupid again, I will disown you," he told them.

He left them crying and saying they were sorry and they would never do it again. They lay there for some time before they could get up and limp to Gad's tent. "How did father find out?" they asked each other. Dan said he thought Naphtali and Asher had been talking about them when Joseph was with them. They knew then that Joseph had reported them to Israel. After that none of the boys of Zilpah or Bilhah would speak kindly to Joseph. They took every opportunity to make his life miserable.

One lazy summer day Mibsam heard a wolf song. It told him that men on camels had passed the lookout. Mibsam gave a wolf song and twenty-five armed men responded. Captain Mibsam told them, "the lookout said men passed him about two fingers of time earlier. We will go toward them and intercept them. We should have about two fingers of time before they get here." They hadn't gone very far when they saw the four men approaching rapidly. They drew up in formation. When the four men were near, they stopped their camels. The leader came forward and introduced himself. "I am Abida, Grandson of Abraham, steward of Job. I have come to see your master Israel. Please take me to him."

"How did you get here so quickly?" Mibsam asked.

"These are deloul camels. They are three times faster than your camels." Abida answered.

Mibsam led the way back to camp. When Israel saw Abida, he greeted him with a kiss. "How is your master, Job? Is he well? Is everything good with him?" Israel asked Abida.

"It is now," Abida told Israel. "Job had a lot of troubles six years ago. One day while the oxen were plowing and the donkeys were grazing nearby, the Sabeans attacked and carried them off. All the servants except one were killed. A storm arose and lightening struck and burned all 7,000 of the sheep and killed the servants in another pasture. Only one servant escaped to tell Job. While he was speaking, another messenger came to tell Job the Chaldeans had come in three large raiding parties, taken all the camels and killed all the servants except him. Another messenger told Job that his sons and daughters were having a party in the oldest son's house when a strong wind blew the house down and killed all his sons and daughters. Then Job stood up and tore his robe, and shaved his head in mourning. He worshiped God by falling to the ground and praying; "I came from my mother's womb without clothes and I will leave this land without clothes. God had given me much; now God has taken it back, blessed be the name of the Lord." Job developed painful sores all over his body. He sat on the ash heap and scraped himself with pieces of broken pottery."

His wife suggested that he curse God and die. Job asked her, "Shall we accept good from God and not trouble?" Again he blessed the name of the Lord. Three of his friends came to tell him that this had happened to him because he was a sinner. Job maintained his innocence. His friends continued to tell him to seek God's forgiveness and all would turn out well. Finally God told Job to make a sacrifice for the friends and they would be forgiven for misrepresenting Him."

Job had put money with lenders in several different cities. He collected some of this. Many of the people who owed money, sheep or other animals to Job came and paid him. His fortune was restored. Two years ago Job's wife died. Job has sent me to you to ask for Dinah to be his second wife."

Abida opened a bag that had been on his camel and poured out the contents. There were jewels; gold and silver cups with jewels in them, a gold bracelet, a bag of gold rings and silver nose rings. "Job has sent these gifts as bride price for Dinah. He heard about her unfortunate problem with prince Shechem and is willing to adopt Shaul."

Israel was taken by surprise. He replied to Abida, "We will talk to the girl and see what she says. We will give you our answer tomorrow. In the meantime let's have a feast to honor your visit."

Leah and Israel called Dinah to see what she wanted to do. Leah reminded Dinah that she had been compromised and it would be very hard for her to find a husband. She told Dinah that Job was very rich, and that he was a kind and generous man.

After much talking and persuading, Dinah was convinced to marry Job. Next morning Israel told Abida of Dinah's decision. Abida was very happy for her and Job. He said he wanted to start back to Edom as soon as possible. Leah asked for a week to get Dinah ready and explain the duties of a wife and mistress of a large house. After much discussion, they agreed on four days.

On the third night Israel threw a party to celebrate the marriage of his daughter with plenty of food, yogurt, wine and beer provided for everyone.

Early the next morning Abida, Dinah and the others from Job's group departed. Israel sent a cart pulled by two oxen with Dinah's possessions. Leah sent a woman as a servant for Dinah. Her family blessed Dinah and said to her, "May you increase to many thousands, may your sons posses the gates of their enemies, may you live a long and happy life and may you hold your children's children on your knees."

Five days later Joseph had a dream. He told his family the dream. "I had a dream that I want to tell you. We were in a barley field binding sheaves. My sheaf stood up and yours gathered around mine and bowed down to it." His brothers ridiculed him and said, "Do you really think we will ever bow down to you, our younger brother? Will you really be our ruler?" That gave them another reason to hate Joseph.

A few days later Joseph had another dream. He told the dream to his family. "Last night I had another dream. In this dream the sun, the moon and eleven stars were bowing down to me."

Israel scolded Joseph, "Do you really think that I, your mother and your brothers will actually bow down to you?" But Israel kept this dream in his heart, wondering what it meant. His brothers were jealous and hated Joseph so much they couldn't say a kind word to him.

Later Israel sent his sons back out with the sheep. They moved the sheep farther toward the great sea. They started for the fields near Shechem. Israel told Joseph, "I am sending you to your brothers. They have left the valley of Hebron and are now around Shechem. I want you to go see them. Bring word back to me of how they and the sheep are doing."

When Joseph arrived at Shechem, he couldn't find his brothers. King Reggy heard that a shepherd boy that looked like one of Israel's sons was wandering around in the fields. King Reggy sent one of his servants to see what the boy wanted. The servant came to Joseph and asked, "What are you looking for?"

Joseph replied, "I'm looking for my brothers, the sons of Israel. Do you know where they are?"

"Yes," the man told Joseph. "The other night they were in the tavern drinking beer and talking. They were overheard saying that they were going to Dothan. They said pasture would be better there. Dothan is a larger town along the caravan route. It is a day's walk from here."

Joseph thanked the man and left for Dothan. He saw the flocks while he was on a hilltop about one finger's walk from them. As he was approaching, Gad saw him and told Dan, "Here comes the dreamer that got us whipped by our father. Dan said, "Let's kill him and throw his body into an empty cistern. We will tell father that a lion ate him." They laughed and Gad said, "Then we'll see what becomes of his silly dreams."

Reuben heard them talking, as the oldest brother he was responsible for them. He told Gad and Dan, "Do not kill him. Throw him in this empty cistern and we can decide what to do with him later." Reuben intended to rescue Joseph and send him back to Israel but he went into Dothan to buy supplies and food for supper.

Joseph came to his brothers and greeted them," Halloo. Father sent me to see if you needed anything."

Gad and Dan grabbed Joseph, pulled his cloak off and threw him into a cistern. Joseph called for them to get him out and to give him back his cloak. "When I get back to camp, I'm going to tell father how you mistreated me," he threatened.

As they were eating the food that Joseph had brought, they saw a caravan of Ishmaelites coming from Gilead with loaded camels.

Judah asked his brothers, "What will you gain if you kill Joseph? If we sell him as a slave we would be richer." They all thought that was better than killing him. They pulled Joseph from the cistern, and took him kicking and screaming to the caravan. The caravan had a Midianite slave merchant with them.

We would like to sell this slave to you," Gad told the merchant.

"He doesn't look like he is a very good worker. I'll give you fifteen silver rings for him." the merchant told them.

"I have heard that the price of a slave this young is thirty silver rings." Dan said.

"Yes," the merchant replied. "For a good slave I would give thirty rings. This slave seems to be untamed and very weak, not used to working. My last offer is twenty silver rings."

Gad and Dan were more interested in being rid of Joseph than receiving money so they accepted the offer. When they got back to the rest of the brothers, they shared the silver rings. "Let's go into Dothan and celebrate the riddance of a great annoyance," Gad suggested. They agreed to go after they ate the evening meal.

When Reuben returned from Dothan, he went to the cistern to release Joseph. When he saw that Joseph wasn't there, he cried, "Joseph isn't here. What am I going to tell father?"

Gad and Dan killed a sick goat and dipped Joseph's cloak into the blood. "We will give this to father. We will not tell him anything. Let him figure out what happened to his spoiled son," Gad told them.

That night the men went into Dothan for some beer and perhaps laying with the women who worked there.

Next morning Reuben started the flocks toward the Hebron valley and their father. When the men reached Israel, they said, "We found this on our way back to camp. Do you recognize this cloak?"

Israel recognized the cloak and cried out, "This is Joseph's cloak! A lion must have caught him and eaten him." Israel tore his cloak, put on a tunic of sackcloth and mourned for Joseph one turning of the moon. His sons and daughters tried to comfort him. Israel would not be comforted. He exclaimed, "I will die and go to my grave mourning my beloved son, Joseph."

CHAPTER 12

— Taken to Egypt —

Joseph fought against the situation his brothers had forced on him. Rasfas, the slave merchant, was a strict master. He had Joseph's hands tied in front of him. He was tied to an ox cart. Joseph kicked and screamed all afternoon. Once he tried running from side to side. He knocked down five other slaves. It took one finger's time to get them separated and moving again. Seegum, the overseer, told Joseph, "if you don't stop being such a pain, I will give you a kiss from the river cow!"

Joseph kept yelling that his father was a rich leader with a large army. "When he finds out his favorite son has been sold into slavery, that army will come and kill all of you. Joseph never let up. All afternoon he up kept a steady stream of curses at Rasfas and Seegum.

When the caravan stopped for the evening, all the slaves, except Joseph, were led away and tied to a tree where they could lay down on grass. They were given a little bread and some water. Joseph screamed about being left tied to the cart. After the meal, two men drove stakes into the ground, one in front and two behind, about two paces apart. Four strong men came to untie Joseph. They carried him over to the stakes and threw him to the ground before he could do anything. They removed his breech clout and tied his hands over his head to one stake. They spread his legs so far apart that they hurt and tied his feet to the stakes. They had thrown him face down in a rocky place. The rocks soon began to punch into his shoulders and hips.

Seegum came over, dressed in his whipping clothes. He had long hair and a curled beard with colored ribbons tied to the curls. He had on a long robe that circled his body. Tassels hung along the bottom of the robe. He carried a whip as long as his outstretched arms. The whip was made of hippopotamus hide. What Joseph hadn't known was that the Egyptians call the hippopotamus, "the river cow". To be kissed by the river cow was to be whipped with a whip made from hippopotamus hide. Seegum had made this whip himself. It was about one finger wide and one finger thick at the handle. It tapered until the end was very thin. Seegum had made it himself. He had polished it with sandstone and rubbed it with olive oil and until it shone. He was a master at bringing pain to his victim.

Seegum danced around Joseph a few times. Without warning he flicked the whip across Joseph's left inner thigh. Joseph let out a yell of pain. Seegum danced around one and a half times to get on Joseph's right side. He snapped the whip down on Joseph's right inner thigh. He danced around again and brought the whip down on the small of Joseph's back. He danced around to give the pain of the last lash time to decrease so that each lash brought new pain. He continued to dance and whip Joseph across the back, butt and inner thighs for thirty-eight lashes. Joseph's back and legs were a mass of painful welts. Each welt was one finger's width from the next. Seegum always relished this last lash. The last lash was delivered to Joseph's right testicle. When the whip hit, Joseph gave a scream of pain, threw up and fainted.

When Joseph awoke, the morning sun was not far from the horizon. Someone was standing near Joseph. His back and legs burned with pain. His testicle had swollen to three times its normal size. The rocks under him felt like sharp boulders. The rocks hurt almost as much as the whipping.

The Being standing at his head called gently to him, "Joseph, Joseph, can you hear me?

When Joseph answered, the Being said, "I am Raguel, I sit on the council of El Shaddai. My name means, Friend of God. I have been sent to tell you why you are here and to give you instructions from God. First, let me make you more comfortable." With a wave of his hands, the rocks felt like a wool pad. The stripes and pain left his body. Now listen to me and pay close attention. God has sent you here! There is going to be a famine in twenty years. You are being sent to Egypt to save your family. You will have to suffer many unjust things. In the end God's plan for you will be fulfilled. You must submit to the yoke of slavery as an obedient slave! Now you are to go to Rasfas and apologize to him for causing trouble. Tell him you were taught by the Egyptian, Jurrad. Explain that you speak four languages and can read and write using the Egyptian hieroglyphics."

"How can I go to Rasfas since I am tied to these stakes?" Joseph asked.

Raguel waved his hand and the ropes untied themselves. Then they retied themselves. "Bow down to Rasfas seven times. Apologize in Egyptian. He is eating his breakfast now. Be humble," Raguel instructed Joseph. Then he disappeared.

Joseph lay there for a short time. He said to himself. "Father always followed the advice given to him when an angel spoke. I had better do the same. I really don't like to do this but I have been instructed by an angel of El Shaddai, so here goes!"

Joseph got up, went to Rasfas's tent and entered. "What do you mean by entering my tent unbidden?" Rasfas snarled.

Joseph fell on his knees and bowed down seven times. In perfect Egyptian he apologized, "Master Rasfas, I have been an unruly slave. I beg your forgiveness and another chance."

Rasfas stared at Joseph's back. "Seegum! Seegum!" he shouted," come here at once!" Seegum came running into the tent.

"Yes master Rasfas, I am here," Seegum said.

"Look at this boy's back. Did you or did you not give him thirty-nine lashes last evening?" Rasfas asked.

"I gave him the thirty-nine lashes you ordered," Seegum replied.

"Then where are the welts?" Rasfas demanded.

"I have no idea what happened to his welts. When I got through, he was striped like all the others. I can't explain this!" Seegum exclaimed. "Let's ask him."

Speak slave" Rasfas demanded. "Why don't you have the welts left by the whipping you got last evening?"

"An angel of God, El Shaddai, the God my father worships, came to me this morning and removed the welts." Joseph explained.

"I suppose he untied you also," Rasfas snarled.

"Yes he released me so I could come and apologize to you for my behavior yesterday. I am also to tell you that I can speak, read and write in four languages. I have also studied poetry, numbers and logic. I was taught by an Egyptian by the name of Jurrad. I was told to be an obedient slave and I will obey from now on," Joseph explained.

Just then the servant that had tied the knots around Joseph's hands and feet came into the tent. "Master, I can't explain how but the slave I tied last evening is gone," The servant said.

"Yes, he is here," Rasfas told him. "How did he get loose?"

"I do not know. The knots that I tied are still tied. Nobody can escape from those knots," The servant exclaimed. Rasfas dismissed the servant.

"What is your name, slave?" Rasfas demanded.

"I am called Joseph," Joseph replied.

"Get up and take a look at the pile of broken pottery. Tell me what they say," Rasfas instructed Joseph.

Joseph got up and went to the table to a pile of pieces of broken pottery. Things had been written on them. Joseph picked up the first one and told Rasfas, "Master this is written in the Hittite language. It says that you spent one night at a caravansary. You rented two rooms on the second floor and space for your animals and slaves. You gave two silver and seven bronze rings for the rooms."

"Tell me what another says," Rasfas demanded.

Joseph picked up another piece. "This one is written in Egyptian hieroglyphics. This one says that you stayed at a caravansary in Ezion-geber. You stayed three days in just two rooms. On the fourth day you rented space in the slave holding pens for fifteen slaves. Picking up another one he said, "This one is a receipt for fifteen slaves bought from Captain Murtl for eighteen silver rings each.

"Very good," Rasfas said. "My scribe got sick just before I left Goshen. I need someone that can put these expenses in order so I can make sense out of them. Are you able to do that?"

"If you will tell me what you want, I can get that information for you, Master," Joseph answered.

Turning to Seegum, Rasfas told him. "Go to the supply wagon and get my new scribe a gown. I can't have my scribe running around naked."

Seegum came back with a white gown. As Joseph was putting it on Rasfas told Seegum to take Joseph to the feeding area and see that he was well fed. Joseph was served a thin gruel made of crushed grain boiled with a little mutton fat and served with barley bread. He hadn't eaten for two days so the food tasted great. When he got back, Rasfas told him he was to be his scribe until they arrived in Egypt. When we get to Egypt, I have a very important client that wants a slave that may be trained as a house slave. On the trip Joseph was given the privileges of a free servant. He could go anywhere within the caravan. He was free to eat and get water any time he was hungry or thirsty. Joseph was given a pallet in the corner of Rasfas's tent. He was to spend most of the day writing down the expenses of the trip. He rode in a cart with a table while he was recording the information.

On the third day, Rasfas called Seegum. "I want to test the loyalty of Joseph," he told him. "How should I do that?"

"Do you remember the slave you trusted three years age?" Seegum asked. "We had a trusted servant take four goats into the hills and sent that slave to find them. When the guard we had following to watch saw the slave take the goats and walk toward the rising sun, we knew he would run away at any opportunity."

"Yes," I remember. Set up that test with Joseph tomorrow."

Next morning Rasfas called Joseph. "Joseph," Rasfas said. "It seems like four of my goats have wandered away. I think they went toward the rising sun. See if you can find them. I think they wandered away about the time it takes the sun to move three finger's width across the sky. Try to catch up with us during the noon break."

Joseph went to the food area and picked up three barley cakes and a small jug of water and departed. He backtracked until he saw where four goats had left the herd and went toward the hills. He found them in three fingers times. When he found them, he sat down and ate his breakfast and drank what water he had brought. He sat for a while thinking. He got up and started the goats on a course that would put him on the caravan trail. The caravan had stopped to rest the animals. Seegum came to Rasfas. "I see a man with four goats walking this way. It looks like Joseph has passed the test."

The caravan was getting ready to move out when Joseph and the goats caught up to them. Rasfas called Joseph to him and asked. "You were a long way from the caravan. Most slaves would think of running away. Why didn't you keep on going?"

"I thought about going back to my father. I knew how great being home would be. I sat and thought about it while I ate my barley loaves. I had almost made up my mind to run. Then I remembered that the angel of the God of my father had warned me to be an obedient slave. I got up and came back here to you."

One of the guards came up as Rasfas continued, "Joseph, you were not alone up there. This man had orders to watch you. If you had run, he would have brought you back in chains. I am glad you came back by yourself."

The next ten days were busy days for Joseph. He listed all the expenses by date. He categorized them by the type of expense. Everything was put in the order Rasfas wanted. On the eleventh morning, Joseph was told to remove the white robe, put a breechclout on and stay with the other slaves. Before noon the caravan came to Memphis. The slaves of Rasfas and other slave merchants were taken to holding pens. They were given durra corn bread made from coarsely ground grain and warm water to drink. Chains were fastened to one wrist, ran through a stout ring attached to the wall, then fastened to their other wrist. "Sleep well," the guard told them. "Tomorrow you will be sold to your new masters." The rings were high on the wall so the slaves could not lie down; they spent a miserable night sitting against the rough, hard, cold wall.

When the sun was two hands high, they were taken onto a platform with hooks into overhead beams. Each slave was taken to a hook and his or her chain was put over the hook. They had to stand with their hands raised over their heads. The position was bad enough but when the guards started removing the breechclouts of both the male and female slaves there was much kicking, yelling and cursing. In a short time all the slaves were standing naked with their hands held over their heads.

Joseph closed his eyes and prayed to God to get him through this. The doors of the sales room were opened. Men and women came in to look over the merchandise. If they had just looked, he could have tolerated the situation better. Suddenly he felt hands on his scrotum and penis. He looked at the two girls who had dared to touch him. He was even more shocked to see that both girls had nothing on from the waist up. He had never seen a woman's breasts before. They didn't know he understood what they said. "This must be an Asiatic that believes in cutting the foreskin from their penis," one said.

A commotion started to the left of Joseph and everyone's attention was turned in that direction. A man wanted a slave girl for breeding purposes. He wanted to feel the girl's genitals. She would not cooperate. He took off his belt and spanked her bare bottom several times. She still would not spread her legs. The owner of the slave market had two of his men go to them. They put ropes around her ankles and pulled her legs apart. The man put his hand between her legs to examine her. After examining her breasts and teeth, he said he would take her.

One of Rasfas's servants came to the owner and told him that Joseph was not to be sold in the auction. The servant unhooked Joseph and led him to Rasfas. A soldier was standing with Rasfas. The soldiers name was Potiphar.

CHAPTER 13

——— FIRST YEARS IN EGYPT ———

Potiphar threw a gown to Joseph and told him, "put this on quickly and follow me! I will take you home and then I must return to the palace." Joseph slipped on the gown and followed Potiphar out of the slave compound. Joseph had never seen, nor could he believe, that so many people could live in such a small area. There were nearly 700,000 people living in Memphis. The crush of people made Joseph confused. Potiphar was walking fast. Joseph tried to keep up but people got in his way and they were rude. "Get out of my way slave," they would yell at him as they pushed him away. In a few blocks Joseph lost sight of Potiphar. He was confused and frightened by all the people. Potiphar heard a pitiful cry, "Master Potiphar, Master Potiphar, where are you?" Potiphar looked around and when he didn't see Joseph he went back. Several rough men were picking on Joseph. They were saying insulting things about him. One said, "You look like dried snot in Seth's nose." Another told him, "You smell like the crud in the crack of Seth's butt." They made a circle around him and were pushing and shoving him, besides calling him names. When Potiphar saw this, he rushed to help Joseph. As soon as the crowd saw a captain of the guard coming to rescue the slave, they ran away.

"I'm sorry master," Joseph said. "I have never seen so many rude people. I come from a small country village."

"You looked like a scared animal," Potiphar said. "You don't know where we are going so I'll walk a little slower." Just then two soldiers came running up to Potiphar.

"Captain," the sergeant said with a salute. "The Grand Vizier has requested that you come before the Pharaoh immediately."

Potiphar turned to the soldier and told him to take Joseph to his house and leave him with the brew master, Hapita. He and the sergeant took off at a run. The soldier took Joseph by the hand and led him several more blocks to Potiphar's house. The guard at the entrance told them the brewery was in a building at the back of the compound. The soldier took Joseph there but no one was in the brewery. This was the day that brewers celebrated a festival to Hathor, goddess of beer. Hathor was also known as the 'Lady of Drunkenness'. Since no one was in the brewery and the soldier wanted to get back to the palace to see what was so important, he told Joseph to go into a small room at the back of the brewery and wait until someone came to get him. After he closed the door, the soldier left in a hurry.

When Potiphar got to the palace, he was taken into the audience chamber of the Pharaoh. He was very surprised when he saw Senusert II sitting on his father's throne. Lord Siese, the grand vizier, told Potiphar, "Pharaoh Ammenemhet II is very ill. He has appointed his son, Pharaoh Senusert II as co-ruler until he is well. Will you swear allegiance to your new Pharaoh? Without hesitation Potiphar dropped to one knee, withdrew his sword and holding it by the blade presented the hilt to Pharaoh Senusert II. "With my life, my honor and my fortune I will do all within my power to protect Pharaoh Senusert II," Potiphar said.

"I am very happy that you will serve me as you did my father," Senusret said. "My father was very pleased with your service. He should have been, seeing that you saved his life twice, once on the battlefield and once when the governor of the Nome of Greater Thebes wanted to take the throne. You are excused to your command Captain Potiphar."

The next morning Potiphar came to the brewery to see how Joseph was working out. He asked Hapita, "How is the new slave doing?"

"What new slave?" Hapita asked.

"Yesterday I sent a soldier here with a new slave by the name of Joseph," Potiphar told her.

"Yesterday the brewery was shut down so we could celebrate a festival for the goddess Hathor," she told Potiphar. "I have not seen or heard of this slave."

Potiphar called his sergeant, "Get the soldier that brought my new slave here."

The sergeant returned with the soldier in about three fingers time. "What did you do with the slave I told you to take to my brewery?" Potiphar asked the soldier.

"No one was here so I put him in this room," he said as he walked across the room to the door. "I told him to stay here until someone came for him." He opened the door, and to everyone's surprise, there stood Joseph.

Joseph looked relieved when he said, "Master I am so glad you finally let me out of this small room."

"Have you been in that room ever since the soldier told you to stay there?" Potiphar asked.

"Yes master. I was getting very hungry, thirsty and lonely in there." Joseph replied.

Potiphar laughed and said, "You are really an obedient slave, Joseph. Hapita, feed this slave and give him some beer to drink. Let him become familiar with the brewery this afternoon. Tomorrow put him to work where you think best."

After Joseph ate some durra corn bread and drank a mug of beer, Hapita took him to each area in the brewery. The first place was the malting area. Several batches of barley were in flat bowls covered with water. "This batch was put in water yesterday," Hapita explained to Joseph. "This next batch has been in the water for three days. See how the grain has swollen. Pointing to another batch she told him, this batch has little sprouts coming out of the grain. This batch is malted. The water will be drained and the grain left to dry."

In the next area two men were grinding the dried, malted grain. They each had a sieve to check the size of the ground grain. If it didn't go through the sieve, it had to be ground smaller. Two women were making barley bread from the ground grain. When the loaves were baked and cooled, they were crumbled into water and boiled for two fingers time. During the boiling, leaven and raisins or other flavoring were added. After the boil had cooled, it was poured into jars with small openings. The openings were filled with mud from the Nile River and a straw was pushed through the mud to allow the beer to breath. That night Joseph was taken to the building where male slaves slept. He was given a blanket and told where to lie on the floor.

Next morning Hapita took Joseph to the grinding area and said, "This is Doofos, you will be working with him until you know enough to work on your own. He knows what to do and how to do it. Pay attention to him."

Doofos told Joseph that he was in charge of malting, drying and grinding grain. "It is a very important job," Doofos said proudly. "Today we will just grind the malted barley. Take one of the baskets of malted grain and come with me." They took the baskets of grain to the center of the malting area. Three large flat stones were there. Doofos put a handful of grain on one of the stones and pushed a rounded rock, about the size of his hand over the grain, until it was small enough to go through the sieve. "There are many small containers stacked here. Fill each container level full with the ground grain. Each container will make one loaf of bread. Master Potiphar is very picky about the flavor of his beer. He demands that his beer be of good quality. We measure everything so that all batches of beer will taste the same."

Doofos and Joseph knelt down by the large stones and began grinding grain. In less than two hands of time Joseph's back and arms hurt. Doofos noticed that Joseph wasn't grinding very fast. He asked, "Have you ever ground grain before?"

"No, I was the favorite son of my father. I never did any work. I studied my lessons and ran errands for my father," Joseph answered.

"Take a short break. Walk around a little. Then come back and grind some more," Doofos said.

Joseph got up to walk around but his legs began to cramp from kneeling so long. He hobbled around and stretched his legs so that the cramps would go away. He walked around for about one finger's time. Then he started grinding again. By the time his hands and back were hurting again it was time to take a noon break. Each slave picked up a loaf of bread and a mug of water and walked into the garden to rest and eat.

Doofos sat beside Hapita and talked to her. "Did you know Joseph has never done any kind of work?" he asked her. "He told me he was the favorite son of a wealthy leader. All he did was study and run errands for his father. In just two hands of time his arms and shoulders were hurting so bad I told him to walk around."

Hapita called Joseph to her. "Come over here, Joseph. I want to talk to you." Joseph came over and sat down. Hapita continued, "Tell me about you. Where are you from and what did you do there?"

Joseph began. "I was the favorite son of my father. He has over 9000 ewes and 5000 she goats. He also owns much cattle and camels. I never had to work. Father wanted me to learn many things. He hired an Egyptian teacher for me. His name was Jurrad. I studied Egyptian, Hittite, Canaanite and Sumerian. I also studied poetry, languages, numbers and the history of many countries."

"This Egyptian, Jurrad, was he a tall thin man that walked with a slight limp? Did he wear his black hair shaved on the left and as a tail hanging on the right side?" Hapita asked.

"Yes," Joseph answered. "Do you know him?"

"I never met him but he was the main teacher for Pharaoh's twenty-three children," Hapita told him. "You were taught by the very best. One of pharaoh's older daughters tried to seduce him. He didn't accept the invitation but pharaoh banished him anyway. "Holding up a piece of broken pottery with hieroglyphics on it, she asked, "What does this tell us?"

Joseph glanced at it and said, "That is the recipe you use to make beer."

Why were you sold into slavery?" Hapita asked.

"Two of my brothers went to worship with temple prostitutes. I overheard them talking about the experience. I told father. He whipped them. After that they wanted to kill me, but my oldest brother wouldn't let them. They sold me into slavery instead," Joseph told her.

"Well it is plain that you can't grind grain. I will try to find something else for you to do until you get used to working," Hapita told him. "When we get back, I want you to clean the brewery."

Another slave, Alita, came to Hapita to tell her they were low on river mud. "Go get some," Hapita said. Then she told Alita. "Take Joseph with you. He has not seen Memphis. A trip to the river to collect clean mud will do him good. It will let him learn more about his new home. It may be something he can do. Tie a rope around his wrist. Master said he gets confused easily with many people around him."

Joseph didn't like having a rope tied to his wrist but as soon as he got on the crowded street, he was glad he was tied to Alita. Some of the black men and women wore only a belt around their waist. Alita told him that the ones who wore nothing didn't wear clothing in their home country and were used to being naked. She kept a running account of what they saw. "The tall really black slaves are Shilluk. The Shilluks make good warriors. The shorter ones are either Dinkas or Mandari. Egypt's entire economy is based on having slaves. They think that the Africans are unlearned and it is their responsibility to teach them to worship Egyptian gods and goddesses. The Africans repay them by becoming slaves and doing the menial tasks that Egyptians do not want to do."

Joseph noticed many young Egyptian women with their breasts bare. He thought what a decadent place God has sent me to live. "Look Joseph, there is a hawk statue. It represents the god Horus. Egyptians think of him as a man with a hawk's head," Alita told Joseph. "They honor him by hawk statues. Horus is the god of the wind. He is the protector of the Pharaoh. Their legend says that he was the son of Osiris and Isis. Seth, another son of Osiris killed his father. Horus and Seth fought to see who would rule earth. In the battle Horus lost an eye but it was restored. Egyptians believe that Pharaoh is a living Horus."

With Alita talking to him, Joseph wasn't as confused in the crowd. "Pay attention to how we get to the river," Alita scolded. "You may have to get mud by yourself later."

"Why do people embalm their cats?" Joseph asked. "I see embalmed cats and cat statues in many houses."

"Those cats represent and honor the goddess Bastet. They consider her a goddess of protection for pregnant women. She is a daughter of the Sun God, Ra," Alita explained. "Look when we turn this corner then you can see the Nile River."

When they came to the river, Alita pointed out several slaves gathering clean mud. "We will go there to get mud. It is the best place. The mud there does not have any sticks or lumps of clay or anything but soft mud in it so we call it clean mud. I do not speak to the other slaves unless they speak first." Alita led them to a quiet place along the river. The mud was very thick and they sank into it past their ankles. Alita sat her basket down and began scooping double handfuls of mud into it. Joseph did the same.

No one spoke to them. All the slaves were busy filling their baskets. If they were gone too long, their masters would punish them. It took about one finger of time to fill the baskets. Joseph could barely pick his up. Alita scooped some mud from his basket and then placed the basket on his shoulder. She picked up her basket and set off at a fast pace. "The longer it takes to get back, the heavier the basket becomes," she told Joseph. There was no conversation on the way back. Joseph was out of breath and very tired when they got back. Hapita came over and told him, "take your time and get your breath."

"Why are you treating me so kindly?' Joseph asked her.

"Master starts all his slaves in the brewery," Hapita told him. "After a few months he gives them another job. I know that you are a very smart slave. You were taught by Jurrad. There is a good chance that you will be a house slave or even the steward in a few years. I want you to remember me with kindness. I have to tell Master how you worked out and how I was able to train you. You aren't used to working but you try to do what you are told. By the time the master gets back, you should be able to handle any job in the brewery."

The next few days were hard for Joseph but he worked diligently and every day he improved in skill, strength and stamina. In an Egyptian week of ten days he had became familiar all the jobs in the brewery and could sit at the grinding stone all day.

One day at the noon break Hapita told all the slaves in the brewery that master Potiphar had gone up river on the Pharaoh's business and would be back in a few days.

When Potiphar returned, he asked, "Hapita, how is the brewery doing?" She told him, "we are producing a good beer in the quantity that you required."

He asked, "Have you talked to Joseph about his former life?"

Yes," she replied. "His father was a very wealthy leader with over 9000 ewes and many goats and cattle. He wasn't used to working when you brought him here but he has worked very hard and now he can do any of the tasks in the brewery.

CHAPTER 14

——— WATCHING SHEEP ———

"Tell Joseph I want to see him," Potiphar told Hapita.

Joseph came quickly to see Potiphar. "Did your father keep sheep?" Potiphar asked.

"Yes master," Joseph answered. "My father was the best shepherd in Canaan."

"What makes you think he was so good?" Potiphar wanted to know.

"Father always took his sheep to pasture as soon as the sun was up. He kept them there until sundown. He said that if sheep get more time in the pasture, they will grow fatter and have healthier lambs."

"How many lambs did your father's ewes have each year?" Potiphar continued.

"Father said that for every 100 ewes you should get 150 lambs." Joseph replied.

"I have a flock of sheep on 500 feddan of land I own in the land of Goshen. I have not been happy with the number of lambs that my ewes are having. If I put you in charge of my sheep as my chief shepherd, can you increase the birth rate?"

Joseph said. "I think that with the right care and attention some of your ewes will have two or three lambs each year. On average your sheep should have one and a half lambs for each ewe."

"The problem is that I don't know the total number of my sheep or lambs. The slaves I have tending the sheep can't count. I have the local butcher count the sheep for me. I don't think he is giving me the correct

information. I am going to take you to be a helper for the three men I have
there. Do not tell them that you can read, write, or know numbers. I will
make arrangements with the woman who sells yogurt in a village nearby
to get a message to me. Do not let them know you are sending messages
to me," Potiphar told Joseph. "They tell me that I have 493 ewes and they
had 506 lambs. I want you to make an accurate count of the ewes, rams
and lambs. Send me a message with the numbers." I had 250 awassi ewes
and twenty-five rams brought to Goshen from Canaan to see if they would
do better than our long horned sheep. I have a friend who has a slave that
can shear sheep. I borrow that slave and take him down river to a landing
about five stadia from my land. I go back in four days and load the fleeces
and the slave on my boat. When we get back to Memphis, I sell the fleeces
for five silver rings each.

Next morning, Joseph rode on the back of Potiphar's chariot. The
horses took off at a gallop. They took the road toward the great sea. Joseph
had never gone so fast. The ground flashed past him so quickly that he
couldn't make out details unless he looked at things in the distance. They
flew past durra cornfields almost ready to harvest. They went past sad
looking slaves using shadofs to bring water from the Nile to the irrigation
ditches that watered the crops. They sped through small villages so fast
Joseph couldn't make out the buildings.

Potiphar had two chariots go with him. The trip took all day. Three
hands time before sundown they were passing through a farming village.
The headman of the village waved them to a stop. "If it pleases the captain,
a large lion with a black mane has been attacking the cattle of this village
and has killed a calf. We do not have anyone to hunt it. Would you take
time to rid us of this killer?"

Potiphar raised his hand in a fist and brought it down fast. The other
two chariots pulled alongside of his. He asked the soldiers in the other
chariots, "are you soldiers ready for a little sport?" When they readily
agreed, he continued, "Á black maned lion has been killing the cattle of
this village. Let's go hunting."

The head man pointed toward the desert and told them, "His last
kill was about ten stadia that way. I will send one of the men to show you
the way."

"That would be a big help," Potiphar answered. "I will leave my slave with you until we return."

They left at a fast trot. The man knew the shortest way to the kill site. In less than one hand's time, they saw the remains of a calf. Potiphar told one of the soldiers to go to the left and the other to go right. He would go straight ahead. He told them "whoever picks up any sign of the lion is to whistle." In two fingers time Potiphar heard a whistle from his right. He waited until the soldier on his left saw him. Then he turned right to find the soldier that whistled.

The lion had been sleeping among some large boulders. A loud whistle awakened him. He was angry about being aroused so he jumped upon a boulder and gave a loud roar. As he was roaring he was beating his sides with the bony spikes in his tail. The lion was surprised to see horses so near. The soldier and horse were startled to see the lion not fifteen paces away. The soldier turned the horses and raced away. The horses were running as fast as they could pull the chariot but the lion was gaining on them. Potiphar saw what was happening and drove his chariot between the lion and the first chariot.

Having another horse run so close to him confused the lion. The lion stopped to see which horse he should chase. The third soldier stopped his chariot fifteen paces from the lion. He quickly shot an arrow into the lion. The lion turned to see who was attacking him. Potiphar and the first soldier had turned their chariots around and were coming back at a run. They stopped their chariots and shot arrows into the lion. The lion gave a roar of pain and fell dead.

Potiphar loaded the lion onto his chariot and returned to the village. The village was very glad to see the dead lion. "Is there a tanner in this village?" Potiphar asked.

"Yes," the headman told him. "We have a very fine tanner. He will be glad to tan the hide of that lion. It was his calf that the lion killed."

"I will leave the lion here," Potiphar told him. "I am on my way to Goshen to check on my sheep. I have a flock about twenty-five stadia down this branch of the Nile."

"Please spend the night with us and continue your journey in the morning," the head man requested. "The village would like to honor you and your soldiers with a festival tonight."

"Thank you for the invitation," Potiphar replied. "It would be better for us to stay here tonight than to try to find my sheep in the dark."

"May I have your name so that we may honor you?" the headman asked.

"I am Potiphar, commander of the Pharaoh's guard." Potiphar answered.

The headman dropped to his knees and pleaded, "Forgive me great captain, but I did not know who you were. I would not have been so bold had I known that you are one of the best of 10,000. Our fare will be far less than what you are used to."

Potiphar laughed and told him, "Rise, we were going to eat traveling rations of durra cornbread and dried goat meat. Whatever you prepare for us will be far better than what we were planning to eat. I did not expect you to know me. You are far from the palace and I have never stopped in your village before."

When the meal was ready, the headman called for the attention of all those in the village, "Men and women of the village by the cliffs we have gathered to honor this great captain and his brave soldiers that have kill the lion that was terrorizing our village. This great captain is commander of the king's guard. He is Captain Potiphar, the man who has twice saved our Pharaoh's life. We are honored that he will spend a night in our village. Let's all make him and his soldiers welcome." Everyone cheered.

The meal was roasted goat, fresh fish baked with leeks, and durra corn, served with sherbet and beer. It is against the custom of the Egyptians to eat with Hebrews so Joseph ate with the other slaves. While they were eating, they heard a loud barking noise. It startled Joseph and the two soldiers. The headman said, "Some dogface baboons live in the cliffs in back of the village. They bark every night, but they are harmless. Occasionally one will come into the village at night and take some corn or something to eat. We consider them to be village pets."

Potiphar and his group found the sheep in about two hands of time the next morning. The men were sitting under a tree finishing breakfast. Joseph heard the sheep lowing. "Master, those sheep are crying for water," Joseph told Potiphar. "They should have been taken to water long before now."

Potiphar didn't say anything to Joseph. He called the three shepherds to him and introduced Joseph to them, "This is Joseph. He is here to help you." Pointing to the largest man Potiphar told Joseph, "this is Cerlu; he is leader of the shepherds. Next to him is Sandow, and the third one's name is Trodo. You are here to help them in any way you can. To Cerlu, Potiphar said, "Joseph's father was a great shepherd. Joseph knows how to take care of sheep." To Joseph, he said, "you are to obey Cerlu."

After giving the instructions, Potiphar left. When Potiphar got out of sight, Cerlu pulled a piece of paper from his tunic and showed it to Joseph, "Do you know what this is?" Cerlu asked Joseph. Joseph could see that it was a receipt for items Cerlu had purchased at the market. But before Joseph could answer, Cerlu continued, "of course you don't. A dumb Asiatic slave like you wouldn't know how to read Egyptian. I'll tell you what it says. This is a letter from Master Potiphar to me. I will read it to you. 'To Cerlu from Captain Potiphar' "he began. I appoint you as leader of the shepherds. They are to obey you and do what you tell them to do. If they do not obey you, you may punish them as you think best. Keep the sheep well fed and watered." He put the receipt back in his tunic. "So you see I am completely in charge here," Cerlu continued. "Don't think I am going to listen to what a dumb Asiatic says about tending sheep. Now take the sheep to water. Then take them to the pasture. We are going to stay here and play Senet." Each of the men had a little bag of bronze rings they used for gambling when playing Senet.

Joseph opened the gate and the sheep rushed out to the river. They couldn't drink because the water was running. Joseph led them down river to a sand bar. He placed rocks in a circle around the downstream end to make the water still. After they were watered, they went up the slope so they could graze. Joseph had time to count them while he was alone with the sheep. He counted 508 ewes, 90 rams and 525 lambs. Joseph was going to keep the sheep in the pasture until sundown but Trodo came to inform him that Cerlu wanted him to get the sheep back in the pen so he could start preparing their meal.

The three men started gambling as soon as the meal was over. They kept occupied by gambling and cursing at each other. After cleaning up the camp, Joseph went off by himself and wrote down the numbers of ewes, rams and lambs.

Joseph got up one hands time before sunup and started preparing breakfast. He had the fire going and the durra corn cakes cooking when Cerlu, Sandow and Trodo came out of the tent.

"What do you think you are doing?" Cerlu demanded.

"I'm preparing breakfast so we can take the sheep out to water and to pasture," Joseph explained.

Cerlu told Sandow and Trodo to grab Joseph and hold him. While they were holding him, Cerlu slapped him across the face several times. He pushed him down snarling, "I didn't tell you to get up so early. You are not to do anything unless I tell you to. We were up late and need to sleep. You had better be quiet so we can sleep." They went back in to the tent and were soon asleep.

Every day was the same except for the slapping. The three would play Senet all day and make Joseph take the sheep to water and pasture. One morning three weeks later the three men got up earlier than usual and Cerlu told Joseph to fix a quick breakfast. While breakfast was cooking, they selected three young rams. He told Joseph to leave the sheep in the pen until they returned. When breakfast was over, they led the rams toward the village. The trip took almost three fingers of time. They took the lambs to the butcher. The butcher gave them two silver rings and six bronze rings for each lamb.

Cerlu gave Joseph six bronze rings and told him to buy anything he wanted. They went to the tavern and bought a large jug of beer with three straws. Each straw had a brass strainer on the bottom. After drinking the beer, they went with the prostitutes to their rooms.

Joseph went to the yogurt seller and ordered a cool yogurt. The woman asked if he had a message for Captain Potiphar. Joseph said he needed papyrus and a writing stick. She took Joseph into the back room so he wouldn't be seen writing. He told Potiphar how the others had beaten him and how they stayed in camp and played Senet and gambled all day and half the night. He told him that after three weeks they had taken three lambs to the butcher and sold them. They spent the money in the tavern on beer and prostitutes.

Potiphar came eight days later with five chariots. When he got there, the three were playing Senet. Joseph was alone with the sheep. One of the soldiers went to Joseph and sent him to Potiphar while the soldier stayed with the sheep. Cerlu, Sandow and Trodo were startled to see Potiphar. Three of the soldiers grabbed them and tied their hands together.

Potiphar was very angry with them. "I gave you a good job. I trusted you and you stole from me. You and the butcher! He is going to jail with you!"

Cerlu asked, "How do you know all this?"

"Joseph can read and write in four languages. He also knows numbers," Potiphar told him. "I knew you were cheating me I just didn't know how. I brought Joseph here to find out. Now that I know your scheme I am going to put you in the jail in the basement of the fort. After you have been there a few years, maybe you will be happy to work in my fields."

Potiphar had brought three Asiatics with him as helpers for Joseph. He introduced them, "Joseph this is Melita, Jasen and Rasup." He said to them, "Joseph is the leader; you three will help him take care of the sheep."

Three soldiers tied Cerlu, Sandow and Trodo to the back of their chariots with about three paces of rope so they could run all the way back to Memphis.

Joseph explained to his helpers how he intended to take care of the sheep. "We will get up one hands time before sunup, eat a quick breakfast and be ready to take the sheep out at sunup." The three helpers were very happy to work with Joseph. They got along well and cooperated. Everyone shared all the work and helped each other.

One evening, several weeks later Joseph suggested, "Let us tell how we happened to become slaves."

Melita began," I came from far away in the land of the Hittite, a little village close to the town of Halab."

Joseph said, "We came by Halab when we left Haran eleven years ago."

Melita said something in Hittite. She was surprised when Joseph answered her in her own language. She continued, "My father drank, gambled and went to the temple to worship with the temple prostitutes. He took our lambs to the temple. He had a run of bad luck at gambling. When the man came to collect, he didn't have enough money to pay him. My father sold me into slavery with the owner of a tavern. I was there to service the men. When I wouldn't cooperate, they tied one of my legs to the bed with a rope and the men forced me so they could have their way with me. I hated it! I hated the owner. One night a drunken man came to my room. As he was taking his tunic off, a knife fell out. I pushed it under the bed with my foot. When he got through with me, he dressed and stumbled from the room, forgetting his knife. That night I cut myself free and ran away to Halab. A man recognized me and said he would hide me if I would service him. I said I would. Two days later he sold me to a slave merchant in a caravan going to Egypt. Working in the field was better than working at the tavern. Working with the sheep is the best yet."

Rasup was the next to tell his story. "I came from a village along the Euphrates River. We made ropes there. I was a servant to a rope maker but I wasn't very good at it. About a year ago a caravan came through our village. The leader wanted to buy rope. He said he needed another man to help take the caravan to Egypt. He told me he would give me two silver rings if I went with him. I didn't like making ropes so I left with him. I worked very hard and he treated me well. When we were almost to Memphis he had some men grab me and tie me with the slaves. I was sold in the auction to Potiphar. I really like working with you, Joseph."

Jasen said her story was different. She said, "I grew up in a loving family. My mother and father worked very hard but we had a good life. Nine months ago a group of raiders came to our village. They killed mother and father and took me captive. I was sold to a slave merchant along with many boys and girls from our village. We were brought to Memphis and sold in the slave market. Caring for sheep is the best job I could have."

Joseph started by telling them of his childhood in Haran and the journey to Canaan. He said, "I was the favorite of my father. My mother made me a fancy cloak with long sleeves that came to my hands, one that hung down to my feet. I couldn't work while wearing that cloak. Father had a tutor to teach me to read, write and speak Egyptian, Hittite, Canaanite and Sumerian. I studied history, poetry, numbers and logic. One day I heard two of my older brothers talking about taking two of father's lambs and giving them to two priestesses of Ba'al to worship with them. I told father and he whipped them for giving his lambs to a false god. My father worships only El Shaddai, the God who created the heavens and the earth. All my brothers hated me but these two wanted to kill me. When my father sent me to check on my brothers, they threw my in a dry cistern planning to kill me after they ate the food I had brought to them.

One of my older brothers suggested that they could profit by selling me into slavery. A caravan going to Egypt was passing by so they sold me."

It was late when they got through telling their stories. They were much closer and got along as good friends. Joseph sent regular reports to Potiphar. The sheep grew fat and were in good health. The season passed from Peret, the growing season, to Shemu, the harvest season.

The four shepherds were talking one evening when Rasup asked, "Joseph how do the Egyptians tell the seasons and years?"

Joseph answered, "You know how we keep time. We use the moon. One moon cycle has 28 days, divided into four, seven day weeks. Every three years we have an extra month called second Adar so our calendar will align with the sun. The Egyptians use the sun. They have twelve months of 30 days, divided into three weeks of ten days each. The sun takes five more days to complete a year so they add five days to make the year come out even. The seasons are Akhet that is when the Nile overflows its banks. They call it the inundation. The inundation gives Egypt the ability to plant crops in the fresh black soil that is left when the water goes down. The season of Peret is the growing season. The season of harvest is called Shemu. Each season has four months. The first month is called First Akhet; the second month is called Second Akhet and so on."

Rasup replied, "I think our way is much smarter. Don't you, Joseph?"

"Our way seems smarter because we are used to it and we don't like changes," Joseph answered.

Jasen said, "They grow something that looks like what we called millet. They call it dhurra corn. It grows larger than our millet. We ate some of the millet and fed some to our cattle and sheep. They say they can get three crops a year and that it can stand dry times."

"It is during the season of third Shemu that our jobs will get harder," Melita told them. "That is the time when the ewes enter their season and the rams fight to get to mount them. After we get through Peret and the corn is harvested, we will put the sheep in the durra corn fields to feed on the stalks."

The seasons passed quickly. It seemed like a very short time until they were taking the sheep to the high ground to keep them from the inundation. That spring the 508 ewes had 769 lambs.

The Grand Vizier sent a message to Potiphar telling him that he would like to see him. He went quickly to see what Lord Siese wanted. As soon as he arrived, he was shown in. Lord Siese began the conversation, "I have been told that you were having trouble with some of your sheep being stolen and that you have an Asiatic slave that can read and write and knows numbers."

"That is correct, Lord Siese," Potiphar replied. "I sent him as a helper to my shepherds. He soon found how they were robbing me. He is now my chief shepherd and my flock is growing fatter and healthier. Perhaps you have heard me brag about this slave?"

"Yes, I was told about your slave. As you know I am also the royal treasurer, and Gatekeeper for Pharaoh Ammenemhet II. As gatekeeper I am responsible for seeing that Pharaoh's necropolis is completed as it was designed. I think we are being cheated by some supervisors. The amount of gold, silver and particularly the bronze they request seems excessive for what they are making. I need someone I can trust to watch them and report if they are stealing. Do you think your slave could do that?" he asked Potiphar.

"My slave, Joseph, is a very honest, trustworthy slave. He is also very obedient," Potiphar told Lord Siese. "I would trust him with my life."

"I would like to borrow him for a while," Lord Siese said. "He will be sent to the necropolis as a helper to clean the room where they are making the gold cart that will take Pharaoh's body into the tomb."

"I will be happy for you to use my slave in any way you want," Potiphar replied. "When do you want him to start?"

"As soon as you can get him here," Lord Siese told him. "Tell me when he is here. I will send him to the Royal Engineer, Lord Khentykhetywer, overseer of the building of the necropolis.

"I will leave for Goshen tomorrow and should be back in three days," Potiphar told Lord Siese.

Potiphar arrived in the afternoon of the next day. The shepherds had separated the flock into four small flocks so they could find better pastures. Potiphar was amazed to see how much better the sheep looked. They were noticeably fatter and had more wool. The first flock he came to was being tended by Rasup. He told Potiphar that Joseph had taken his flock over the hill into a valley because the grass was better.

Potiphar left his chariot and walked to Joseph. Joseph was surprised to see him walking towards him. He ran to meet him and bowed down when he approached.

"Arise, Joseph and walk with me," Potiphar told him. "The sheep are very fat. You have done a good job. I have another job for you. I have been bragging about how you caught the butcher and the three former shepherds. The overseer of the necropolis wants you to watch some workers. He thinks some of the workers are stealing. Take your flock back to the pen I will tell the others to do the same. When all the sheep were in the pen, Potiphar said to the shepherds, "you have done a very good job of taking care of the sheep. I am taking Joseph back to Memphis with me. He has recommended Melita to be your leader. I want to reward you for a job well done. Here are five brass rings for each of you. You may go into the village one at a time to spend them."

As they were riding back to Memphis, Potiphar told Joseph that Lord Khentykhetywer was the overseer of the necropolis. He has the responsibility of seeing that the necropolis he designed for Pharaoh Ammenemhet II is completed before the pharaoh dies.

Potiphar went on talking about Lord Khentykhetywer, "He is also the royal engineer. Years ago one of the Pharaohs built a canal from the Nile into a low area called the Fayoum depression. Some think it was Pharaoh Senusret I who built the canal. Others say it was built earlier and that Pharaoh Senusret I only improved it. The canal was constructed to improve farming in Egypt. Water flows from the Nile into the depression from First Akhet until the end of second Peret. Then the water flows from the depression into the Nile the rest of the year. Lord Khentykhetywer designed and built two dams that divert more water from the Nile into the depression. He also improved control of the flow by designing and building locks that are adjusted by water. Before the canal was built, a pyramid was built in the center of the depression. The pyramid stands about 175 royal cubits above the water level and about 175 royal cubits below the water. The surface area of the lake is 17,000 feddan."

"If the Lord is so smart, why does he need me?" Joseph asked.

"He wants you to work in the crafts area and listen to their talk," Potiphar answered. "You are to watch to see if they are stealing gold or silver."

Even though they got back after dark, they went directly to Lord

Siese's' palace. He was waiting for them. The Lord offered them cold beer to drink. The beer was welcome after the long dusty chariot ride.

Lord Siese gave Joseph a sheet of papyrus and told him to explain it

Joseph took a quick look and said. "This is a request from the supervisor of the craftsmen to the treasurer for 100 deden of gold and 300 deden of silver."

"You read that very quickly. I am going to send you to Lord Khentykhetywer," Lord Siese told Joseph.

Lord Khentykhetywer spoke to Joseph in the Hittite language. He asked Joseph, "What languages can you read and write?"

Joseph answered in the Hittite language, "I can read and write in Canaanite, Hittite, Surmerian and Egyptian."

"Very good," Lord Khentykhetywer said. "I want you to write in Hittite. Years ago when I was an apprentice engineer, the engineer I worked for took a job building a bridge for the king of Hittite. We built a bridge over the river on the caravan route toward the sunrise from Haran. Do you know the place?"

"Yes," Joseph answered. "My father worked for his uncle Laban for twenty years near Haran. I was born there."

"The scoundrel I worked for took the money for building the bridge and left us stranded there. I worked for a fleece buyer in Haran for two years. I remember a shepherd named Laban selling fleece to me. I left there 30 years ago and came home," Lord Khentykhetywer told them. "I am going to put Joseph in charge of cleaning the craft shops. You are not to tell them you speak anything but Canaanite. The person in charge of slaves can speak that language. Look at every paper you see. Listen to their talk to see if they are cheating me on the amount of gold and silver they are taking from the treasury. You will stay here tonight and tomorrow I will take you to meet Inteb. His family was rulers of part of Egypt years ago. Strong drink and gambling has reduced them to a lower estate today. I have heard that Inteb still gambles and still loses. He is a fair Senet player but many are better. He bets he can beat them and then loses."

"How will I contact you?" Joseph asked.

"Captain Potiphar will have a soldier talk to you each evening during the meal. He is able to speak the Canaanite language. Most people won't understand, but be careful what you say. If you have any information, write it down in Hittite and give it to the soldier. He will have a fast chariot to bring the news to me."

CHAPTER 15

—— THE NECROPOLIS ——

Captain Potiphar had one of his ships take them to the necropolis. When Lord Khentykhetywer and Joseph reached the pyramid, they walked up the causeway to the east entrance. Entering, they went down a hallway and turned right. They walked down this hall until they were about the middle of the pyramid and turned left. At the end of this hall, they came to a large chamber with a vaulted roof. That chamber would be the Pharaoh's burial chamber but for now it was the gold craftsmen's work shop. Just before they got to the burial chamber, there was a smaller chamber. On one of the walls of the small chamber a picture of Thoth had been painted. Thoth, the Ibis headed god, was the god of truth and knowledge. He had a balance in his hand. The Egyptians believed that he would put the heart of the deceased on the scale. The heart was be weighed against the principles of his wife, Ma'at. If the scales did not balance, it was thrown to Sobek, the Alligator God, who would eat it. The Egyptians believed that one could not go to the western fields of Paradise unless the body was whole.

Lord Khentykhetywer introduced Joseph to the supervisor as a new slave from Canaan. He told them he could not understand any other language. He told the supervisor of the slaves "Joseph is to keep the crafts area clean. Get the cleaning material and show Joseph how to use them. Joseph is not to leave this area except to eat and sleep."

When Lord Khentykhetywer left, Joseph was given a broom, a mop, a bucket and some rags. The supervisor of slaves showed him how to sweep and how to mop and then that supervisor left. Inteb and another supervisor named Thasd were talking, Inteb said, "I don't like having that slave here. What if he can understand us and tells Lord Khentykhetywer?"

Thasd, Inteb's assistant, told him to watch and learn. He motioned for Joseph to come to him so Joseph went to him. Thasd said to Joseph, "You smell worse than the crud in Seth's buttocks and you look uglier than a bugger in Seth's left nostril." He was smiling while he said that to Joseph. Joseph smiled back and nodded his head, yes, yes.

Turning to Inteb he said, "You see, if he could understand, he would not have been happy with what I called him but since I was smiling he took it as a compliment. As you know, any reference to Seth, the god of the underworld and evil, is the worst insult you can make to another person."

After that they felt comfortable to speak freely in Joseph's presence. Joseph pretended not to hear them but he listened very carefully. Two weeks later he sent a letter to Lord Khentykhetywer telling him that the supervisors were saving the floor sweepings but not accumulating enough gold for concern. Every two weeks Joseph sent a letter to Lord Khentykhetywer telling him what he had heard and seen. After he had been cleaning the chamber for seven weeks, three supervisors from the silver and jewelry shops came in to talk with Inteb.

Inteb asked, "Do you think enough time has elapsed so we can send another load of dirt to Memphis?" They all laughed and agreed. Inteb continued, "This load will give each of us 150 dedens of gold and 450 dedens of silver."

A slave pushed a cart load of dirt into the work area. The supervisor of the slaves told Joseph, "put the dirt into sacks. It is for Lord Khentykhetywer's garden." As he filled each sack, one of the supervisors tied the sack shut. Joseph noticed that some of the bags had another small bag dropped in before it was closed. The sacks with the small bag inside were marked with a white stripe. When all the dirt was bagged the supervisor of slaves told Joseph, "push the cart to the dock and load the dirt onto the boat waiting at the dock. Then you can go eat." After loading the dirt, Joseph went to his quarters and wrote a note to Lord Khentykhetywer telling him of the gold and silver in the bags with the white stripes. He also told him that he had heard the five supervisors saying they each would have 150 dedens of gold and 450 dedens of silver hidden in their houses. When the soldier came by, Joseph slipped him the note and told him to get it Lord Khentykhetywer quickly.

The soldier left immediately. He drove the chariot most of the night to reach Memphis. The soldier went to Lord Khentykhetywer as soon as he got there. When he arrived at the palace, the guards were reluctant to allow him to pass. When he told them his orders were to report to the Lord any time day or night, they let him through. The guard at the door asked, "Are you the soldier from the necropolis?" When he said "yes" the guard went into the bedroom and roused Lord Khentykhetywer. As soon as the Lord read the message he called for the sergeant of the guard. The sergeant came quickly.

Lord Khentykhetywer told him, "get Captain Potiphar as quickly as you can." The sergeant left at a run. He came to Captain Potiphar's house and called for Captain Potiphar. He told Captain Potiphar that Lord Khentykhetywer had a message from Joseph.

Captain Potiphar went to see Lord Khentykhetywer and was told, "take three ships and head upstream. Stop all boats coming down river. Capture the ship with a load of dirt. The sailors probably don't know what they are carrying in the bags so arrest them but treat them kindly. Question the captain of the boat to see if he has any idea about the contents of the sacks. If you are satisfied that they knew nothing of the gold or silver in the sacks, put them in jail for two days. Then turn them loose with a silver ring each for their troubles."

Captain Potiphar left with the three ships and went up river stopping all boats and making sure they were not carrying a load of dirt. Close to sunset he found the boat with a load of dirt going to Lord Khentykhetywer's palace. The sailors on that ship were arrested. Soldiers from Captain Potiphar's ships took off their uniforms and put on regular clothes and manned the boat. The captain of the boat with the dirt complained that there was no reason to arrest them. Potiphar opened one of the sacks with the white stripe and showed him the bag of gold inside. The captain didn't know anything about the gold. After much questioning Captain Potiphar decided that he was not in collusion with the thieves. The captain and the crew were told, "You are under arrest for transporting stolen goods."

The sacks with the white stripes were taken to Lord Siese. When they were opened, the gold and silver were weighed. There was 50 dedans of gold and 150 dedans of silver. Lord Siese was furious. At first light he went with Captain Potiphar to see Pharaoh Senusret II. When he explained the situation to the king, he asked for permission to search the supervisors' houses. The Pharaoh was just as angry as the others. He asked, "Is Captain Potiphar here?"

The vizier answered, "Yes, Mighty Egypt, he is in the outer chamber awaiting your pleasure."

The Pharaoh took off his ring and gave it to the vizier. "Give this to him. He will go as my agent. The vizier gave Potiphar the ring and told him to search the houses and to bring back anything he found. Captain Potiphar, four soldiers and a scribe went to search the houses belonging to the supervisors. The steward of the first house would not grant entrance until Captain Potiphar showed him the Pharaoh's ring. Upon seeing the ring the steward bowed and allowed them to enter. Potiphar asked if his master had a chest with a lock on it. "Yes Captain," the steward answered. "He keeps it in his bedroom in a storage space under a rug."

The steward led the way to the bedroom. He pulled back the rug to expose a trap door. The door was locked but the Steward went to a hidden drawer in the wall and got a key to unlock the door. In the hole was a large chest. When the chest was removed, they saw that it was sealed with the impression of the owner's ring. Captain Potiphar had a scribe write a receipt for the chest and give it to the steward.

"Do you have an impression of your master's seal?" Captain Potiphar asked the steward.

"Yes, Captain." The steward replied. "I will get one for you." He went to a desk and got a letter his master had sealed. The impression was the same as the one on the chest.

With minor variations the same things happened at the other four houses. When all the chests were collected, Captain Potiphar took the chests back to the vizier. The vizier went into the audience hall of the king and told him what they had done. Pharaoh commanded them to bring the chests to him. Soldiers brought the chests to the king. Pharaoh looked at the seals and at the impressions on the papers and knew they were owned by the same people.

"Open those chests," Pharaoh commanded. The vizier had men standing by with mallets and chisels to open the chests. With the locks broken off, the king raised the lids and looked in each chest. "Can you identify any of the articles in these chests?" The king asked the vizier.

"Yes Mighty Egypt," the Lord Siese answered. "I cannot identify all of the gold and silver items, but I know that some of the items were made for your father's necropolis. This gold bar should have been on the handle of the sled. This piece is a foot for one of the tables in the entrance way. These jewels were for decorations for the Pharaoh's cloak. They have reduced the number of jewels that were to be put on the cloak." He went through each chest picking out pieces that he could identify.

"Bring those thieving rascals to me immediately!" Pharaoh ordered Captain Potiphar "Take Lord Khentykhetywer with you."

Captain Potiphar and Lord Siese went to Lord Khentykhetywer's palace to get him. Captain Potiphar sent a sergeant to get three ships ready to depart as soon as they arrived.

The party arrived in about three fingers time and boarded the first ship. Captain Potiphar called for all the soldiers to listen. "We must get to the Pharaoh's necropolis very quickly. We have two teams of rowers on each ship. The first team will row for one hand of time, and then the second team will row. The first team will rest while the second team is rowing. We will continue changing teams until we reach our destination."

The sun was beginning to rise when they reached the harbor that served the necropolis. Breakfast was served to Lord Khentykhetywer and Captain Potiphar. After the crews began working, Lord Khentykhetywer sent a servant into the pyramid to tell the supervisors that he wanted to talk to them about changes and also to bring the slave, Joseph. In about one hand of time the servant came back with the supervisors and Joseph.

The supervisors sat down and began talking. They told Lord Khentykhetywer that the necropolis would be completed in six more weeks. While they were talking, Captain Potiphar and ten of his soldiers walked around the deck encircling the supervisors to keep them from trying to escape.

Lord Khentykhetywer said, "The biggest change we are going to make is that you five are under arrest for stealing gold, silver and jewelry from the Pharaoh."

They started to protest their innocence. Lord Khentykhetywer stopped them. "We intercepted the last shipment of dirt you sent. We confiscated the gold and silver in the sacks with the white stripes. Captain Potiphar went to your houses and picked up your chests filled with gold, silver and jewels."

"He did not have the right to enter our houses without our permission," they yelled together.

Captain Potiphar came forward and showed them the Pharaoh's Egyptian blue ring. When they saw the Pharaoh's ring they shut up. The five were separated and three were taken to different ships. The two remaining were put in separate rooms.

Lord Khentykhetywer and Captain Potiphar came into the first room. Three soldiers were with them. They had a brazier of burning charcoal. Captain Potiphar told the prisoner, "As you know, we interrogate prisoners by stripping their clothes off and tying them to the ceiling by their feet. In that position we shove burning charcoal up their rear end if we don't like the answers we get. Since you are a respected supervisor I will give you a chance to tell me everything you know about the thefts of the gold, silver and jewels."

The prisoner replied, "I have helped interrogate prisoners. I will tell you what you want to know."

Lord Khentykhetywer asked, "Who came up with the plan for the theft?"

"Inteb made the plan and told us we could get the gold, silver and jewels to our homes if we could get you to approve building a garden in the rocks in back of your palace. We told you we wanted to build you a garden as a thank you for giving us our positions."

"Yes," Lord Khentykhetywer remarked. "I remember that conversation. You were to bring a boat load of dirt every season. I have seen how much dirt you have brought and how you have placed it but go on with your confession."

"We cut corners in the amount of gold we used by putting bronze centers in things. The round rails on the sledge were to be of solid gold, two fingers thick. We made a bronze pole one finger thick and put enough gold around it to make the rail two fingers thick. When we shipped a boat load of dirt for your garden, we put the dirt in sacks to make it easier to load and unload. We put gold, silver or jewels into some of the sacks. We marked those sacks with a white stripe. None of the sailors or workers knew of our plan. We told the captain of the boat to send the sacks with the white stripes to Inteb's warehouse and to take the rest to your garden. The sacks remained in the warehouse until we came to Memphis. After we sent a boat load of dirt, we made some excuse to be in Memphis. We usually came to ask you to clear up some problem. While we were home we would divide the gold, silver or jewels. How did you catch us? No one knew what we were doing."

Lord Khentykhetywer called Joseph over to him. "This young man can speak, read, and write four languages. He also knows and can calculate numbers. Captain Potiphar had a soldier walk through the workers' area during the evening meal. The soldier stopped and talked to several workers. Joseph was always one of those workers. Every two weeks Joseph sent a report to me which was written in Hittite."

The interviews with three of the other prisoners were much the same. Inteb's was much different. "I am entitled to all the gold and silver I can get," Inteb began. My grandfather was a Pharaoh as was his father, grandfather, and great-grandfather. The Intebs have been cheated out of all our wealth and power. We were the richest family in all Egypt. Now I am reduced to working for a mere pittance. Anything I took should have been mine by inheritance."

He continued this tirade for a half a hand of time before Lord Khentykhetywer cut him off. He was locked in a cabin again and the three ships started back to Memphis. Lord Khentykhetywer told Joseph that Inteb I had been Pharaoh of the Greater Thebes and was the first Pharaoh to say he was a Horus man.

When they reached Memphis, they started for Lord Siese's palace. They noticed that the entire palace was draped in black cloth. Calling a servant to them they asked, "Why is black cloth covering everything?"

"My Lords," the servant began. "Didn't you know that Pharaoh Ammenemhet II passed away in his sleep last night? Pharaoh Senusret II and the royal wives are in the temple of Ra mourning his passing."

Captain Potiphar said, "I will put the prisoners in jail until after the funeral. Then Pharaoh can decide the punishment for them. Before Captain Potiphar left with the prisoners he was summoned to see Lord Siese. Potiphar gave the prisoners to a sergeant and told him, "put them in secure rooms in the fortress. They have been accused but not judged guilty by Pharaoh. They are to be allowed visitors and if they desire, a servant may stay with each one."

Lord Siese told Captain Potiphar to ready six ships for a fast run both north and south to carry the announcement of Pharaoh Ammenemhet II's death. The entire country must be told.

Captain Potiphar sent four ships south. Two would stop at all the towns and villages on the east side of the Nile and the other two would stop at all the towns and villages on the west. When the first ship stopped, the other continued on. The second ship stopped at the next village. They continued leapfrogging each other until they arrived at the southernmost village on Elephantine Isle. Two ships were also sent north. One took the east channel and spread the news on both sides. The other took the west channel. When they reached the great sea, they turned along the coast and then back up the two middle channels. Then they traveled up two more channels and finally down the seventh channel and returned to Memphis. They continued sailing up different channels until the towns on all seven channels were notified. As they were walking from the palace to the fortress, Joseph asked Potiphar, "Master, what is the reason for the announcement and how do they make a mummy from the dead body?"

Potiphar answered Joseph, "the reason for the announcement is to tell everyone about the death and to give them time to get ready for the mourning period and the burial ceremony."

"In answering your question about mummification, Pharaoh's body will go to the embalmers work shop. There the priests, who are the embalmers, will get the body ready to be mummified.

The chief priest will wear a mask of the god Anubis, the jackal headed god, to impersonate him. Anubis is also the guardian of the scales Thoth uses. Anubis is the god of the embalmers and the protector of the necropolis."

"The first step is to remove the brain. This is accomplished by pushing a special spoon, or wire, through the nose into the brain cavity and removing a little of the brain at a time. We do not know the purpose of the brain. We think of it as a pudding to hold the head bones in place. As the brain is pulled out, it is put in water to dissolve. They will continue pulling a little at a time until they have pulled the entire brain out. Sometimes the water is thrown out; other times it is put in the burial chamber. Since this is the Pharaoh, the water will be put in his burial chamber".

Potiphar continued, "The next step will be the removal of the organs. A slit is cut in the left side of the stomach and the liver, lungs, intestines and stomach are removed. These organs are mummified separately and placed in canopic jars. There are four jars; each contains the head of one of Horus' children. Qusenubehse, a falcon headed god, is protector of the intestines. Duamutef, a jackal headed god, protects the stomach. Imsety, a human headed goddess, protects the liver, and Hapy, a baboon headed god protects the lungs. We believe the heart is the center of a person's being so it is never removed from the body."

"After the organs are removed from the body, the inside of the body is washed with palm oil and natron salt that will help preserve the body. The body is then stuffed with material to keep it in its normal shape. The body is placed on a diorite slab and covered with natron salt. The slab has a tilt to it so the fluids will drain into a collecting basin. The body is covered and taken outside to dry. The body is left outside for forty days. During this period, people walk past and pay their respects to the deceased."

"Once the body has dried, it is wrapped. Wrapping the body is a long hard process. The body is first rubbed with oils. A gold piece with a picture of the 'eye of Horus' is placed over the slit in the stomach. Each finger and toe is wrapped separately. Many hundreds of cubits of linen are used to wrap the body. The chief priest will also wear a mask of Anubis. Between each layer of wrapping the priests will stop to write a prayer to be covered by the next layer or to place a good luck charm. Many eye of Horus gold pieces or pictures are wrapped with the body. We believe these items to be magical and will give good luck to the body and protect it in the afterlife. After many layers of strips are wound around the body, it will be wrapped by a shroud to keep the strips together. The shroud is dipped into to solution called 'mummia', to hold everything together. The reason we call the protected body a mummy is that mummia is used. The Pharaoh had a death mask made of gold eighteen months ago. The mask looks just like him. The eyes are of black stones and the lips have been painted red. We use a coffin that is shaped like the human body. His coffin has been made of gold with a likeness of Pharaoh Ammenemhet II sculpted into the head. Cosmetics are applied to the face and a garland of flowers will be placed around the neck of the coffin. The person's Ka, his essence, needs to recognize the body. The more lifelike they can make the face look the easier it will be for the Ka to find his body. Then the mummy is put into its gold coffin."

"After all this has been completed, the mummy is taken through the streets. The family and friends walk behind the coffin on the way to the burial site. Mourners are hired to wail and cry loudly. They want the gods of the nether world to hear how much the person was loved while alive. We believe that the more people cry and wail the more the nether world will think he was loved and admired. His chances of going into the western fields of paradise are much improved by our crying and wailing. We will load the coffin of Pharaoh onto a ship and take it to the landing near his necropolis. His family and friends will accompany him. Slaves and servants will follow the sled to the pyramid carrying the gifts of sacrifice. Furniture, food, drink, jewels, and a freshly killed calf's leg, still spouting blood, will be offered to the dead. As soon as they reach the Pyramid, a purification ritual using salt and cow's milk will be performed."

"At the pyramid the coffin will stop at the entrance. The coffin will be stood upright, facing south, and a very important ceremony called, 'Opening of the mouth', will be preformed. A close family friend will burn incense and a priest will be reading from the 'Book of the Dead'. Other priests will be chanting potent spells. At this time the Ka cannot speak, hear, see or eat. The opening of the mouth ritual is conducted by an embalming priest in an Anubis mask. A special tool is used for this important ceremony. The priest will touch the mouth with a gold spoon with a handle shaped like a cobra for Pharaoh. When he touches the mouth, the family and friends will chant,

> 'My mouth is opened by Ptah,
> My mouth's bonds are loosened by my god.
> Thoth has come fully equipped with spells,
> He loosens the bonds of Seth from my mouth.
> My mouth is given me, so I can
> Eat of the food of the Western Paradise.'"

"The priest will then touch the eyes and another blessing is chanted by family and friends.

> 'Ptah has opened his eyes,
> By gently rubbing the lids open.
> Ptah wanted him to see the wonder,
> And beauty of the Western Paradise.'"

The priest touches the nose with the spoon, and another chant was recited.

> 'Ptah has opened his nose,
> To allow him to smell
> the wonderful food, and the beautiful flowers that are in
> the Western Paradise.' "

"The priest will touch the ears and the family and friends will recite an appropriate chant,

> 'Ptah has unplugged his ears, so he can hear wonderful music.
> He will be able to join the, choir of the Western Paradise.'"

"The coffin will be lowered and taken into the burial chamber. The coffin will be placed in a sarcophagus. The Canopic jars with the heads of the four protecting gods will be put in a canopic box and placed beside the sarcophagus. A jar with a copy of the book of the dead will be placed on the other side of the sarcophagus. The entrance of the chamber will be sealed."

"The most important ceremony will be conducted after the pyramid is sealed. It will not be seen by anyone. The ceremony of the 'weighing of the heart' is required by anyone wanting to achieve immortality. Thoth, the god of truth will bring out scales to weigh the heart of the deceased. This judgment is to see how the person conducted himself while alive. The balance scale will have the person's heart on one side and the feather of truth on the other. Anubis, the god of the underworld will be the judge. Thoth, the god of scribes, will record the results. For the person to be granted immorality the scale must balance. If the scale does not balance, if bad things outweigh the good, the Ka of that person is condemned to a horrible existence. That person's heart will be thrown to the god Sobek, a crocodile headed goddess, called the 'devourer of the dead.'"

As they reached the fortress Potiphar said, "I hope that explained our beliefs about the dead. It takes forty days to embalm some people, but for Pharaoh and other high officials it takes seventy days"

"Thank you master," Joseph replied. "My teacher, Jurrad, had told me a little about those beliefs but I had forgotten them."

Potiphar told Joseph that he was going to take him home. "I am going to put you in my house as a helper to the steward. I think he is an honest person but it pays to make sure. Don't tell him that you know other languages or that you can read and write."

After doing some work, Potiphar took Joseph home and introduced him to Ahani, his steward. Ahani wasn't happy to have a helper, "Master I have gotten along by myself for all these years," Ahani said. "Why do I need a helper now?"

"You have done a good job Ahani," Potiphar told him. "I wanted to lighten your load a little. I have been told that Joseph is a very obedient slave. He will do anything you tell him. At first he might not know what to do but if you will show him I think he will be able to do it. I am going to be busy with the funeral for the next two months. I know you will take care of things while I am gone."

Ahani showed Joseph around the house and explained how the master wanted the furniture arranged and cleaned. "You will start by dusting the furniture, sweeping and mopping the floors each morning. In the afternoon you will help in the garden." Ahani didn't like having Joseph for an assistant. Joseph was always respectful and obedient. After three months Ahani got used to having him around. In fact, he liked that Joseph did all the hard, time consuming jobs so he had more time to play Senet.

Every two or three days the head jailor, Mibzar, came by to play Senet and drink beer. Mibzar usually won. One day he asked Joseph to play against him. Joseph asked Ahani if it was alright if he played a game. Ahani gave him permission. Ahani and Mibzar were amazed that Joseph beat Mibzar so quickly and easily.

Senet is played on a board with thirty spaces in three rows of ten each. Space number fifteen is a restart space, any piece going forward landing on that space must go back to start. Number twenty six is a safe space while number twenty seven sends the piece back to number fifteen. Each player gets seven pieces. Play is started with all fourteen pieces on the board. Spaces twenty-eight, twenty-nine, and thirty are marked three, two, and one, meaning that the player must have that many sticks with the flat side up. Moves are determined by throwing the sticks. There are four sticks with a flat side and a round side. Players hold the sticks in one hand about two hands high and drop them. The number of flat sides turned up, allows the player to move a piece that many spaces. Luck and skill is needed to win in Senet.

"Who taught you to play senet?" Ahani asked.

"In my spare time I have been watching you play," Joseph answered.

Ahani wanted to play a game with Joseph. Luck and skill seemed to be on Joseph's side. Mibzar and Ahani didn't know that Joseph had gotten a book from Potiphar's library about how to 'Win at Senet', by a master player. He had studied the plays in that book.

After that Mibzar and Ahani wanted to play Joseph every time they set up the board. With the knowledge Joseph had gained by studying the masters, Joseph could easily beat them every time but he lost many games so they would not know how much he knew. Ahani began to like Joseph.

After five months Ahani told Joseph to come with him to the market to help carry the supplies. Joseph had never been to the market so he was eager to go. The market was about one hand's walk from Potiphar's house. When they got to the shop where they would get the supplies, several other stewards were there. Joseph was so interested in the shop that he didn't pay any attention to the buying. Ahani was happy that he didn't have to carry all the supplies. Following that trip he took Joseph every time he went to the shop.

Joseph had lost interest in the items in the shop. He paid more attention to the other stewards. He noticed that the shopkeeper gave each steward two silver rings when they signed the receipt for their supplies. Three or four of the other stewards would leave their supplies in the shop and go across the street to a tavern. When Joseph had been working with Ahani for almost a year, Ahani gave Joseph a list of items he wanted, "just give this list to the shopkeeper and he will get the supplies ready I am going with my friends to get a beer," he told Joseph. Joseph looked at the list before he gave it to the shopkeeper. The shopkeeper got most of the items in the quantity on the list. Joseph noticed that some of the quantities were a little short. He thought he would tell Ahani that the shopkeeper was cheating him. When Ahani and the others came back, the shopkeeper gave each two silver rings so Joseph remained silent.

CHAPTER 16

——— THE STEWARDS ———

When Joseph got to his room, he wrote down the items and the quantities ordered. In the next column he wrote down the quantities received. When he added the values of each column he saw that the difference was about four silver rings. He knew that the stewards were cheating their masters every time they went shopping. After that he made a list of the items ordered and of the items received each time they went shopping.

Pharaoh Senusret II went on a military campaign through the southern part of Canaan. Captain Potiphar went with him. They expected to be gone nearly two years. During that time Joseph kept records of what was ordered and what was received. One night after Potiphar had been gone for over a year, Ahani came into Joseph's sleeping quarters. Joseph was writing down the quantities ordered and what was received in Hittite.

Ahani asked, "What are you doing?"

Joseph replied, "I am trying to learn how to write in my language. These are my lessons."

"What good is knowing how to write in anything other than Egyptian?" Ahani scowled.

"I have no one to teach me the Egyptian letters," Joseph replied.

As he turned to leave, Ahani remarked, "Slaves do not need to know how to read or write. All they need to know is how to obey the master. Stop wasting your time on that nonsense and pay attention to your work." Ahani left and Joseph gave a sigh of relief.

Pharaoh Senusret II and the army came home after being gone thirty months. They brought much booty including many slaves. Captain Potiphar brought twenty five new Asiatic slaves from Canaan. Ahani reported to Potiphar on the state of the household. He had maintained the house in good condition and had been able to keep the expenses within the amount Potiphar had allowed.

Captain Potiphar told Joseph to train the new slaves since he spoke their language. Joseph spoke to the new slaves and told them they were lucky to have Potiphar as their master because he was kind and treated slaves better than most masters. If they did what they were told to do, they would be treated well. All the new slaves were from an area close to Egypt. Joseph was very glad to know that the army had not gone near his family.

Two weeks later Potiphar called Joseph to ask him how the new slaves were doing. Joseph told him that most had been shepherds or had kept cattle. He recommended that three be sent to help the shepherds. Then Joseph presented Potiphar with the records he had kept. He told him the merchant was cheating all the owners by giving short supplies and giving each steward two silver rings and keeping the other two for himself. Potiphar said, "I will look into the charges and get back with you. Do not tell Ahani of this conversation."

Potiphar took the records to Lord Siese. Joseph had written in Hittite which Lord Siese knew. After looking at the records, Lore Siese said, "My steward uses the same merchant as yours, as do many of our friends. We need to check this out. Send me ten of your African soldiers that can read and write. We will set them up as stewards for ten houses. One will go to the market with an order each morning and another will go each afternoon to see if this merchant is cheating everyone."

When the soldiers arrived, Lord Siese took them to a house he owned, a few blocks from the market. He gave each of the soldiers a steward's gown and told them, "each one of you go to the market on different days each week, one in the morning and one in the afternoon with an order that I will send you each week. Tell the merchant you heard that he gave special deals to stewards and then give him the list of items"

If he gives you two silver rings but not all the items on your list, keep the rings and make a list of the shortages." Each soldier would name a prominent person as his master. Lord Siese would have that person go by the market and arrange to pay for the items purchased. Their masters would pay at the end of each month.

Joseph did not know of these arrangements. Potiphar told Ahani that he had other duties for Joseph. He took Joseph to his office and told him to clean the office in the fort every day. One month later Potiphar called Ahani and Joseph into his office in his house. There were two soldiers in the office with him. As soon as Ahani and Joseph entered, Potiphar told the soldiers to arrest Ahani.

"But master," Ahani began. "Haven't I have done everything you told me to do?"

"I thought you were a very good steward until I caught you cheating with the merchant. For the past month ten of my soldiers have been posing as slaves and stewards for ten prominent men. During that time they have observed you and many other stewards accepting two silver rings from the merchant. You and the other stewards go to the tavern across the street for beer and a prostitute. I don't know how long this has been going on but you are going to jail with the merchant and the rest of the stewards. You will be tried in court by Lord Siese," Potiphar concluded. "Take him to jail," Potiphar told the soldiers.

The soldiers left with Ahani. Potiphar turned to Joseph. "You are now my steward. You have been with me for around five years and you have proven to be loyal and trustworthy. You will assume you duties now."

Joseph hated to see Ahani go to jail although he knew he deserved jail time. He put on the gown of a steward. He moved his things from his small room into the steward's rooms. He started making his rounds of the estate to check on everything. When he entered the brewery to check on the beer for the master's dinner, Hapita came up and said, "Joseph, didn't I tell you that someday you would be the steward? What happened to Ahani?"

"I remember how kind you were to me," Joseph said. "I was afraid and I didn't know anything about being a slave. You were kind and helped me. You worked with me and taught me all I needed to know about making beer. Ahani was cheating the master through a scheme with the merchant and many other stewards. They were all doing the same thing. They have all been arrested and taken to jail. Do you have the beer ready for the master's diner?"

Joseph watched as the cooks prepared the evening meal for Potiphar and his guests. The cooks were slaves who had been taught how to cook. Joseph didn't need to know how to cook. His presence there made them careful of how they prepared everything. Joseph observed the meal. He was able to anticipate the needs of the diners.

Lady Zuleikah Potiphar was much younger than her husband. She was the spoiled youngest daughter of the governor of the Nome of Thebes. Zuleikah had been given to Potiphar as his wife after he saved the Pharaoh from the assassins. She was still young and very beautiful. She was still very spoiled and demanding.

Joseph liked his new duties. What he didn't like was the way young women dressed. It embarrassed him to see women with one or both breasts bare as they walked down the street. He realized that this was their custom but he still didn't like it. He was really annoyed when he was doing his duties and Zuleikah Potiphar was lying on her couch with both her breasts uncovered. She seemed to know that he didn't like to be in the room with her. She was fond of wearing a white skirt with a split up the side. She would twist so that one of her thighs was uncovered whenever Joseph came in to do his work. When she saw how it embarrassed him, she would laugh and make a crude remark to him.

The year passed quickly and Joseph was busy and happy. Mibzar came by to get instructions from Captain Potiphar, or so he said. He knew that Joseph was a very smart person so he came by to play Senet with him. Mibzar would come by four or five times a week. They became good friends.

Joseph had been steward for almost two years when Pharaoh Senusert II took his army to Ethiopia to stop a rebellion that had started. The Ethiopian king refused to send the required tribute. Captain Potiphar was ordered to go with him. Potiphar told Joseph he thought they would be gone five or six months.

Joseph carried out his duties as if Potiphar was there. Zuleikah became even more embarrassing to Joseph. She started making suggestive remarks to him. In the fourth month she asked Joseph, "Do you think I am beautiful?" He replied, "I am sure the Egyptian men find you beautiful. Emboldened by his remark, she asked, "Do you want to feel my breasts?" Joseph said "no!," and hurriedly left the room.

A week later she ordered Joseph, "come to bed with me!"

He refused, "With me in charge," he told her, and my master does not concern himself with anything in the house. Everything he owns he has entrusted to my care. No one in this house is greater than I am. My master has withheld nothing from me except you, because you are his wife. How could I do such a wicked thing and sin against God. And although she spoke to Joseph day after day, he refused to go to bed with her.

One day he went into the house to attend to his duties and none of the household servants were inside. She caught him by the gown and said, "Come to bed with me!" But he left his gown in her hand and ran out of the house.

When she saw that he had left his gown in her hand and ran out of the house, she called for her household servants. "Look," she said to them, "this Hebrew has been brought to us to make sport of me! He came in here to sleep with me but I screamed. When he heard me scream for help, he left his gown beside me and ran out of the house."

Eight days later Potiphar came home. Zuleikah told him the same lie she had told the servants. Potiphar called Joseph in and told him, "I am disappointed with you. You are no longer my steward." He had a soldier arrest Joseph and take him to Jail. Mibzar was amazed to see Joseph arrested. Joseph told Mibzar what had happened. Mibzar said, "I believe what you have told me. There are rumors about how Mrs. Potiphar carries on when the captain is gone." The Lord was still with Joseph. Mibzar made him a trustee and allowed him to go with him to the market. They played several games of Senet every day. Mibzar put Joseph in charge of taking care of the prisoners. A year later Mibzar had a bad case of gout in his right foot. He could hardly walk. Joseph went to the market alone. After that the only thing Mibzar concerned himself with was trying to beat Joseph at Senet. Joseph improved the food for the prisoners. He got news about their families and passed it on to them. Because of the way he treated the prisoners there were not as many problems. Two years passed swiftly. Joseph had been a slave for ten years.

Pharaoh Senusert II became suspicious of some of his court. He had his cupbearer and the chief baker put in prison. Captain Potiphar came to the prison when these two officials were taken there. He assigned Joseph to take good care of them. They were confined in a room on the first floor of the fort. They had been suspected but not found guilty. Joseph became their personal attendant. When he went to the market, he bought the foods they liked. He put fresh water and fruit in their room every day. Joseph brought them a Senet board to help them pass the time.

When Joseph came into their room a year later, he saw that they were sad of face. He asked them, "Why are you so sad?"

"We each had a dream last night but there is no one to interpret the dreams for us," the cupbearer told him.

Joseph told them, "Interpretations belong to God. Tell me your dreams."

The cupbearer told Joseph his dream, "I saw a vine with three branches on it. The branches budded, leafed out and bloomed. The blooms turned to grapes which ripened. I took the grapes and squeezed the juice into a cup and placed the cup in Pharaoh's hand."

"This is the interpretation," Joseph told him. "The three branches that had three clusters of ripe grapes are three days. Pharaoh will restore you to your position as cupbearer in just three days. Once again you will put Pharaoh's cup into his hand just like you did. I ask you to remember the way I treated you while you were here and remember me to Pharaoh. I was sold into slavery even though I had done nothing to deserve being sold."

When the chief baker heard the interpretation Joseph had given the cupbearer he told his dream to Joseph. "I also had a dream. I was carrying three baskets of white breads on my head. The baskets had many types of baked goods for Pharaoh but birds were eating the breads from the baskets."

"This is the interpretation," Joseph told him. "In three days Pharaoh will take you from prison and lift up your head and hang you on a tree after you are beheaded. The birds will devour the flesh from your body."

Pharaoh's birthday was three days later. He restored the cupbearer to his position as cupbearer but he had the chief baker's head cut off and his body hung on a tree. Joseph had given correct interpretations of their dreams. The cupbearer forgot Joseph and his kindnesses. Joseph stayed in prison for two more years.

Pharaoh dreamed that he was standing by the Nile when seven healthy river cows came out of the Nile and began eating the stalks of standing papyrus. Then seven other river cows came up. These river cows were very thin and poor. He could see their ribs very clearly. The second cows ate the first cows, but they were still just as thin and poorly. The dream troubled Pharaoh.

He finally went back to sleep but he had another dream. In this dream a stalk with seven big full heads of grain grew on it. Seven other heads came on the stalk. These heads were ugly and blighted. The ugly heads swallowed the good heads but they were just as thin and blighted as before. Pharaoh woke up troubled even though he knew it was a dream.

When he awoke the next morning, he was still troubled. He called for the wise men and magicians. After he told them his dreams, they had no idea what the dreams meant.

Then the cupbearer remembered Joseph. He reminded Pharaoh of his imprisonment two years earlier. He told Pharaoh that while he and the chief baker were in prison they had dreams. One of the prisoners, a young Hebrew, and a slave of the captain of the guard, had interpreted the dreams correctly for them. Pharaoh called for the captain of the guard. Captain Potiphar was in his office in the fort. A guard was sent to get him. As soon as he arrived at the palace, he was shown into the king's audience chamber. Potiphar bowed to the Pharaoh. Pharaoh told him to rise.

The Pharaoh asked, "Do you have a Hebrew slave named Joseph, in jail?"

"Yes, my Pharaoh," Potiphar answered.

"Do you think he can interpret dreams?" Pharaoh asked.

"Joseph has many talents, but I have not seen him interpret dreams," Potiphar answered. "But if he says he can, then I would believe him."

"My cupbearer told me he can interpret drams," Pharaoh told Potiphar. "Get him and bring him to me."

Potiphar told a sergeant to run to the prison and get Joseph. Joseph was in the back of the prison on the lower level when the sergeant came running in.

"Where is Joseph?" the sergeant demanded of Mibzar.

Mibzar sent one of the other prisoners to get Joseph. As soon as Joseph arrived, the sergeant grabbed his hand and ordered, "Come with me slave!" With that he pulled Joseph from the prison and they ran to a barber shop for a bath, shave and a haircut.

The sergeant told the barber, "Pharaoh wants to see this slave immediately. Give him a bath, a shave, a haircut and get him a new gown quickly." By the time they had cut his hair, shaved him and given him a bath, the barber had gotten a new gown.

The sergeant told the barber to give him a bill and Lord Siese would send the payment. He and Joseph ran back to the palace. Joseph was shown into the king's audience chamber immediately.

Joseph bowed seven times to Pharaoh and said, "How may I serve you my Pharaoh?"

Pharaoh asked Joseph, "Can you interpret dreams?"

"No I cannot," Joseph answered Pharaoh. "But my God will give Pharaoh the correct interpretation."

So Pharaoh said to Joseph: "I was standing on the bank of the Nile and seven river cows came up from the Nile. These river cows were well fed and fat and began to graze among the papyrus plants that grew there. Then seven other river cows came up. These cows looked like they hadn't eaten in months. They were the ugliest cows I have ever seen. The second cows ate the first cows but they were just as thin and ugly as before. Then I woke up.

I went back to sleep and had another dream. In this dream a stalk with seven heads grew up. These heads were full and ripe. Seven more heads of grain grew on the stalk. These heads were blighted and thin as if scorched by the east wind. The second heads swallowed the first seven heads but they still looked just as blighted and bad.

Joseph said, "The seven good cows and the seven good heads of grain are seven years. The seven poor cows and the seven blighted heads of grain are seven years. God has shown Pharaoh that he is going to send Egypt seven years of great harvests followed by seven years of famine. This is what I think Pharaoh should do. During the seven years of plenty one fifth of all the harvests should be gathered and put into storerooms and kept to be used during the years of famine. Two dreams were given to Pharaoh to reveal that God has determined to do this and he will soon begin the years of plenty. Pharaoh should appoint a wise and trusted person to oversee this project."

The proposal pleased Pharaoh and all his servants. Pharaoh said to all who were gathered there, "Can we find anyone as wise as Joseph? The spirit of his God lives in him." Then Pharaoh told Joseph, "Since God has given you so much wisdom and knowledge, I know of no one as wise as you. Therefore, I appoint you to the task of gathering the grain during the seven good years. You will build storehouses in every city. You will be over my house. You will be second only to me on my throne in all the land of Egypt. I am placing you over all the land of Egypt, and I give you the title of 'Lord of Egypt'. Pharaoh took off his Egyptian blue ring and gave it to Joseph. "Any person who sees this ring must obey you as they would obey me," Pharaoh told Joseph. Pharaoh changed Joseph's name to Zaphenathpaneah and gave him Asenath as his wife. She was the daughter of Potophera, priest of the temple of On.

Servants brought a fine linen gown and a gold collar for his neck. Then Pharaoh placed the Gold of Praise around Joseph's neck. Turning to Lord Siese, Pharaoh said, "Draw up the marriage contract between Lord Joseph and Asenath. I want the marriage as soon as possible."

Lord Siese sent a message to the Priest of the temple at On instructing him and his daughter to appear before the Pharaoh immediately. He then wrote the marriage contract. This contract was dated in the month of fourth Shemu, in the ninth year of Pharaoh Senusret II. The contract named Lord Joseph, age thirty, as the husband and Lady Asenath, age fifteen as the wife. It stipulated that the priest would be compensated with thirty gold rings for the loss of the services of his daughter. Normally the amount paid to compensate for a bride was the price of a slave but Pharaoh was generous in this case. The contract stated that Lord Joseph was Lord of Egypt and would be able to provide for a wife. The contract mentioned that Lady Asenath would be head of the house and servants.

Lord Siese talked to Pharaoh about a home for Joseph. "My Lord as you may remember, Lord Palkert was dishonored. You had him strangled and took all of his property for yourself. Lord Joseph needs a proper palace. If I may make a suggestion, give him Palkert's property as a wedding present."

Pharaoh Senusret II answered, "Make it happen. If it can be done, do it before the wedding."

Lord Siese wrote the bill of transfer that afternoon. He went to see Lord Joseph. "Lord Joseph, if you will accompany me, I have something to show you." He had brought two sedan chairs, each carried by four strong slaves. "Since I know where we are going, I will lead." The bearers moved a slow trot. The slaves ran down the road toward the great sea. After one hand of time they turned away from the Nile and went down a dirt road to a large palace. When they stopped, Lord Siese got out and asked Joseph to come with him.

When all the servants had assembled in front of the palace, Lord Siese told them "This is Lord Joseph, Lord of Egypt." Then to Joseph's surprise he announced, "Our beloved Pharaoh Senusret II has given all the property that belonged to Palkert to the honorable Lord Joseph as a wedding present. You will work for him as you worked for Pharaoh."

As soon as they got back to town, Joseph went to the fortress. Potiphar came out to meet Joseph. Joseph said to him, "Captain I would like to see you in your office now!"

CHAPTER 17

—— THE HIPPOPOTAMUS HUNT ——

Joseph and Potiphar walked quickly to Captain Potiphar's office, when they entered, Joseph said, "Please take a seat, Captain. I am in desperate need of your help. I feel just like I did the first day I was your slave. Several rude people were pushing me and you came to my rescue. I have no idea what I am to do. Can you help me?"

Potiphar said skeptically, "You are the most powerful man in Egypt and you need my help?

"Yes," Joseph said. "I know that I have to visit all forty-two gnomes and get the governors to build the storehouses but I don't know how to do that. What would you suggest? Would you be my assistant?"

"Why would you want me as your assistant?" Potiphar asked.

"I have seen that you are an honest, hard working, officer. You know the ins and outs of the Egyptian government. I trust you," Josephs replied.

"You have offered me a great honor. Being your assistant would make me a great man. I had you put in jail when I knew you were not guilty. So why honor me?" Potiphar asked.

"You think you put me in jail but my God had you put me in jail so I could meet the cupbearer and the baker. Through them I met the Pharaoh and interpreted his dream. It was all in the plan God told me about when I was on my way to Egypt. Since it was my God that had you put me in your jail, why would I have any hard feelings toward you?"

"You are as kind as you are wise," Potiphar told Joseph. "I think we should go talk to Lord Siese. He is very smart and wise in the ways of the court."

Joseph took the papers that Lord Siese had given him and gave them to Potiphar. "Do you know what these are and what do they mean?" He asked Potiphar.

Potiphar read the papers and told Joseph, "These papers give you all the possessions that Lord Palkert once owned. Lord Palkert was involved in the plot to assassinate Pharaoh Ammenemhet II. I was the guard that killed one of the assassins and I gave a sword to Pharaoh and he killed another. That is when he promoted me to captain of the guard and gave me the gold of valor. What it means is that you are a very rich man. You own all the property that Palkert once owned, including 1500 feddans of land, 64 slaves, and a large palace."

Captain Potiphar sent a sergeant to Lord Siese's asking for an audience with him for Joseph. Lord Siese sent a message back almost immediately. It read, "Joseph is my superior, he does not need an appointment to see me. If he wishes, I will come to him. If he wants to see me in my palace, I will welcome him."

Potiphar sent a message back to Lord Siese, "If it is not inconvenient, he would like to see you now."

When Joseph and Potiphar entered Lord Siese's palace, Lord Siese came to meet them. He bowed and said, "How may I help you Lord Joseph?"

Joseph was amazed at being called Lord. He said, "I am like a fish out of water. I know what to do but I don't know where to start. I think I should visit all the gnomes and tell the governors to start building the storehouses but I don't know the proper way to do that."

"If I may offer a suggestion" Lord Siese said. "We are in the month of fourth Shemu. At the end of fourth Shemu we have the five epagomenal days. These five days are to align our calendar with the sun. During these five days we have festivals honoring five gods. The first god we honor is Osiris. We have a large celebration. All the Nomarchs will attend. I can arrange for Pharaoh to hold a banquet for them. At that banquet you can tell them what you want them to do. With Pharaoh sitting at your side, they will not argue with you."

"That is an excellent idea," Joseph replied.

"I will have the royal engineer invite engineers from all the gnomes to a banquet," Lord Siese told Joseph. "He will give them plans for the storehouses at that time. In six or seven months you can go to each Nome and inspect the work."

"I think you have an excellent idea." Joseph told Lord Siese. "Let's do it."

Lord Siese told Joseph, "Your wedding is to take place in four days, We must make the arrangements. The priests of the temple of On will weave a canopy of river rushes. The Canopy will be put under a large tree so that it will be in the shade.

On the day of the wedding Asenath and her father waited under the canopy for Joseph. Asenath was wearing a skirt that reached to her feet and had been dyed with the juice of shellfish, to the color of fine wine, to show that she was a virgin bride. A bridal wreath of long stem water lilies had been placed on her head. Her hair hung down and to her waist. The blooms of the water lilies were a cerulean blue with bright yellow centers.

As Joseph approached, he saw lines of musicians playing the lyre and the harp. The cymbal and the drums were being beaten loudly. Others were shaking the sistrum and the rattle. Many were blowing on the curved horn of the wild goat and the strait horn of the ibex. When Joseph reached a certain point, all the music stopped except the drums. The drums played a slow steady beat so that Joseph would walk at dignified pace. When he arrived under the canopy, Potiphera, the High Priest of On, took Asenath's hand and put it in Joseph's. One of the senior priests washed the feet and hands of Asenath and Joseph with water drawn from the Nile. This was to tell everyone that both of them were pure. One of the jugs that had held wine for the wedding feast was placed in front of Joseph. The groom was supposed to pull his sword and break the jug. Potiphar presented his sword to Joseph. Joseph took the sword and smashed the jug, returning the sword to Potiphar. Potiphera told Joseph, "Take her into your home. There will be much music and a lot of partying but you and Asenath will not attend."

Joseph said, "In my country when a man weds he is not to do anything for at least one week. Then for the next three weeks he does very little." The wedding was just as Lord Siese had planned it. Joseph moved into his new palace. Joseph and Asenath spent the week getting to know each other. She said it would be a good omen if she got pregnant during that week.

After the wedding week, Joseph spent much time in the office Potiphar had prepared for him or conferring with Lord Siese. They planned the banquet and information Joseph would share with the Nomarchs. Captain Potiphar had been busy with the hippopotamus hunt. The annual hippopotamus hunt was twenty-five days prior to the celebration for Osiris. He had special arrows made. These arrows had a cord attached to the arrows. The other end of the cord was tied to a wooden ball, and when an arrow was shot into a hippopotamus, the ball would pull away and would float above the animal. That allowed the hunters to follow the movement of the hippopotamus. He was also overseeing the making of special crocodile spears. These spears had razor sharp points with a barb to keep it lodged inside the crocodile's head. A rope was attached to the point. The point was made so that a twist of the shaft would loosen it from the head. The rope was used to drag the crocodile to the back of the boat.

A week later he came into Joseph's office. "My Lord, have you ever been on a hippopotamus hunt or tasted a hippopotamus steak?" he asked Joseph.

"No," Joseph answered. "I didn't know people hunted hippopotamus nor did I know we ate them."

Tomorrow I am taking my squadron to Elephantine Isle. We are going to the lagoon in front of the Temple of Hapi on Elephaine Isle. The priests have given permission for us to kill 73 hippopotami. There are 373 hippopotami in the lagoon. The priests want to keep 300 alive to keep the papyrus plants from choking the channel. We will use the hides to make shields for the army. We will also kill many crocodiles and use their hides for shields for the officers." "Would you like to go?" Captain Potiphar asked.

"I would like to go but I haven't any clothes to wear," Joseph replied. "The only clothes I have is this gown Pharaoh gave me."

"Let's go to a shop that sell the best robes, sandals and other things you will need." Potiphar said to Joseph. "You won't need money. You are the king's representative. We will tell the merchants to send the bills to Lord Siese. Lord Siese is the king's treasurer. He will pay for anything you need or want. Put the Gold of Praise on before we leave. When the merchants see it, they will know the king honors you."

In a few minutes they were in the market. Potiphar led Joseph to the most prestigious merchant. When they entered, the owner came up and spoke to Potiphar. "Captain Potiphar how may I help you?"

"This is Lord Joseph. The king has placed him over all of Egypt. He is going with me to hunt hippopotami at Elephantine Isle. He will need at least five outfits by ten tomorrow morning," Potiphar told the owner.

The owner clapped his hands several times. Five assistants ran to him. He told them, "This is Lord Joseph, he needs five complete outfits by ten tomorrow."

The chief assistant came to Joseph, bowed low and asked, "Are you the slave that interpreted the dreams for Pharaoh?"

Potiphar spoke rather angrily, "It doesn't matter who he was! He is now Lord over Egypt!"

"My Lord, I meant no disrespect. We are slaves and to hear of a slave gaining his independence and becoming a great Lord makes all slaves happy." The assistant bowed to Joseph. "We are happy to get to meet you and to serve you, my Lord."

Captain Potiphar sent a message to Lord Siese asking him to bring Joseph's wife when he came to the hippopotamus hunt.

Next morning when the sun was four hands high, thirty ships hoisted their sails and started south. Captain Potiphar had a canopy and a sleeping pad placed on the deck for Joseph to sit under during the day and to sleep on at night. These were fighting ships and had no comforts. The men ate traveling rations of durra corn bread or barley cakes. Joseph didn't mind the food or the lack of comforts. He was enjoying seeing the country side and the towns as they passed.

Captain Potiphar signaled for Lieutenant Sorbek to bring his ship along side. When the ships were side by side, Potiphar threw a bag of silver rings to Lieutenant Sorbek. Potiphar told Sorbek, "Take your ship at attack speed to the next town. Buy two roast goats and ten large jugs of beer for each ship. Get a receipt for the purchases."

Lieutenant Sorbek's ship quickly pulled ahead of all the other ships. When the rest of the ships reached the next town, Captain Potiphar signaled for all the ships to stop. Lieutenant Sorbek had made the purchases. He went by each ship and passed the meat and beer to them. The ship's crews rested for one hand's time to eat drink and rest. The men respected Captain Potiphar for his kindness. No other captain treated his men as well as Potiphar did. They would follow him anywhere even if he attacked the gates of Seth's kingdom.

Joseph was watching the changing scenery as the ships went toward Elephaine Isle. Both sides were green for a little way. Then the landscape changed into desert. The high hills were coming closer to the river. They came to a place where the sides of the river were narrowed and the river rushed rapidly through the narrow strait. "We call this 'the gate of Hapi' in honor of the god that created the Nile," Potiphar explained to Joseph. Joseph looked at the high granite cliffs. The Nile had been compressed into a narrow gorge. Joseph thought that if a bridge could be built from one side to the other, it would take 400 paces to cross it. After passing through the gate of Hapi, they came to a series of small islands followed by the larger island called Elephantine Isle. The island got its name from the large gray boulders that lay on the island. From a distant the rocks looked like the backs of a herd of elephants. Joseph noticed trees on this island. Potiphar told him, "This is the only place in Egypt that has trees. The seeds were brought down from the upper Nile by the floods. I have been told that there are around 100 kinds of trees on this island."

Before the ships pulled into the harbor, Potiphar gave a chest to Joseph. "This chest contains bags of silver rings," Potiphar told Joseph. "I will have the ships pass by and you will throw a bag onto each ship. There are enough silver rings for each soldier to get two, the sergeant to get five and the Lieutenant to have ten. I am going to give the men the night off."

Who gave these silver rings for this purpose?" Joseph asked.

"You did," Potiphar answered.

"And where did I get the silver rings for this?" Joseph wanted to know.

"Lord Siese loaned them to you," Potiphar said. "You will be rich when you get your share of the profits from selling the hides we get from the hippopotami and crocodiles. Pharaoh takes half of the profit but Lord Siese gets one fifth of that. This year Lord Siese is going to give you his share. That should be around 250 gold rings."

The men were very happy to have the silver rings and a night of freedom. They all headed to the taverns for beer and women Next morning the ships were spaced around the outside of the lagoon. Potiphar had his personal standard ran up the flag pole. Only an officer with the rank of

'Best of 10,000' could have a personal standard. The raising of the personal standard was the signal for the hunt to begin.

The crew of Potiphar's and Lt. Sorbek's ships each killed three hippopotami. Seven other ships got two each. By the time the third hippopotamus was killed, the first had filled with gases in its stomach and was floating with its feet sticking straight up. They pulled the ship next to the dead hippopotamus and one of the soldiers jumped onto its stomach and tied a rope around its neck. The rope was tied to the stern and it was pulled to the shore. As soon as they got close to the shore, several men took ropes and pulled it to shore.

Joseph thought he had seen large crowds in Memphis but they were nothing to compare with what he saw here. Almost all of the poor people of Egypt seemed to be there. The people of Egypt were the best fed people in the world, but they seldom, if ever, ate meat. The chance to eat meat, particularly the sweet meat of the hippopotamus, drew them to this area. During the festival of Osiris, all restraint was cast aside. Every type of passion was released. Pharaoh sent hundreds of Haqats of beer for the populace to drink.

As soon as a hippopotamus's body was dragged on shore it was cut up by men and women wielding knives to get meat for their families. As a piece of meat was cut out, it would be thrown to one of their children. The child would run to a fire and throw the meat on it. Before it was warmed through, the children would take it off the fire and eat it. As soon as they had eaten that piece, they would run back screaming for more.

When all the dead hippopotami had been taken to shore, the ships formed a semicircle around the area, bow to stern. With all the blood in the water, every crocodile for miles around was lured to the feast. Six soldiers stood on the shore side of each ship. The crocodiles slipped under the ships and surfaced a few feet from them. The soldier nearest to the crocodile leaned over and with a quick thrust of his spear sunk the point into the crocodile's head. The sharp point severed the spinal cord just behind the head. Other soldiers would drag the crocodile to the back of the boat to be tied to the stern. Occasionally a crocodile moved his head and the javelin missed the vital spot. A fight raged for several minutes until the crocodile was pulled close to the ship where it was soon killed. Soldiers on the ships killed 87 crocodiles that day.

The servants of the rich were there getting portions of meat for their masters. Members of the quartermasters corps were there skinning the bodies and salting the hides. The grand viziers' bailiffs were there to collect the teeth. The teeth were as valuable as elephant tusks.

The soldiers were given the night off so as soon as the ships were docked. They ran back to the festival area. They found women who were there to share pleasures with anyone who wanted to be with them. In the evening twilight men and women could be seen coupling everywhere. No one paid any attention to them. This was the festival where everything happened.

A tent had been set up for Joseph and Asenath. Hippopotamus steaks had been slow cooked and the wine was chilled. Joseph thought that hippopotamus meat was too mild and sweet. It was good, but to his taste, it was not as good as roast lamb. Lord Siese came by and asked Joseph and Asenath to join him in his pavilion to watch some entertainment and share some wine. Acrobats doing all types of amazing feats and dancing men and women entertained them.

Potiphar told Joseph that he had to go back to the ships to check on the repairs. Several ships had been rammed by hippopotami and needed minor repairs to stop leaks.

Only twenty-nine ships were ready to go the next morning. They had taken forty-one hippopotami the first day so they were supposed to kill only thirty-two more That day was a repeat of the day before. They killed thirty-six hippopotami and forty-nine crocodiles. The people on the shore were the same unruly crowd as the previous day. This festival was the only time most would get to eat meat all year. Only the priests of Hapi could kill and eat a hippopotamus any time they desired.

The soldiers were given the next day off. Again Joseph gave each soldier two silver rings, the sergeant five and the lieutenant ten. He was generous with Lord Siese's money. The quartermaster's corps had skinned all the hippopotami and crocodiles and it took most of the day loading them on the ships. They put a box of hippopotamus teeth on Potiphar's ship for Joseph. The ships lay heavy in the water on the way back due to the load of salted skins and meat pickled in brine. The meat was supposed to feed the army and other government officials. But most would be sold and half the profits would go to Pharaoh with Joseph getting a share. The soldiers were much happier on the way back. They hoisted the sails and the current was with them so they didn't have to row. The trip from Elephantine Isle took over nine days.

They arrived in Memphis on the first day of the festival of Osiris. This was the day when a play about the origins of Egypt and the gods and goddesses was presented. Pharaoh was brought to the temple of Osiris on his great gilded sledge pulled by twelve yoke of white oxen. A canopy of finely tanned antelope skins covered the sledge and had been painted with images of all the gods and goddesses of Egypt. The Pharaoh wore the double crown of Egypt. One was the red crown of Lower Egypt with the cobra head of the goddess of the delta, Buto. The other was the white crown of Upper Egypt with the head of the vulture goddess, Nekhbet.

After speeches by many nobles and Lord Siese, Pharaoh started his speech. He droned on for three fingers of time telling the people how much better things were now that he was Pharaoh. He ended by telling them about his dreams. He told them all the wise men in Egypt could not interpret the dreams. He had Joseph brought to him and Joseph was able to interpret the dreams. Joseph had explained that the two dreams were the same dream. God had given it to him twice because the matter was settled and would happen. His wise men thought that Joseph was the right person to oversee the saving of the grain for the next seven years. He had made Joseph Lord of Egypt and had given him the Egyptian blue hawk ring.

The great hall of the temple was crowded. When Pharaoh concluded his speech, trumpets sounded and the director of the play began his oration on the beginnings of the world. He told how Ammon Ra, the sun god created Egypt. He told them that Ammon Ra stroked himself and his emission created the earth and the stars and the Milky Way. Amon Ra created Geb and Nut. Geb and Nut coupled and brought forth the gods Osiris and Seth, and the goddesses Isis and Nephthys.

The play started with the flooding of the Nile that brought forth the golden grain. The actor playing Osiris came on stage and acknowledged the river Nile. As Osiris wandered around the stage that had been made to look like a field of ripe grain, an actor portraying Seth came running onto the stage and bellowed in rage because Osiris had created a beautiful world without his help. An argument followed. Seth drew his sword and after a long fight hacked Osiris to fourteen pieces. The first act ended with the actress playing Isis singing a lament over the death of her brother, Osiris.

The second act began with Isis and Nephthys gathering all the pieces but one, the scrotum, which is called the talisman of Osiris. Osiris was restored to life by Isis coupling with his dead body. This act ended with Isis holding a baby and introducing the god, Lord Horus, god of the wind and sky, and the falcon of the heavens.

The final act started with Horus walking through the paradise he had created. Seth came to him and accused him of exceeding his authority by not allowing him to help in the creation. An argument followed. Seth drew his sword and attempted to kill Horus. In the fight that followed, Horus defeated Seth and banned him from the earth assigning him to be the god of the underworld and evil.

After the play ended, the actor who played Horus made a long boring speech about the greatness of Pharaoh. He extolled the virtues and goodness of Pharaoh. He told how much Pharaoh had improved the lot of the common person. After three fingers' time he ended the speech and everyone left the temple.

As the sun was setting, Lord Siese sent a very ornate litter to carry Joseph and Asenath to the banquet. The litter was carried by eight strong slaves. As they were carried to the banquet, people all along the way bowed down and saluted them as they passed. They were taken to Pharaoh's audience hall. Pharaoh was waiting for them. After they bowed to him, he rose and Lord Joseph and Lord Siese escorted Pharaoh to the banquet. Joseph was on Pharaoh's right side and Lord Siese was on the left. The Governors of the forty-two nomes and their wives were there. They noticed that Joseph was on the side of greater honor.

When Pharaoh entered the hall, everyone stood up. Pharaoh sat down and then Lord Joseph and Lord Siese sat. After they were seated, Pharaoh told everyone else to be seated. Joseph was wearing only a white skirt with the Gold of Praise on his bare chest. Lord Siese had advised him to dress in the Egyptian fashion.

Pharaoh Senusret II told them about the dreams he had that had troubled him so much. None of the magicians or wise men had been able to interpret the dreams. Joseph was brought to him. He was able to interpret the dreams. He said, "Joseph told me that the dreams were the same. God had sent the dream twice as he had settled the matter and it would happen. Seven years of abundance has started and will be followed by seven years of severe famine. When I asked the wise men what to do, they did not know. Joseph told me that I should build storage facilities and collect and store one-fifth of all the harvests during the years of plenty and have it to feed Egypt during the years of famine. My advisors suggested that I select Joseph for the task of overseer for collecting the grain. I appointed Joseph, Lord of Egypt. I gave him the blue hawk ring to show his authority."

Lord Siese introduced Joseph and shared his background. He told how Joseph had helped Captain Potiphar capture three slaves and a merchant who were stealing his sheep. Then he told about Joseph's help in catching the supervisors that were stealing gold, silver and jewels from Pharaoh Ammenemhet II's tomb. He told other things about Joseph and his wisdom. Then he presented Lord Joseph.

Joseph began to speak, "You have had to endure two lengthy speeches already. I'm sure you do not want another." Everyone applauded. "At this time the royal engineer is meeting with your engineers and giving them the plans for your storehouses. I am expecting you to give them your full support and co-operation in building them. You are to store one fifth of the harvest in these buildings. My God has promised to increase your crops so that you will not miss the one fifth. In a few months I will come to your Nome to see how you are doing. Now I hope you will enjoy your meal."

Pharaoh had provided the food and drink, and the party lasted until well after midnight.

Soon Joseph and Lord Khentykhetywer started the buildings for the great storehouses to be built near the fortress. Joseph knew that the famine would be from Egypt to Haran. He wanted to be able to sell grain to the whole area and in particular to his father's people.

Lord Siese gave Joseph a box containing 438 gold rings. He said, "This is your share from selling the hides and the teeth of the hippopotamus. I have kept the amount of the silver rings I loaned you.

They conscripted over 1000 slaves and supervisors to do the work. One day about two months later Joseph ran into Potiphar's office and he was very excited. He danced around shouting, "A father, a father, I'm going to be a father!"

Potiphar told him, "calm down and tell me what you are trying to say."

Joseph responded, "Asenath is going to have a baby, my baby. I'm so happy for her. She wants a boy. I don't care as long as she is safe and happy." Joseph gave her everything she wanted and placated every whim. When she wanted a steak from a young hippopotamus, he sent Captain Potiphar to a lagoon to find and kill a young hippopotamus. If she wanted a young gazelle steak, he sent one hundred hunters to slay a young gazelle.

Five months after the festival to Osiris, Joseph and Captain Potiphar made a trip up the Nile to visit all the Nomarchs and see how the storage facilities were progressing. Most of them were almost finished.

A baby boy was born nine months and twelve days after the wedding. Joseph named the boy, Manasseh, "because God has made me forget all my troubles and my entire father's house," he said.

When the harvest was over, large quantities of grain had been stored. Joseph levied a tax of one fifth of all the stored grain to be brought to the storehouse near the fortress. God had sent an abundance of grain in every field. By the end of three years all the storehouses were full.

When Manasseh was almost three years old, Joseph went to see Lord Siese. "Lord Siese, in my country when a boy is weaned we have a celebration and invite all our relatives and friends. Asenath is weaning Manasseh and I would like to have a party. How should I do that and whom should I invite?"

"How large a party are you planning?" Lord Siese asked.

"I want a very large party. Egypt has been kind to me and I would like to show my gratitude," Joseph answered. "The party should be a family affair."

"I do not know if he will come, but you should invite Pharaoh," Lord Siese said. "I would hope that I am included among your friends. You could invite all the Nomarchs and their families, all the Lords and their families and the high ranked military officers, at least those who are in the rank of 'a Lion of Egypt'. Do you think that is enough?"

I would like to invite Captain Potiphar but he is only at the rank of 'best in 10, 000," Joseph told Lord Siese.

"That is easy to solve," Lord Siese responded. "Just promote him to a general with the rank of 'a Lion of Egypt'. He happens to be here on business. All you have to do is tell him that he has been promoted. Should I send for him?"

"Yes, please do. I owe him so much for all the help he has given me." Joseph said "I would like to repay him by promoting him."

Lord Siese sent a servant for Captain Potiphar. When he arrived, Joseph looked stern and to tease him he asked, "Potiphar, why are you out of uniform?"

Captain Potiphar was astonished, "but my Lord, this is the prescribed uniform of the commander of the guard, and one of the best in 10,000.

"You are no longer one of the best in 10,000." Joseph paused for a few seconds and then continued. "I hereby promote you to the rank of a 'Great Lion of Egypt'. Last week we were traveling down the Nile and you pointed out 160 feddans of prime farmland and told me that it would make a fine summer place for me. I give that land to you as a promotion gift."

"Thank you, Lord Joseph," Potiphar began. "You have become the best friend I have ever had!"

Joseph suggested, "Why don't you go tell you wife and get in the proper uniform."

Lord Siese sent some of his servants to Joseph's palace to help make arrangements for the party. Lord Siese's servants had planned parties for Pharaoh so they knew how to contact the right person to get everything that was needed. The party went flawlessly. Pharaoh and almost all the nobility and important people of the kingdom and their families were there. The servants had been trained and put in new uniforms. The food was excellent with a wide selection of choices. Canopies had been set up so that everyone sat in the shade. Just before the meal was served, Joseph stood and holding up Manasseh he said, "This is my firstborn son. He was weaned last week. This party is to celebrate his passage from being a baby to being a boy." Everyone applauded. The party lasted three days.

That year Asenath had another baby boy. Joseph named this boy, Ephraim. He said, "God has made me fruitful in the land of my suffering."

Joseph had a large area paved with rocks and piled the grain in the open. The pile grew larger every year. At the end of the seven years of plenty grain was piled everywhere.

CHAPTER 18

— JOSEPH MEETS HIS BROTHERS —

Shortly after the famine started, the people cried to Pharaoh for food. He told them to go see Joseph. Joseph sold grain to all Egyptians. People from all over that part of the world came to Egypt to purchase grain. Israel sent ten of his sons to Egypt for grain. He would not let Benjamin go with them. Israel was afraid that harm would come to him.

When the ten brothers came to Joseph to buy grain, they did not recognize him. He was dressed as an Egyptian with most of his head shaved and the rest of his hair tied into a long tail hanging to the right side. When the brothers saw Joseph, they bowed down with their faces to the ground. Joseph was reminded of his dream that his brothers would bow down to him.

Even though they did not recognize Joseph, he recognized them. He spoke harshly to them, "Where did you come from?"

"We came from the land of Canaan. The famine is severe there. We came to buy food for our families," Reuben replied.

"I think you are spies!" Joseph replied. "You have come to see the weakness in our defense."

"That is not so," Reuben answered. As the oldest, he spoke for the ten.

Joseph asked, "How old is you father, and how many sons does he have?"

"Your servant, our father is 129, and had twelve sons," Reuben answered. "He would not let us bring the youngest and one brother is dead."

Joseph said to them angrily, "It is just as I said. You are spies! This is how I will test your words. As surely as Pharaoh lives, I will keep nine of you in prison and one will go get your younger brother. General Potiphar arrest these men and put them in jail."

Joseph kept them in jail for two days but he said to himself "my father's family needs grain. I must let them take the grain to their families." On the third day Joseph had them brought from jail and told them, "I also fear God. To prove that your words are true, nine of you may take food to your families. This man, he pointed to Simeon, will stay in jail until you return with your younger brother. I will not see you or sell you any more grain unless your youngest brother comes with you."

The ten brothers started discussing their plight. "Surely this is our punishment because we sold our brother into slavery. We saw how he cried for mercy and pleaded to be free, but we didn't pay attention to his cries," Levi said.

Reuben replied, "Didn't I tell you not to sin against the boy? But you didn't listen to me! Now we must give an accounting for his blood. Do you remember how I told you not to kill him and to put him in a dry cistern? I intended to take him back to father. While I was gone to buy supplies, you sold Joseph to the Midianite trader. Then you killed a goat and dipped his cloak into the blood. You gave the cloak to father so he would think a lion had killed him."

Gad turned to Dan and said. "I still remember the whipping we got when Joseph told father we gave two lambs to the prostitutes of Ba'al so we could worship with them. At the time I was still angry and wanted to get even but now that I think about it selling him was very harsh."

Gad replied, "At that time you and I wanted to kill him. That was twenty-one years ago. Now I don't think we should have been so angry with him."

They did not realize that Joseph understood what they were saying. He had been talking to them through an interpreter. Now he turned away and began to cry.

Joseph had his workers fill their bags with as much grain as the donkeys could carry. He had their silver put back into one of each man's sacks. He provided provisions for the trip back to Canaan. Each of Joseph's brothers had brought three donkeys. Joseph told the men loading the donkeys,

"Their donkeys are small; they cannot carry a full khar for a trip that long. Give them a khar about two-thirds full." After the donkeys were loaded, they left with Simeon's donkeys tied behind the other donkeys.

General Potiphar came to Joseph and asked, "Lord Joseph, why did you treat those men so harshly? I have never seen you be so unkind to anyone."

Joseph answered, "Those men are my brothers. They are the ones who sold me into slavery. I thought I had forgiven them but now I am not sure. I need to test them to see how much they have changed."

Joseph commanded the guards, "Put Simeon in one of the rooms on the first floor and allow him to go where he wants as long as a soldier goes with him." Joseph also sent food from his table to Simeon every day.

The nine brothers discussed the evil that had befallen them. They felt sorry for Simeon being in the hand of such a fearful man, the Egyptian that put him in jail. They kept trying to figure out the situation until they came to an oasis. They got a drink and then gave water to their donkeys. Reuben said, "I do not know why these things are happening to us. The best thing for us to do is to get this grain back to our families as quickly as possible." As the day was almost gone they decided to stay at the oasis for the night. They unloaded the donkeys and Judah untied one of the khar from his first donkey to give grain to his donkeys. He was surprised to see the bag of silver in the sack of grain. "Look," he exclaimed. "My silver is in this sack of grain."

The others quickly opened their sacks and found silver in one of each brother's sacks. "How did this silver get into our sacks?" Levi cried. "We are undone. What do we do now?"

Reuben said, "We cannot go back because the Lord that sold the grain said we would not see him again unless Benjamin was with us. We shall go to father and he will tell us what we should do."

When they arrived at Israel's camp they left the donkeys for the servants to unload. They went directly to Israel to tell him all that had happened to them. Reuben started, "The Lord who sold grain said that we were spies and that we had came into Egypt just to discover the weakness in their defenses. We tried to convince him that we were true men who came only to buy grain. He questioned us very closely about you and our family. We told him that you had twelve sons but one was dead and the youngest was at home with you. He told us that we could not buy more grain unless the youngest brother came with us. He put us in jail for two days. Then he let us out of jail. He had Simeon tied up to be kept in jail until we returned. When we came to an oasis in the evening, we untied our sacks and found our silver in our sacks."

"Oh what evil has befallen me," Israel cried out. "Joseph is dead. Now Simeon is in jail in Egypt and this evil man wants me to send Benjamin to Egypt. NO!"

In a year the grain they had bought in Egypt was nearly gone. Israel called his sons together and told them they would have to go back to Egypt and buy more grain.

"Father," Reuben said. "You know we cannot see the man unless Benjamin is with us. We will not go unless you allow us to take him! Father, put Benjamin into my hand and I will bring him back safely. If I do not bring him back, you may kill two of my sons."

"Why have you dealt so evilly with me?" Israel wailed. "Why did you tell him you had a younger brother?"

Levi answered, "Father, the man asked us directly if there were any more brothers at home. We did not know he would say," 'bring your youngest brother with you or you will not see my face.'

Judah told Israel, "Father, if you send Benjamin with us, I will go surety for him. If he is not with us when we return, I will bear the blame the rest of my life. If you had not kept us from taking him, we would have been to Egypt and back by now."

Israel looked very sad when he said, "If you must take him, you must. Do this. Take the man a gift of some of the best things we have and twice the amount of silver you paid the first time. Take it to the man and tell him it must have been an oversight. Take Benjamin and go to Egypt. May El Shaddai give you mercy before that man? Maybe he will send all my children back to me. If I lose my children, I lose them."

The men were on their way before the sun was up the next morning. They traveled as fast as they could because their families had very little food. When Joseph saw Benjamin with them, he said to the steward of his house, "Take these men to my house and slay a calf and make ready. These men are to eat with me at noon." The men were very afraid when they were taken to Joseph's house.

Water was brought for them and a servant washed their feet. Servants fed the donkeys. Dan spoke about what they were all thinking. "We are being brought to this man's house so he can accuse us of stealing the silver. He wants an occasion to take our donkeys and force us into slavery."

Reuben went to the steward and said, "My Lord, we don't know how it happened but when we opened our sacks after we were here the first time we found our silver in them. We have returned the silver and have more to pay for the grain we get this time."

The steward said, "Peace to you, fear not. Your God gave you back your money. I had your silver." Simeon was brought to them. They asked about his well being and his treatment.

"I don't know why it happened but I was treated very well." Simeon told them. "I had very good meals. Anything I asked for was prepared for me. I was allowed to go anywhere I wanted to go as long as a soldier went with me and if I wanted anything the soldier bought it for me. It was more like I was a guest than a prisoner."

Reuben told them, "Strange things are happening to us. We must be on our guard. I don't know why we are being singled out for this honor but it worries me greatly."

"Does everyone have a knife hidden in his cloak?" Judah asks. "If they try to take us as slaves, we will go down fighting!"

When Joseph came home, they brought the gifts to him and bowed down with their faces to the ground. Joseph told them to rise. They stood and presented their gifts. Reuben gave Joseph a jar of honey saying, "I don't know of any honey sweeter than the honey from the bees that live in a cliff near our home." Next Levi presented same balm, "This balm is made from trees in Canaan. I think it will help heal the little cuts and scratches your boys get." Judah offered Joseph some almonds, "These almonds were grown close to the camp of our father," he said. Issachar gave Joseph some more balm, "This balm was made by our esteemed mother. She makes it for her grandchildren when they get scrapes or cut," he explained. Zebulon was the last of Leah's sons to make an offering, "Here are some pistachio nuts from our trees, I hope you enjoy them," he said.

The two sons of Bilhah came forward and presented some spices to Joseph without saying anything. The two sons of Zilpah came to give Joseph a gift, "Here is some more honey for your table." Last of all

Benjamin came with a decorated box full of Myrrh. "My Lord, please keep this for a long time before it is used," he said.

Joseph accepted the gifts. He had almost been overcome with emotion when Benjamin came up to him. Joseph had told his steward how to seat the brothers with the oldest first and the youngest last. He asked them about the welfare of their father "Is your father still alive and is he in good health?"

Reuben answered, "Your servant, our father, is still alive and in good health." Then they all made obeisance to Joseph and bowed down with their face to the ground. Joseph told them to rise.

Joseph looked intently at all of them but when he looked at Benjamin his emotions got the better of him. He looked directly at Benjamin and asked them, "is this your younger brother, about whom you spoke?" Then to Benjamin he said, "God be gracious to you, my son."

Joseph could not hold in the tears any longer so he went into his bedroom and cried. When he finished crying, he washed his face, reapplied his makeup and went back into the dining room. "Set on the meal," he ordered. Joseph ate at a table by himself. The Egyptians ate at another table and the brothers sat at a different table.

The brothers marveled that they had been seated in the order of their age. All the food was put on Joseph's table. He carved the meat and served the vegetables and sent portions to everyone. Everyone got a generous portion and a good meal but the portion sent to Benjamin was five time as large as all the others. The brothers ate and drank and had a good time and were reasonably happy.

Joseph commanded his steward saying, "Give them as much as their donkeys can carry and put each man's money in his sack. Also, put my silver cup, the one I use to divine, in the mouth of one of the youngest man's sacks."

As soon as it was light enough to travel the next morning, the brothers started home with each leading his three donkeys. When they were out of the city half a hand's time, Joseph told his steward, "go after those men and when you catch them, search their sacks. When you find my cup you are to ask them, 'why have you repaid the kindness of my master by stealing his silver cup?' This is the cup he drinks from, and also the one he uses to divine. You have repaid kindness with evil by doing this."

When the steward overtook them, he explained what he was going to do and why. Then Reuben protested. "Why do you say such wicked things about us? God forbid that your servants would steal anything from your master. Didn't we return the money from our first trip? We are honest men. Why would we steal anything from The Lord of Egypt, either silver or gold. If the silver cup is found, whoever has it in his sack should be put to death and we will all become your master's slaves."

"Let it be as you have said," the steward answered. "If the silver cup is found, the person who has it will be my servant and the rest of you may continue to Canaan."

They quickly took the sacks from their donkeys and opened them. The steward started with Rueben's sacks and continued with each until he had searched all the sacks. The cup was found in one of Benjamin's sacks. The brothers tore their clothes, quickly loaded the donkeys and started back to Memphis to confront Joseph.

Joseph had stayed at his house as he knew they would be returning. When they arrived, they fell prostrate on the ground. Joseph told them to rise and then spoke harshly to them, "Why did you steal my cup? Didn't you know that I can discover everything that happens?"

Judah, who had given surety for the safe return of Benjamin, started talking, "I don't know what we can say to you, my Lord? How shall we clear ourselves? God has seen our iniquities and has judged us fairly. We are my Lord's servants, all of us, both we and the one in whose sack the cup was found."

Joseph answered Judah, "God forbid that I should take all of you as servants. The man in whose sack the cup was found will be my servant and the rest may leave in peace and take food to your families."

Judah came to Joseph and said, "Oh my Lord, allow me to speak to you, please, and do not be angry with me, your servant, for you are even as Pharaoh. The first time we came to buy food, you, my Lord, asked us if we had a father or brother. We told you that we had an aged father and a younger brother. We told you that our younger brother was born to our father and his favorite wife in his old age. His mother died giving him birth. Our father's life is tied up in the boy. His favorite wife had two sons, one is not, and the other is the apple of my father's eye. My father loves him very much."

Joseph said, "I know all this. Please tell me something I do not know."

Judah continued, "My Lord, you told us that you would not see our faces again unless our younger brother came with us. You accused us of being spies and said that to prove our words we had to bring our younger brother. We told you that the boy could not leave our father because if anything happened to him it would bring our father to the grave in great sorrow. You were very clear in your demand that we bring the lad with us next time we came to buy food. We relayed your demand to our father that the boy must come with us."

"Why did your father think something bad would happen to Benjamin if he came with you?" Joseph asked. "Did he normally get into trouble?"

"No my Lord, "Judah continued. "The boy is a very honest respectful man and has never gotten into trouble. Our aged father loves the boy so strongly that he didn't want anything to happen to him. Last month our father told us to go to Egypt to buy more grain. We told him we would not go unless the boy came with us. We told our father if you will let the boy go with us we will go buy more grain but if you do not allow him to go, we will not go. Your servant, our father, said to us, 'you know that my wife bore me two sons, one is not and has been torn to pieces and is lost to me. If you take this son from me and mischief falls on him, you will bring my gray head down to the grave in great sorrow.'"

The steward went to Potiphar and asked, "General Potiphar, Joseph is normally kind and gracious to everyone. Why is he being so harsh with these men?"

Potiphar answered, "These are his brothers. They are the ones who sold him into slavery because he told their father that they had gone to a prostitute of Baal. Their father whipped two of them soundly. He is testing them to see if they have changed."

Judah said. "I, your servant, went surety for the safety of the boy. If we return without him, I shall bear the blame to my father forever. After much persuasion our father allowed us to take him with us. Now I beg you my Lord take me as your servant and let the boy return to his father. How shall I go to my father if the boy is not with me? If I do not return him I will see the evil that shall come on my father."

Joseph asked the brothers, "Why do you call Benjamin a boy. He is a man of twenty-five years.

They were startled that Joseph knew that. Judah explained, "Benjamin is much younger than the rest of us, and we have always called him the boy. But how did you know how old he is?"

"I know a lot more about you than you do of me." Joseph told Judah, "You are thirty-nine. I know your mothers, Leah, Zilpah and Bilhah and I knew Benjamin's mother, Rachel." This really worried the brothers. They wondered what else he knew about them.

Talking about his mother and the others brought memories flooding into his mind. Joseph could not bear the emotions any longer. "Let everyone go out of this room except these men and me!" Joseph cried out. After they had left, Joseph said to his brothers, "I am Joseph, whom you sold into slavery" Then he wept very loudly.

Joseph called them to him and said, "Come near to me." As they came near he continued. "I am Joseph, your brother, whom you sold into slavery. Do not be angry with yourselves that you sold me to the Midianite trader. It was not you but El Shaddai sent me here to save lives. The famine has lasted two years and for five more years there will be neither plowing nor harvesting. God sent me before you to preserve you and your families by this great deliverance. It was not you but God that sent me here and He has made me a father to Pharaoh. I am the Lord of Egypt."

Joseph embraced Benjamin and kissed him. Then he kissed all of his brothers. They were surprised that Joseph was alive and that he was the lord of Egypt.

The Egyptians heard Joseph say that he was their brother. They told Pharaoh that Joseph's brothers had come to buy grain.

The brothers were astonished to know that Joseph was alive and doing so well. They all cried on his shoulder and told him how happy they were that he was alive. After Joseph had comforted them, a messenger arrived from Pharaoh.

The messenger told Joseph, "Pharaoh has heard that your brothers have come to you. He said you are to say to your brothers." 'This is what you are to do. Take carts and oxen to your father's family and bring them to Egypt. Do not worry about your possessions. Joseph will provide you with all the good thing that Egypt has to offer. Take as many carts as you need to carry all the children and wives, and send twenty female donkeys and ten male donkeys with grain and supplies for the trip.'"

Joseph told the steward to load their donkeys with as much grain as they could carry and send twenty additional female donkeys and ten male donkeys loaded with grain, bread and wine for the trip to Egypt. He gave them each a change of clothing but to Benjamin he gave five changes of clothing and 300 silver rings. Joseph said to his brothers as they were ready to leave, "Do not get into an argument over who was at fault for selling me into slavery. Remember it was not you but God that sent me here. You were just an instrument in God's hand. Be friendly and have a good trip."

As the brothers traveled, they talked about how God had used Joseph and how fortune had smiled on them, their father and the whole family. They praised God for the blessing he had given them. There was about 300 miles from Memphis to Israel's camp. They could travel about twenty miles each day. They enjoyed the trip. Joseph had sent the twenty female donkeys, ten male donkeys and twelve carts with them. The carts were pulled by white oxen. Potiphar had sent soldiers along with them for protection against bandits.

They were still four days from home when Leah said to Israel, "The boys have been gone a long time. Why don't you send one of your servants to see if he can find them?"

"That is a very good idea," Israel answered. He called his steward to him and said, "Send one of the young men on a camel toward Egypt to see if my boys are coming. When he sees them, he is not to go to them but to return to me as fast as he can.

Two days later the young man reported to Israel, "My lord, your boys are over a day's travel from here, but they are not alone."

"What do you mean they are not alone?" Israel demanded.

The young man excitedly explained, "Besides the donkeys they are leading, there are more donkeys that are loaded and are being led by Egyptians. Also, they are being followed by twelve carts each pulled by two white oxen. That's not all! They are being protected by Egyptian soldiers."

"What does this mean?" Leah asked. "Do you think something has gone wrong?"

Israel answered, "We will find out tomorrow or the next day."

CHAPTER 19

—— LAST YEARS IN EGYPT ——

At noon the second day Israel saw the group coming. When they got closer, Benjamin gave his donkeys to a soldier and ran ahead.

"MY BROTHER JOSEPH IS ALIVE!" He shouted as he ran. "Joseph is alive and is ruler of Egypt!"

When the others drew near they all shouted, "Joseph is alive and he is the governor of Egypt!"

Israel did not believe them. The commander of the military detachment informed Israel, "What they are telling you is true. Lord Joseph is governor of Egypt."

Reuben told Israel all the things Joseph had wanted to tell his father. He showed Israel the carts and extra donkeys. With the good news Israel's spirit revived. He said, "It is enough that my son Joseph is alive. He has sent these carts to carry us to Egypt, so, to Egypt we will go. Everyone start packing for the trip."

Israel sent his flocks and herds toward Egypt that day. They loaded all their possessions on the carts and were on their way just after noon the next day. They were a very happy group. They sang songs and praised God as they walked. At night they talked about how good it would be in the land of Goshen. When they came to Beersheba, Israel had the carts stop while he offered sacrifices to God. That night God spoke to Israel in a dream.

"Israel, Israel," God called.

"Here am I," Israel answered.

"I am the God of your father Isaac, and of your grandfather, Abraham,"

God said. "Do not be afraid to go to Egypt, for I will be there to make your descendants into a mighty nation. I will go to Egypt with you, and I will bring your descendants out of Egypt to Canaan. Joseph will put his hands on your eyes to close them when you die."

Israel got up and they traveled on toward Egypt. Israel's family included his sons, his son's wives, grandsons, and their wives, daughters and granddaughters. In all 66 Hebrews and the nine Canaanite wives of Israel's sons went to Egypt. Including Joseph, Asenath and their sons who were already in Egypt there were 70 in Israel's party. Israel took most of his servants with him.

With the soldiers guarding them, they were not bothered by bandits. They completed the trip in fifteen days. While they were still two days from Goshen, Israel sent Judah to Joseph to tell him they had arrived. Joseph got in his chariot and drove out to meet his father. He kissed his father and fell on his neck and wept for a long time.

Israel said to Joseph, "Now I can die in peace since I have seen your face and know that you are alive."

Joseph told his father, "I will tell Pharaoh that my family has arrived in Goshen. My father and brothers have come to me from Canaan. I will tell Pharaoh that you are shepherds and that you have tended sheep and cattle all your lives. When he calls you and asks your occupation, you are to tell him that you are shepherds. If you tell him this, he will allow you to live in Goshen. The Egyptians think shepherds are an abomination."

Joseph went back to Memphis and reported to Pharaoh Senusret III. He said, "My father and brothers and their flocks and herds and all their families and all they possess have come out of Canaan and are in the land of Goshen." He had taken five of his brothers with him to Memphis. He presented them to Pharaoh. Pharaoh asked them their occupation. They answered as Joseph had instructed them saying, "your servants are shepherds, both we and our fathers. We have come to stay in your land as long as the famine endures. The pastures in Canaan have all dried up and blown away. With your permission, we would like to live in Goshen, mighty Egypt."

Pharaoh spoke to Joseph and said, "Your father and your brothers have come to you. The best land of Egypt is open to them. If they want to live in Goshen, let them. If any of them is a man that knows cattle, put them in charge of my herds."

Joseph brought Israel in and sat him before Pharaoh. Pharaoh asked Israel's age. Israel told him, "The days of my journey on earth have been 130 years. Few and evil have been the days of my life. I have not lived as long as my fathers." Then Issac blessed Pharaoh.

Joseph gave his father and brothers 1200 feddan of land in Goshen just as Pharaoh had commanded. Joseph gave them enough grain so that all the families had plenty to eat as long as the famine was in the land.

The famine was very bad in Egypt and Canaan. Joseph sold grain to the Egyptians until they had no money left. Then he took the money to Pharaoh. When the money was gone, he gave them grain for their animals and fed them the next year. When all their money and animals were sold to buy grain the people came to Joseph pleading for mercy.

The people cried to Joseph saying, "You have all our money and all our animals. All we have left is our land and our bodies. Why should we die in front of you and our land lie desolate? Buy us and our land and feed us until the famine is over." All the land in Egypt became Pharaoh's except the land of the priests. Pharaoh gave them a food allotment each year so they did not sell their lands.

Joseph passed a law providing the people with seed to plant after the famine was over and requiring one fifth of the crops and animals to be given back to Pharaoh. They would have four firths to feed their families and animals.

The people answered, "You have saved our lives, Let us find favor in your sight, my Lord. We will be Pharaoh's servants."

Joseph continued as Lord of Egypt until the famine was over. He went to Pharaoh Senusret III and said, "Live forever Pharaoh. I have led Egypt these last fourteen years as vizier for your father and for you. Now I would like to give you back the Egyptian blue hawk ring and resume a normal life."

Pharaoh Senusret III agreed but before he dismissed Joseph he gave him another Gold of Praise. Pharaoh ordered him to retain the title of Lord. "You will always be my counselor and advisor," Pharaoh told Joseph. "As long as you live, I will give you and your family an allotment of food and you will receive 100 gold rings each year for your invaluable service to Egypt."

Israel lived in Egypt seventeen years. He called Joseph to him and told him, "I am about to die. Put your hand under my thigh and swear to me that you will bury me in the cave at Machpelah, where Abraham and Issac are buried. Joseph swore that he would do as his father asked.

Later a messenger came from Reuben to tell Joseph that Israel was very sick. Joseph took Manasseh and Ephraim and went to his father. Israel told Joseph and his brothers, "God, the creator God, El Shaddai, appeared to me at Luz before I left Canaan. He blessed me there and told me that I would become the father of many peoples and nations. He gave the land to my descendants forever."

Because his eyes were getting dim due to his advanced age, Israel could not see well. Israel looked at Manasseh and Ephraim, and asked, "Who are those two men?" Joseph answered, "These are my two sons." Joseph brought his sons to Israel and Israel kissed them and embraced them. Then he said, "I did not think I would ever see you again but now I have seen your sons." Israel told Joseph, "Now I take your two sons that was born to you in Egypt and claim them as my own. They will be ranked with Reuben and Simeon and the rest of my sons. They will be given the inheritance as if they had been born to Leah and me. If you have any more sons, they will be yours." In doing this, Israel gave Joseph a double portion.

When Joseph took his two sons to Israel to be blessed, he put Manasseh, who was thirty years old, on his left so that Israel's right hand would be across from him, and he put Ephraim, who was twenty-seven years old, on his right. When Israel reached his hands to bless the men, he crossed his arms and put his right hand on Ephraim's head and his left hand on Manasseh's head.

Israel blessed Joseph and his sons, "I bless you in the name of El Shaddai, before whom I walked and the God my fathers, Abraham and Isaac, did walk. He is the God which fed me all my life until this day. May the angel who saved me from all evil, bless these two boys, and let my name be named on them. Let them grow into a multitude of people." In this way he adopted both men. Israel told Joseph, "I am giving you the mountain slope that I took from the hand of the Amorites with my sword and bow.

"Father, you have your right hand on the younger brother's head,"

Joseph said. This displeased Joseph and he tried to move Israel's hands. Joseph told Israel, "Father, this is my firstborn, please put your right hand on his head."

Israel answered, "I know, my son, I know. Manasseh will be a great people but the younger will be much greater. Ephraim's seed will become many nations. Then he blessed them saying, "All your brothers and their descendants shall bless each other saying, God make you prosper as He did Ephraim and Manasseh." By blessing them in this way he put Ephraim ahead of Manasseh. Then he said, "Look at me, I will soon die. When you have become a mighty nation, God will visit you and He will take you back to the land He promised to give you."

Israel rested for a while and then he continued, "I am giving you the first son's inheritance. You will have one portion more than your brothers." Israel raised Joseph to the position of firstborn to solve a family problem. As a young man Reuben had lain with Israel's wife, Bilhah. Israel had heard of this and had taken away Reuben's right of being the firstborn. By giving Joseph the position of firstborn, he was telling Reuben that he was not considered the firstborn son.

Then Israel called his sons and said, "Gather around so I can tell you what will happen to you in the days to come."

Assemble and listen sons of Jacob, listen to your father Israel."

"Reuben, you are my first born, my might, the first sign of my strength, excelling in strength, excelling in power. Turbulent as the waters, you will no longer excel, for you went up onto your father's bed, upon my couch and defiled it."

"Simeon, and Levi are brothers, their swords are weapons of violence. Let me not join their assembly. For they have killed men in their anger and hamstrung oxen as they pleased. Cursed be their anger, so fierce, and their fury, so cruel. I will scatter them in Jacob and disperse them in Israel."

"Judah, your brothers will praise you, your hand will be on the neck of your enemies, your fathers sons will bow down to you. You are a lion's cub, O Judah, you return from the prey, my son. Like a lion he crouches and lies down, like a lioness, who dare rouse him? The scepter will not depart from Judah, or the ruler's staff from between his feet, until He comes to whom it belongs and the obedience of the nations are his. He will tether his donkey to a vine, his colt to the choicest branch; he will wash his garments in wine, his cloaks in the blood of grapes. His eyes will be darker then wine, his teeth whiter than milk."

"Zebulun will live by the seashore and become a haven for ships; his border will extend toward Sidon."

"Issachar is a rawboned donkey lying down between two saddle bags. When he sees how good is his resting place and how pleasant is his land, he will bend his shoulder to the burden and submit to forced labor."

"Dan will provide justice for his people as one of the tribes of Israel. Dan will be a serpent by the roadside, a viper along the path that bites the horse's heels so that its rider tumbles backwards."

"I look for your deliverance, O Lord."

"Gad will be attacked by a band of raiders, but he will attack them at their heels."

"Asher's food will be rich; he will provide delicacies fit for a king."

"Naphtali is a doe set free that bears beautiful fawns."

"Joseph is a fruitful vine, a fruitful vine near a spring whose branches climb over a wall. With bitterness archers attacked him; they shot at him with hostility. But his bow remained steady, his strong arms stayed limber, because of the Mighty One of Jacob because of the Shepherd, the Rock of Israel because of your father's God who helps him, because of the Almighty who blesses you with blessings of the heavens above, blessings of the deep that lies below, blessings of the breast and womb. Your father's blessings are greater than the blessing of the ancient mountains, than the bounty of the age old hills. Let all these rest on the head of Joseph, on the brow of the prince among his brothers."

"Benjamin is a ravenous wolf, in the morning he devours the prey, in the evening he divides the plunder."

Israel blessed all twelve of his sons. He gave each the blessing they deserved. Then he charged them to bury him with his fathers in the cave Abraham bought from Ephron the Hittite, the cave in the field of Machpelah. After Abraham bought the field, he, Sarah, Issac, Rebeckah and Leah were all buried there. Israel finished blessing his sons and telling them where to bury him. Then he drew his feet into the bed and died.

Joseph and his brothers wept because of the death of their father. Joseph threw himself on his father's face and wept and kissed him. Joseph sent for the physicians and told them to embalm his father. After the physicians had removed his lungs, kidney, intestines and stomach, they covered him with natron salt and left him to dry for forty days. His sons and the Egyptians mourned for Israel for all forty days. After the days of mourning were over, Joseph said to the Grand Vizier, "If I have found favor in your sight, I pray that you will tell Pharaoh Senusert III that my father made me promise to bury him in the family cave in Canaan. Please let me go and bury my father as he requested of me."

Pharaoh answered Joseph, "You are to take your father to Canaan and bury him as he made you promise. All of my servants that want to go with you may go."

Joseph, his brothers, many of the servants of Pharaoh, and some of the elders of Egypt went to Canaan for the burial. They went in their chariots, on camels and in carts. When they reached the threshing floor of Atad, east of the Jordan, they stopped to mourn Israel. At Atad they stayed seven days and mourned Israel with loud lamentations. The mourning and the weeping was so loud that the Canaanites and other peoples living in that land knew that a great person had died. "This is a grievous mourning for the Egyptians," they said. So they called the place Abelmizraim.

The Egyptians returned to Egypt and Joseph and his brothers took their father to the cave and buried him. Then Joseph and his brothers returned to their families in Egypt. The brothers thought that now that father is dead Joseph may hate us and deal harshly with us.

"Let us go to Joseph and apologize so that he may deal kindly with us," Reuben said. So they went to Joseph and said, "our father commanded us to say to you," 'forgive the trespasses of your brothers and their sins against you. They meant to do you harm, but God meant it for saving lives.' "So please forgive the servants of Father's God. We will be your servants" They fell down with their faces to the ground.

Joseph wept when he heard them. He said to them, "Rise, fear not, I am not in the place of God. But as for you, you planned evil for me, but God planned good for everyone. You have seen how many lives I saved because you sold me into slavery. Again I say, fear not! I will give you and your families grain so that so that you may continue to live."

Joseph lived in Egypt with his brothers and all their families. Joseph held Ephraim's sons, Shuthela and Beker and his great grandsons, Tahan and Eran on his knees. He also saw Manasseh's son, Makir, and his grandson, Gilead. Joseph lived to be 110. Then he called the Israelites together and said, "I will soon die. God will visit your descendants and take them back to Canaan to the land God swore to give to Abraham, Issac and our father. When you go, I charge you to take my body with you."

Joseph was embalmed and his coffin was put in Memphis. Even though the ruling Pharaoh, Queen Sobekneferu, had never known Joseph she had heard how Joseph had saved Egypt. After Joseph's mummy had lain in the public square on the diorite slab to dry out, she declared a national month of mourning for Joseph and had his coffin put in the main chamber in the temple of Horus. During that month the people of Egypt passed by the coffin and paid their last respects to the man who saved Egypt.

Israel's descendants remained in Egypt until they had become a mighty nation. When the time came, God sent Moses to fulfill His promise to Israel and Joseph.

Bibliography

"Past Worlds" by Harper Collins Atlas of Archaeology:
    Ground Looms -- Page 41
    Cultivated Plants -- Page 78
"Great Events of Bible Times" by Doubleday & Company
    Life Among the Nomads--Page 21
    Map of the Route Abraham Traveled--Page 21
    Wheat Harvesting and Thrashing--Page 71
Great People of the Bible and How They Lived
    Picture of Bedouins Camp--Page 25
    Abraham and His Family Traveling--Page 37
    Picture of Lion Stealing a Lamb--Page 41
    Issac Plowing--Page 47
    Canaanite Worship--Page 46
    Isaac's Altar--Page 47
    Watering Sheep--Page 51
    Pitching Tents--Page 53
    Family Sitting Around Campfire--Page 56
    Egyptian Nobleman Inspecting Beer Making--Page 61
    Buying Grain from Joseph--Page 65
Biblical Archaeology Review; Did the Ancient Israelites Drink Beer, by Michael Homan (September/October, 2010 Issue)
Manners and Customs of Bible Lands, by Fred H Wright; Copyright by Moody Press, 1953
"River God" by Wilbur Smith, St. Martin's press, copyright 1993

Printed in the United States
By Bookmasters